MW00333197

THE BLEEDING EDGE

Dark Barriers, Dark Frontiers

Edited by
William F. Nolan
and

Jason V Brock

THE BLEEDING EDGE
Dark Barriers, Dark Frontiers

Anthology © 2009 by Cycatrix Press

Editors: Nolan, William F. and Brock, Jason V

100 Deluxe Hardcovers, Signed and Numbered
ISBN:

978-0-9841676-0-9
0-9841676-0-9

400 Trade Hardcovers, Signed
ISBN:

978-0-9841676-1-6
0-9841676-1-7

First Edition, First Printing

Printed in the United States of America
using vegetable-based inks. Bound in the USA.

Printed by B&B Print Source
USING 100% WIND POWER

Published by:
Cycatrix Press

http://www.JaSunni.com

Email/Contact: *JaSunni@jasunni.com*

JaSunni Productions, LLC
16420 SE McGillivray Blvd.
Ste 103-1010
Vancouver, WA 98683
USA

~Distributed in conjunction with~

DARK DISCOVERIES PUBLICATIONS

http://www.DarkDiscoveries.com

THE BLEEDING EDGE

Dark Barriers, Dark Frontiers

Cycatrix Press

~ CONTENTS ~

※ ※ ※

FOREWORD

by S.T. Joshi

❈ ❈ ❈

This volume is a snapshot of the extraordinarily rich and varied modes of writing that have dominated weird fiction over the past fifty to seventy-five years. Without any intention of doing so, the twenty-plus contributions to this book make clear that the literature of terror and the supernatural can encompass the widest possible array of human emotions -- from sardonic humor to cosmic tragedy -- and do so by manipulating the widest possible diversity of styles, themes, and subject matter. In these days when "theme" anthologies all too often produce a monotonous sameness in motif and treatment, it is refreshing to come upon a volume as multifaceted as this.

To gain a sense of the directions weird fiction has taken over the last half-century or so, a good place to start is Frank M. Robinson's touching essay on his early readings of the pulp magazines, including *Weird Tales*. In the 1920s and 1930s, H. P. Lovecraft was the dominant writer for the magazine -- not only in his own right but by way of the many friends and colleagues who formed what came to be called the "Lovecraft Circle," including such writers as Robert E. Howard, Clark Ashton Smith, Henry S. Whitehead, E. Hoffmann Price, Robert Bloch, Fritz Leiber, and many others. It is of course unjust to regard these writers as somehow dependent on Lovecraft, for many of them evolved distinctive styles and themes of their own, as witness Howard's Conan and King Kull and Smith's exotic tales of Zothique and Hyperborea. Indeed, it was not so much Lovecraft himself as some of his frankly less talented disciples -- of whom we are forced to number August Derleth, his chief advocate and champion after Lovecraft's early death in 1937 -- who, in their attempt to write homages to their lost mentor, unwittingly produced parodies of Lovecraft's own work and manner.

Accordingly, the generation that came to literary maturity after Lovecraft -- including such writers as Ray Bradbury, Richard Matheson, William F. Nolan, Charles Beaumont, and Ray Russell, several of whom are represented here with work both old, though unpublished, and new -- revolted from what they felt to be the now hackneyed "Lovecraftian" tale, the tale of some erudite professor battling cosmic monsters in obscure corners of the earth. That this was in reality a caricature of Lovecraft's densely textured tales is of no consequence; what this new cadre of writers sought to do was to bring the weird and the supernatural down to the level of daily reality, and in this task they were wondrously successful. Bradbury, along with Fritz Leiber, perpetually danced on either side of the thin dividing line between horror and science fiction, and his contribution to this book, brief as it is, shows keenly how imaginative fiction can serve to address complex social issues such as racism and moral conservatism.

As Bradbury, Matheson, Beaumont and others were making horror (and science fiction) more accessible to the average reader, writers like Robert Bloch were broaching the equally thin partition between horror and psychological suspense. Bloch's classic novels *The Scarf* (1947) and *Psycho* (1959) definitively made psychological terror a key component of weird fiction writing, and that tendency has continued to the present day, as the grim tales by John Tomerlin and Joe R. Lansdale attest. It was during this period, too, that media -- especially film and television -- significantly influenced the writing of weird fiction. The complex interplay of writing and media is most clearly evident in George Clayton Johnson's unpublished *Twilight Zone* script, "The Grandfather Clock." Johnson, in his brief author's note, observes that his script was purchased by Rod Serling but that it was subsequently "changed quite a bit." We can perhaps elaborate on this tactfully restrained remark. What happened was that William Froug, a new producer, disapproved of Johnson's script and commissioned another writer, one Richard deRoy, to rewrite the story. Although the central idea is preserved, the general consensus is that deRoy's version -- aired on December 20, 1963, as "Ninety Years Without Slumbering"-- is substantially poorer than Johnson's. The collaborative nature of media makes this type of result all too common. Such veterans of film and television as Norman Corwin and Dan O'Bannon, with their widely varying but equally distinctive unproduced screenplays, can attest to the truth of that dictum.

Weird fiction was changed irrevocably when it became a best-selling phenomenon, beginning with Ira Levin's *Rosemary's Baby* (1967) and continuing on with William Peter Blatty's *The Exorcist* (1971), Stephen King's *Carrie* (1974), and the many works that have followed in their wake. In a sense, this development was also intimately tied to the media, for the new mass audience for weird fiction might never have been created if horror in film and television had not been laying the groundwork for fifty years or more. Indeed, some of the novels that became best-sellers only did so when blockbuster film adaptations appeared. This "horror boom"-- which finally exhausted itself by the early 1990s -- left a very mixed legacy. To the extent that many more readers than previously would seek out horror fiction, the field was broadened in a way that could encompass both the quiet lyricism of a Peter Straub and the noisy pyrotechnics of a Clive Barker, with all manner of gradations between. But many writers strove merely to duplicate the worst aspects of literary bestsellerdom in a quest for quick riches, and the appalling plethora of subliterary rubbish that emerged made it difficult for the work of superior writers to get a hearing. What is more, it is by no means clear that the weird works best in the novel form; indeed, if this volume is any testimony, it is almost uniformly better in shorter compass. But stories, then and now, are a harder sell than novels, and accordingly many of the best writers of this period were relegated to the small press.

Nevertheless, the expansion of range in weird fiction to cover nearly every style and manner of writing is now evident. The weird can now take the form of the erotic tale (Nancy Kilpatrick's "Hope and the Maiden"), the satirical parable (Christopher Conlon's "Triptych"), the gruesome comedy ("Madri-Gall" by Richard Matheson and Richard Christian Matheson), the tale that draws upon ancient myth (Cody Goodfellow's "At the Riding School") and age-old fears and phobias (Earl Hamner's "The Death and Life of Caesar LaRue," Lisa Morton's "Silk City"). At the same time, even such venerable supernatural motifs as the ghost can, as John Shirley's mordant tale attests, be given new life through a distinctively original vision. And Gary A. Braunbeck's tale shows that the Lovecraftian idiom can also be revitalized by an appeal to contemporary advances in science. The stories by James Robert Smith and Kurt Newton approach the realm of fantasy in showing that even the possession of wondrous supernatural abilities cannot ward off horrific tragedy.

Fear and terror have definitely been brought down to earth. What we learn from such tales as Steve Rasnic Tem's "Red Light" and Jason V Brock's "The Central Coast" is that the most unremarkable events -- driving a car at night, throwing a house party -- can lead to unthinkable results. The very fabric of daily life provides all the seeds for the most bizarre of scenarios; and now that horror writing has returned to its proper venue, the small press, writers have rediscovered the monumental impact that a trenchantly written short story can have.

We may well be entering a new golden age of horror writing. A century or so ago, such titans as Arthur Machen, Lord Dunsany, Algernon Blackwood, and H. P. Lovecraft absorbed the best of the weird literature that preceded them and raised supernatural writing to its heights through a dark vision that looked upon literary terror as far more than a momentary shudder: these and other writers realized that the supernatural could be used symbolically to express their deepest beliefs about the fragility of humankind in a bafflingly inscrutable cosmos. Today, a new generation of writers seems to be following their lead, writing vibrantly and at times explicitly about the terrors of science, of sex, of society, and of the simple act of living from day to day. Are we alone in the universe, the creatures of a day, the victims of our own tragic flaws, or are we the pawns in some enigmatic game played by forces incalculably superior to anything we can imagine? The writers in this volume would not presume to answer these questions, or even to maintain that these questions can ever be answered; they are content to provide intriguing hints, with a few shivers along the way.

✳ ✳ ✳

S. T. Joshi is a widely published critic and editor. He is the author of such critical studies as *The Weird Tale* (1990), *H. P. Lovecraft: The Decline of the West* (1990), and *The Modern Weird Tale* (2001). He has edited the standard corrected editions of H. P. Lovecraft's collected fiction, revisions, and miscellaneous writings (Arkham House, 1984-95; 5 vols.), as well as *The Ancient Track: Complete Poetical Works* (2001) and *Collected Essays* (2004-06; 5 vols.). He has prepared three annotated editions of Lovecraft's tales for Penguin Classics (1999-2004). His exhaustive biography, *H. P. Lovecraft: A Life* (1996), won the British Fantasy Award and the Bram Stoker Award from the Horror Writers Association.

He is co-editor of Ambrose Bierce's *Collected Short Fiction* (2006; 3 vols.), and has edited several editions of the work of H. L. Mencken. He is co-editor of *Supernatural Literature of the World: An Encyclopedia* (2005; 3 vols.) and the editor of *Icons of Horror and the Supernatural* (2006; 2 vols.). He is the author of *God's Defenders: What They Believe and Why They Are Wrong* (2003) and *The Angry Right* (2006). He edits the journals *The Lovecraft Annual, Studies in the Fantastic,* and *Dead Reckonings*. Visit his website: *www.stjoshi.net*.

WELCOME TO THE DARK SIDE... 1

That's what this anthology is all about: bad deeds, bizarre revelations, troubled characters. Oh, there's humor here, also, but it's *black* humor.

It is our intent as editors to boldly go where no editors have gone before. With this book, we established an initial goal: to open some very special doors into the human condition. We feel that the pieces gathered here (all new, unpublished, provocative) deliver on the promise of our subtitle -- breaking down "Dark Barriers," assaulting "Dark Frontiers". You will find fresh surprises on nearly every page, as the respective authors unspool challenging tales of murder, isolation, sex, urban restlessness and satire.

We freely admit that we have set out to stun you, disturb you -- but most of all to entertain you. If we succeed in that enterprise, then we have done our job.

So, partake of this harrowing feast, as our contributors (new names and old alike) gleefully ply you with intoxicating jolts of shock and suspense, accompanied by doses of blood and grue, and a dash of wry laughter.

It's a meal we're sure that you'll never forget...

--William F. Nolan
Vancouver, WA
2009

WELCOME TO THE DARK SIDE... 2

❋ ❋ ❋

All books are collaborative, anthologies especially: there are artists, writers, editors, publishers. With this volume, we hope to startle, amuse, violate, inflame, disquiet; at times all at once. Quite ambitious, I know, but if Man's reach doesn't exceed His grasp...

Regardless, the tome you're reading came about in latter 2008, the result of much kvetching and brainstorming about the lamentable state of the Publishing Industry. It was originally envisioned as a comment on the best that the field had to offer -- old or new -- so long as it had never seen the light of day. Nolan and I wanted to push the envelope of what was presented, so there were no limits on the type of story (or its presentation), it just had to be modern and intense. Also, we wanted to *edit* a book, down to the line; neither of us likes the trend toward compiling things.

That's how everything got so precarious: it's been a race to the bottom, not an aspiration to higher calling. Enough. We hope to change that in some small fashion with this effort, and others like it. The very concepts of "modernity" and "horror" are both somewhat antiquated: one person's gory excitement is another's ennui. We have cast the net wide, therefore: some stories are straightforward, others more esoteric, even bordering on the *avant-garde*. The point being that there is no *one* way to interpret the genre or tell a story. You will not find any of the stale tropes currently infecting the (ever-shrinking) market, such as vampires, zombies or insightful serial murderers. If that is what you seek, you will be disappointed. This was intentional on our part: the world is saturated with such fodder. No doubt, especially skillful writers can (and do) deliver the goods with these stereotypes, but we chose to avoid them right from the outset.

Edge is what we desired: the Outsider, the alternative viewpoint, the unheralded idea. Of course, not all of these stories will succeed; try though we might, our tastes as editors *will* diverge from our intended audience from time to time. That's okay: what a boring place the world would be if we all agreed on everything...

As to the rest, the illustrations (for the Deluxe Edition only) and cover are by an up-and-coming artist named Kris Kuksi. Kris is not only a wonderful artist, but a really nice guy, and we are pleased to have him as a part of this project. Visit his web site at *www.Kuksi.com* for more.

Kris Kuksi

Bill Nolan and I had a great time editing the book, and are already working on a 2010 follow-up (all cross-genre fiction, with never-before-published-works from a surprising and diverse lineup). Additionally, while we did not mean for this to be a kind of *"Twilight Zone/*Califor-nia Sorcerers" reunion, it is nonetheless; a fitting tribute, we feel, to commemorate the 50th anniversary of that landmark series. So, 'Happy Anniversary!' *Twilight Zone* (And Rod, you're really missed...). Within these covers are true horror, humor, erotica and everything in between... Your task is to investigate these landscapes unknown.

What does the world want?

A great story, well told...

--Jason V Brock
Vancouver, WA
2009

"Some of My Best Friends Are Martians..."

by Ray Bradbury

Marlo Stevens announced her engagement that night.

"Eeel and I are being married next week," she said.

"What?" cried Mother.

"Oh my *God!*" exclaimed Father.

"To a -- *Martian?*" asked Grandfather.

"You can't do that," said Grandmother.

"Goodbye, everybody," said Marlo.

The door slammed.

Father was on the televisor an hour later, his face like a badly photographed sunset. "Marlo, you come home right now!"

"Sorry, father, I've made up my mind: I love Eeel!" Her hair was like fresh spring dandelions and her mouth the newest hydroponic cherry.

"You can't love a Martian: it's obscene!"

"I like his green skin, it's different."

"Oh, my God. This'll cost me six months psychiatrical treatment... It might even split me down the middle," Father stammered.

"Then they'll bury you in two coffins," said Marlo to her father.

"You're heartless... What are your plans?"

"We're honeymooning on the planet Mars, of course, and then a little trip through the meteor swarms and on out of the solar system."

"What do you see in him? I mean, a man with four arms."

"Oh, come off it Papa! I'm twenty-one years old and know enough to realize that a man with four arms can be twice as good a lover, and besides, he has -- *other* qualities."

"I won't stand for it! You come home right now!" Father demanded.

"I'll send you a colour film of our honeymoon," she threatened.

"I'm going into my depressed phase," moaned Father, shutting his eyes. "You're obviously psychopathic and somewhat -- *perverted.* But I'll forgive you if you come home now."

"Furthermore, did you know--,"she began telling him a few things which sent the old man raging from the televisor.

"Why don't you marry an iguana lizard!" he screamed. "I'll have the law after you!"

"Ta ta." And she rang off.

●●●

"Father," said Mother. "You shouldn't be so prejudiced. Remember what my parents said when they found out you were Black, rest their souls..."

"My dear," said Father, trembling and seething and boiling by turns. "I have been a member of the Society for the Advancement of Coloured Peoples... I have been against vivisecting dogs and cats... I have lectured at the Booker T. Washington Institute and aided the stricken Tibetan Buddhists... I have put up with Southern Democrats and Yankee Republicans... Look! Here is my Labor Union ticket and my receipt for money I sent to help the hungry boll weevils of Neeraphut; but when my daughter, my lovely little sweet fine child marries a green man with four arms and pink eyes, then it is time to wrap me in a cold wet sheet, tie my arms behind my back and dump me into a rubberoid cell with a piece of adhesive over my raving mouth! Four arms! Good *God!* The one time we met him, it took us half an hour to shake hands!"

"I say *shoot* the son-of-a-Martian," said Grandpa, blowing the chambers of an old gun with his tobacco breath, lining up the sights with an oystery eye.

"We must act as a unit of four," said Grandma. "I once had a crush on a man from India. But then he wasn't -- *green.* He wore bright purple, and was rather pretty if you got him in a yellow room... Of course, he had only two arms, but I soon got over my crush when I realized that a girl on a moonlight ride with a man with the normal allotment is really quite defenseless: I can only imagine *four!* Heavens, I looked like a damaged fingerprint file when I got home that night! And then --"

"Shut up, woman!" cried Grandpa. "We've got a problem here!"

"I'll go one better, dear... I, too, once fell in love with a man from another planet -- Mercury," Mother confessed. "Mercury's a warm planet, as you know, and he sort of, well, 'steamed' all the time... It was most flattering until he explained this was only natural to him, and was not due to my company. He was sort of a cherry-red, looked like a big hunk of molten steel fresh out of a kiln. But then you came along,

Henry, and I forgot all about him."

"That's it! Of course," said Father, uneasily. "If we could find one of her *own* kind, at least... a big strapping Earth lad, a big ton of gristle and brontosaurus bone, perhaps not an ounce of brains --"

"I wonder if it's the arms?" mused Grandma.

"What?"

"I wonder if it's the *idea* of four arms that attracts Marlo so? If it is, why maybe we could graft a couple of extra arms on an Earth man and --"

"You talk like a busted jet-wash," snapped Grandpa.

They all rushed out of the house.

❂❂❂

Three months went by. At last, Marlo rang up on the televisor.

"Where are you?" asked Father.

"Venus."

"Who are you with? *Eeel, the Martian?* Thought they were at war? Damn Martians are always at war!"

"No, a Venusian, and he's very nice. Eeel felt that I would hamper his career as a writer, as I needed a lot of -- *fondling...*"

"What *colour* is this Venusian?" Father queried, sweat on his brow.

"Sort of a... cobalt blue, and - oh!- he has the *cutest* gills! Say something, Foosha!"

There was a gurgling noise on the televisor.

"No, *no!*" screamed Father, and fainted dead away.

Ray Bradbury, acclaimed novelist, short story writer, essayist, playwright,

screenwriter and poet, was born August 22, 1920 in Waukegan, Illinois. He graduated from a Los Angeles high school in 1938. Although his formal education ended there, he became a "student of life," selling newspapers on L.A. street corners from 1938 to 1942, spending his nights in the public library and his days at the typewriter. He became a full-time writer in 1943, and contributed numerous short stories to periodicals before Arkham House published a collection of them, *Dark Carnival*, in 1947. With a catalog that includes *The Martian Chronicles; Something Wicked This Way Comes; The Illustrated Man* and *Fahrenheit 451,* suffice it to say the rest is history…

Among his many honors, Mr. Bradbury has received the French *Commandeur Ordre des Arts et des Lettres Medal*, the National Medal of Arts, as well as the World Fantasy, Stoker, and SFWA Grand Master Lifetime Achievement Awards. He has also received an Emmy Award and a Pulitzer Special Citation for "…his distinguished, prolific and deeply influential career as an unmatched author of science fiction and fantasy."

What the author says about this story:

" 'Martians' is from my *Martian Chronicles* era. It captures my feelings about race relations."

Just a Suggestion

by John Shirley

This is a for-real story about me and the Holiday family. I figure they're a good example of what I can do, and what can happen. I'm going to talk all about the shooting, and where the people who got shot went after they died, to the extent I know, and why I'm still ghosting up this house. I'll tell you that part right now. I'm trying to put it on the tape recording this Ghost Seeker boob is using to get his EVP that he's hoping will get him on a TV show. That *EVP*, it's Electronic Voice Phenomena. They play a tape recorder when no one's talking and later on, see, they play it back, turn it up loud, and there's a message on it. Anyway that's what they think. Really, it's just some noise, and they interpret the noise any way they want. I know this from watching a show about this stuff, when I was haunting the Costco store in Tustin. They had all those TVs turned on for people to buy, and I watched a show about this EVP business. Think they're hearing ghosts when the tape goes, "Bzzguhbuzzgukbuzz." And they tell each other they're hearing, "Be gone, good bye!" Right.

People know so little about ghosts, spirits, what have you. Ghosts and spirits aren't even the same thing.

The chubby dumbass with the male pattern baldness and the dirty glasses, he's sitting here right now running the tape recorder -- hey if he actually hears this, later on, me talking about how he's dumbass and chubby, ha, nothing personal buddy! He painted "Ghost Seekers" across the side of on an old white cargo van, in orange paint, with a stencil. The bottom of the *ee* in 'Seekers' is runny. Looks stupid. I don't think this guy is going to get on TV.

But he had an ad in *The Orange County Register*, I guess, judging from what I heard Lucille say when she called him on her cell phone. She called him because of what Lindy said. Lindy's the only one who seemed to know I was there. She's more sensitive or something. Not "a Sensitive" like they say on the *Psychic Channel* -- but more *sensitive*. That's how it works. I mean, if you're a live person paying attention, if you're really *with it*, you see the dead around you. No special talent. But it helps to be sensitive -- and just pay attention to the right things.

I'm sitting here talking right out loud, into the little microphone he's got set up in the room, but judging from the look on his face and the fact that he's digging in his nose every so often, when he isn't scratching his crotch, I don't think the dumb son-of-a-bitch hears me. No clue I'm here. Maybe the machine'll pick me up, though. I'm talking as loud as I can. I don't exactly have lungs or a, what you call it, a voice box, or a tongue, but then again I kind of do, in a fuzzy way. I can move air around a bit, and I can make sounds. When I whisper *to* people, though, it's more to their minds. They hear it, but then again they don't. I don't understand the whole process that much myself.

We'll see if anyone can hear this. I think I can see that little needle on the tape recorder moving a tiny, real-tiny bit when I talk. I'll give a shout out to the world, just in case. *Go Lakers!* I'm still a Lakers fan. And my name is Murray Samuel Mooradian. Kind of a mouthful. My dad was being cute with the Murray Moora sound. I'm Armenian American. Or I was. I guess I don't have any DNA anymore. Don't you need DNA to be some ethnic type?

After my old man died of that blood clot thing, I went into his convenience store business. One of those stores attached to a gas station on Culver Avenue. Never was interested in the convenience store business as a career. I wanted to spend as little time in the store as I could. Because he was there morning to night -- and I didn't want to be around him. He always seemed disgusted with me, no matter what I did. I got a B plus, he was disgusted it wasn't an A. "You always got to fall short, huh? Push harder next time." Disgust came rolling off him like a bad smell.

I wonder where his ghost went. I've never seen it, not my mom's ghost either, or the ghost of anyone I knew in life, unless you want to count someone like Blondo and I don't. All the ghosts I know are strangers. Most dead people don't seem to stay around -- just some of them. Where are all the ghosts of all the millions and billions who've died?

Fact is, I haven't seen anything about God or Heaven or Hell or angels since I've been dead, these last ten years. But I picked up on some pretty mean spirits that you might call devils. Sometimes I hear them and I almost see them.

About my death, I was two days short of my forty-sixth birthday and walking the two blocks home from work about midnight, crossing the street with the light, and some tweaker ran a red light, smacked me like a two-ton baseball bat, his car spun out, and stopped -- and he sat there babbling in his car the way they do. And then the son of a bitch drove off. I saw that much because I was already dead. Just like that, bam. Floating a few feet over my body -- which was twisted all kinds of wrong ways.

Didn't yet have it together to follow the hit-and-run tweaker. So I never got the chance to take revenge on that asshole. But pretty soon I was watching a couple paramedics, a Cholo and some surfer-looking dude, loading my mashed body into the back of an ambulance. They were laughing about it, "You go ahead and do some CPR on him, he's got one lip left there, Blondo." Like they'd even do CPR that way. Just liking to laugh at the dead guy. I saw one of those blown glass pot pipes sticking out of "Blondo's" pocket, too. I know exactly what it was; we sold them at the convenience store. That pissed me off more than the hit and run. I don't know why -- just him treating me like that. Wrinkling up his nose with disgust while he's talking about my body. They drove off and now I wish I'd gotten in the ambulance, taken care of them right there. Only, I didn't know how to do it, back then. I was new to being dead.

So I started walking. I walked for miles till finally I was in Tustin, and there were those old blimp hangars, historical somethings, and there was the Costco. I waited till a security guard went in, and I went in with him... and just stayed. The store was big enough to wander in but also it was shelter from the sky. Now that I'm dead, the open sky always makes me feel like something's going to reach down and grab me and take me somewhere. Maybe somewhere bad. So I stayed put, puttering around in Costco for years. You lose track of time when you're dead. But I knew about how many years because of the seasonal products; Halloween stuff in bulk would come, Christmas decorations in bulk, Easter junk in bulk, July 4th decorations, Halloween crap again, Thanksgiving turkeys, and there you have one year.

I should tell you how I picked the Holiday family. I was getting sick of haunting Costco. Sick of the other ghosts, especially the Mexican landscaper who used to work around there. Died right outside of a heart attack. His ghost was always wandering around asking where his family was; asking me had I seen them. He would ask *"Where are they? What's going on?"* over and over in a pitiful way. "Que pasa, que pasa?" *You* pasa, dude, you pasa away. Most ghosts are confused, see. Me, I got clarity, though. I can think. I'm clear on what I want to do, given, you know, the choices I've got. Which aren't that many. I mean, it's all bullcrap about how a ghost can walk through walls. No sir. You have to wait till someone opens a door and then you follow them through before it closes. You can ride along, on their shoulders, piggy-back like as they go through the door. They don't usually feel it. Ghosts do that a lot, and people never know.

I stayed in the Costco for a long time because it was big, and there are a lot of people to look at. A lot of housewives. You can have fun checking them out in ways they never figured on. But after a while, the Muzak, the lights, the other ghosts who lived there -- dud conversationalists, all of them -- it was Hell. I'd *just* been thinking, "Maybe there *is* a Hell. And maybe it's Costco," when I saw the Holiday bunch.

They were walking around the store in a kind of family conga line, up and down the aisles, Dad leading the way, pushing that giant basket. "Dad", that's Boyd Holiday, chunky guy with a space between his front teeth, his eyes a little too far apart, nose flattened like the tip of a hammer; he was about the same age I was when I died. Then comes his wife, Rema Holiday, almost small enough to be a midget, wears short dresses maybe to make her tiny legs look longer, her brown hair bobbed, bruised-looking eyes but no one had hit her; then Boyd's goofy sister Lucille, same space in the teeth and wide apart eyes, dyed-black hair looked to me like a mop, but she calls it dreads because she's got some Jamaican boyfriend. Weak chin. Lucille was staying with them while she studied to get her chiropractor license, like that's ever going to happen. Then, trailing after Lucille, the kids: Lindy, the eleven year old girl, and Franklin the teen boy. Franklin was shaped like his old man, and he could've been the poster boy for snotty teens. Mouth stayed open, always texting -- took me awhile to figure out what texting was, it wasn't big till after I died. And he's got those droopy-ass pants like his hip-hop heroes. Makes me glad I never had any kids -- 'course I never had any women to get knocked up, hardly, no women except if I paid, to be honest, so how would I... Wait, do I want to say that about paying? Okay, shit, so what, it's on there now. I can't make the rewind button work. And it's nothing compared to some of the stuff I'm going to tell you about. Stuff that I did.

I followed them, the Holiday family, not sure why I was doing it, just thinking that there was potential of some kind. Maybe I could really get *involved* with a family, besides just whispering this and that to the people in Costco. Wait -- I know what it was! It was that "I'm mad but I'm not going to admit it" look on Boyd's face. Charging along like he was trying to challenge his family to keep up. Looking, hurt, mad -- disgusted. I just thought, "There he is, Mr. Powder Keg! It's playtime!"

And then I slipped into their slipstream, you might say, followed them around as they bought groceries and the boy hassled them into buying a game about Grand Theft, the little girl got some concert DVD to do with somebody named Hannah Montana, the mother picked out food and a big bag of socks, and then out the door of Costco, and out into that endless sunny parking lot, and up to their SUV. Passed a fading old ghost I know who presents himself in an Army Air Force uniform from around World War One. One of those blimp-hangar guys, died in an accident, likes to natter about preparedness.

When they opened the back of the Chevy SUV to cram in the big containers of taco beans and dip and Mountain Dew and several jars of barbecue sauce big as buckets and huge Styrofoam trays of frozen pork chops and chicken legs, that's when I climbed in, and crowded myself into the back, curling up on top of some groceries, kind of chortling, loving the novelty of this.

"Let's go on a family drive!" I yelled, as they got in the big car. They couldn't hear me, of course, not talking that way. Come to think of it, though, I think Lindy did glance around a bit.

So we drove out of the lot, and out of Tustin, to Southeast Irvine.

This was in the more affordable Irvine, East of the 405. West, now, you got your rich people, some movie stars, some grandsons of movie stars: your Turtle Rock, your Shady Canyon, your tony beach houses. East Irvine, you got a lot of people working for the high tech outfits, chipmakers, all that stuff. That's where old Boyd worked, assistant supervisor in some department of the microchip plant.

They got a pretty okay split-level four-bedroom house. There's a pool but it's dried out and covered over.

Lucille spent most of her time in a bedroom that Boyd called his "den" but there was nothing left of him in it but a locked rack of guns-- mostly rifles, one shotgun. Boyd belonged to a gun club. Went out there to shoot skeet and drink.

When we came into the house, everyone went their separate ways, Lucille scurried off to hole up in her room and talk to her boyfriend "Droppy" on a cell phone; Franklin, he holed up in his room to play the Grand Theft thing. Lindy went to her room to watch the DVD on her little television. Boyd threw himself into a big chair in the living room to watch Encore's *The Western Channel* on cable. He was watching an old George Montgomery picture, a real stinker. Drinking a Tequila Sunrise. Little wifey was in the same room, flipping through *Sunset Magazine*, but as far as Boyd was concerned, she was somewhere else. I was sitting between them on the sofa, looking back and forth and kind of grinning to myself, that first day.

Rema wasn't going to let him just stay in his Western Channel -Tequila Sunrise world though. "It's kind of early to start with the Sunrises," she said.

"That's funny, Rema," I said. "How can a sunrise be too early? Get it?" They couldn't hear it, of course. But I appreciated my own wit. "Hey and you know what else, you're reading *Sunset Magazine* while he's drinking a Sunrise. Hey lady, you guys are in different time zones!" I started singing, "Sunrise, sunset, swiftly flow the yearrrrrrs!'"

"It's my day off, Rema," Boyd said. "And it's almost four."

"Are you going to that gun club tomorrow?"

"You bet your sweet patootie I am. Not that your patootie has been sweet to me, any time lately."

"You see, Boyd? You drink and say unfortunate things. And what if Lindy heard you?"

"She's up to her neck in that Hannah Montana. Let me watch my show now."

"We don't have that much chance to talk, with you on that shift now. It's unfortunate." That was one of her favorite words, *unfortunate*.

"I can't argue with them about the shifts, I haven't got enough seniority, I told you this."

"I'm just saying that we don't have much time to talk, Boyd, and I'm worried about Franklin."

"What else is new? The kid's a loser. Straight Ds. Does no work of any kind, anywhere. Listens to criminals singing about how they killed cops and sold crack. Great! Lucky enough to be white, wants to be black."

"Don't be racist. Your own sister has an interest in black culture."

"She's got an interest in a black something."

"Ha, Boyd," I said, "Good one."

"That's definitely one Tequila Sunrise too many, Boyd," Rema said, "when you talk like that."

"One too many," I said, and this time I leaned close to him and whispered it with my mind as much as my mouth. *More like one too few -- she should have one with you. Then you might have something to talk about. You might get lucky there, Boyd.*

He heard me, in a way. When I do that kind of special whisper, they don't seem to hear every word, but they get some part of it, or the sense of it.

"You ought to have one, and loosen up," Boyd said, as if it were his idea.

"I think Franklin is depressed," she said, flipping moodily through her magazine. "He doesn't go out much. Just stays in his room. Internet, videogames. Texting. That's all. He's got that friend Justin, but apart from that..."

"The kid that lives in Tustin?"

"Justin in Tustin!" I crowed, slapping my knee. If I visualize slapping my knee while I do it, I can almost feel it. "Ha, Justin over in Tustin!" Boyd wasn't hearing me anymore. I wasn't doing it the special way.

"I don't like that Justin around here," Boyd said, frowning, clinking the ice in his glass. "I always feel like he's laughing at me. The two of them, I hear them rapping together for some MySpace site. It's disgusting. You get disgusted with your own son, something's wrong. And I think Franklin was trying to pick the lock on my gun cabinet. Kid's not honest."

"If you would take him to the gun club..."

"I asked him if he wanted to go. Insisted he had to take his friend along too! Why? I'm so boring he's got to bring entertainment?"

"That's just being a teenager. You forget what you were like."

"Not like *this*, isolated in that room with his Internet..."

"You didn't have the Internet when you were a kid, Boyd," I said.

But I wasn't really focused on Boyd now. He got me thinking about the boy. Depressed, isolated. Maybe I'd picked the wrong powder keg.

"If we could just put some water in the pool," Rema said, "Franklin thinks that if he could have a pool party..."

"Costs way too much. I'm having to support Lucille…"

"Maybe she really ought to…" She lowered her voice. "Move in with her boyfriend."

"That guy? I won't have her move in there, I got anything to say about it. She needs to get a part time job, sure, but…"

I was already wandering away from them, looking for Franklin's room. I had to wait outside a while, till he went to the bathroom. When he came back I followed him in and looked around. It was a little bedroom with clothes all over the floor, socks and underwear, the moldy remains of a half-eaten Subway sandwich (I was glad I didn't have a sense of smell), a magazine called *Hip Hop Hard*, the open magazine like a run-over bird on the unmade bed, posters all over the wall, mostly of hard-looking black guys including one called Lil Wayne and one called Fifty Cent. Franklin was on the computer at a white desk that looked too small for him, and, after glancing to make sure the door was closed, he started to look at Internet porn.

"Kid," I said, "Normally I'd be into it, but we've got business."

He was looking at something called "Tranny Fanny" and just starting to touch himself. I leaned near him, and whispered into his ear, in that special way, with my mind: *"Your dad's about to come in and catch you."*

His back straightened and he turned really quick in his seat to glare at the door. And lucky for me, someone -- probably Lucille -- was walking by just then, outside the closed door. He heard the footsteps, thought it was his dad.

Franklin closed the porn pretty quick, I can tell you.

Then he sat there, shaking. "No fucking privacy," he said. Teeth all clenched.

"You get things like privacy when people respect you, kid," I said, knowing he wouldn't hear it. Then I bent near him again and whispered the opposite with my mind, *"You deserve their respect -- all the crap you put up with…"*

He nodded to himself. "Deserve more respect."

Internet stuff was just starting to get really big when I died. I knew about the worldwide web. I used to stand behind an Assistant Manager in Costco when he was supposed to be working in his little office, and watch him do a lot of the stuff Franklin was doing. So I whispered, *"They made a movie about those Columbine guys. Everybody knows about them… How about check out some websites on that…"*

It was a little too early for that, though. He seemed to consider it and shook his head.

I heard a car roaring down the street outside, somebody showing off their big noisy engine. That gave me an idea. I leaned close and whispered into his mind, *"You can do a protest your own way."* The first time I made the suggestion he just sat there and chewed his lip, frowning. Snorted to himself. Kind of laughed. Then muttered something about "Fucking cops..."

This would take some work. But I had to prepare him for later. First thing, I figured, was to get him in a more suggestible state. I leaned over and whispered with my mind, over and over, every ten seconds or so, *"The only way out is to get drunk and high."* Ten seconds. *"The only way out is to get drunk and high..."*

He resisted a little. Apparently he'd promised his mom he'd do some kind of homework and he sort of esteemed his old lady. But pretty soon he was calling his friend Justin on one of those tiny little cell phones. "What up, dog. Hey we got to kick it..."

This was some kind of code between them for get all fucked up. And it wasn't an hour later that Franklin was 'chilling' with Justin, a fox-faced teen with several piercings and a tee-shirt that said, *World of Warcraft.*

Justin didn't exactly come to the house, they agreed by cell to meet down the street, in a construction site for another house more or less like the one Franklin lived in. The foundation and the frame of a house, in raw yellow wood, were already there. Franklin and Justin squatted in a half-walled room with a pint of something brown that Justin had stolen from his pop's liquor cabinet, and what I thought was a cigar but after a while I realized it was stuffed with dope. These kids, they call it a *blunt.*

So they were drinking and smoking and talking about all kinds of stuff, neither one listening to the other much. Franklin talking about how he thought his mom was flirting with an airline pilot who lived across the street, how he wished she'd leave his dad for the pilot, he could get a free trip to Hawaii or something, and how the guy knew how to party, because a girl who'd been over there told him this pilot, Mr. Burford, liked to get hammered. Which was something I took note of.

Justin brought out his iPod, and they each took one "ear bud" -- I think that's what they're called -- and listened to some band that Justin said was from Norway, said it was a "Death Metal Rap" band, and they were bobbing their heads like a whore giving a quick BJ, and when they were done, oh baby, were they ready to listen to me. Mostly it was the dope and the booze and just being pissed off. It turned out Justin's dad had smacked him around, the night before, and he was still mad about it, so that helped.

"You could probably get that car away from the house, real quiet, and drive if off and go for a cruise and get it back without anybody noticing," I told Franklin. *"You know where the keys are..."*

The kid was primed and ready to go. A few more suggestions and he and Justin were pushing the SUV down the driveway slope in neutral and onto the street, not to make too much noise. And then they were driving it off literally into the sunset -- with me wedged between them on the front seat. Franklin drove west toward the ocean, faster and faster, on surface streets, and I was there, riding along, whispering with my mind. *"You can push it a little faster, a little faster, this'll make Justin respect you more, he makes fun of you like your dad does..."*

The car was still barreling along -- faster and faster -- and the boys were whooping and the radio was on real loud, something about diving from a mountain of cocaine, and then they didn't quite make a corner, they swerved, the car spun around, and they were both going *shiiiiit!* but I was going "Ha, this is more like it!"

And then wham, bam, but no-thank-you-ma'am, we're wrapped around a telephone pole.

The Justin kid didn't make it. He'd gone right through the windshield. No seat belt, see. Cut all to ribbons. I saw his ghost standing around mewling to itself, and I said, "Hey fuck off, kid!" And he got scared of me and backed away and kind of melted into himself. That's what happens to a lot of them, they melt into themselves, like they're going down a drain that's in their heart. Then they're just gone.

Maybe it'd be better, to be just gone that way. Wherever they go.

Anyhow, Franklin had smacked his head on the steering wheel and his left arm was pinched into place by the door. He was crying like a bitch when the cops got there. Some firemen used the "jaws of life" to cut him out, and they lugged him to an ambulance. There was Blondo, working that ambulance! "I'll find a moment to deal with you, Blondo," I said, as I got into the ambulance, in back. Squatting in there with Franklin, I rode along to the hospital.

"Your dad's going to say you killed Justin," I whispered, to the moaning Franklin, in back. *"He'll imply it even if he doesn't say it."*

Turned out to be not far from the truth, too. Boyd was pretty damned mad. By the time he talked to Franklin the next morning, in the hospital, he'd already had the threat of a lawsuit from Justin's family. "They're saying it's your fault," his dad said angrily. "And that makes it my fault. And the car is totaled. That much car insurance I haven't got. Do you know what the deductible is?"

"It was just so *unfortunate*," said his mother.

Franklin was lying there listening to this and moaning, and finally he begged them to leave him alone.

Once they'd gone, I whispered to Franklin with my mind, *"You see? They're not concerned about you, or even Justin, only about how much damn money you cost them. Somehow there must be a way to teach them respect..."*

Turns out Boyd's insurance wasn't so great. Deductible too big again. Boyd and his wife argued about keeping Franklin in the hospital longer. I whispered hard at Boyd to get him out of there. *"He's fine! He doesn't deserve to be catered to in here! You can't afford this!"* So the kid was rushed out of the hospital against the advice of doctors. They wanted to do an MRI or something. Concussion, and so on...

Franklin's left arm was battered up but not actually broken, his head was thumped a bit but not actually cracked right open. So finally they let him go home.

I suspected something else was going on, though, because I'd been watching Franklin closer than the doctors, who maybe spent ten minutes with him total.

Meanwhile, when I followed the family out the hospital, who did I see outside but Blondo. He was just getting back into an ambulance, having dropped some dying old lady off. And the Cholo was with him, too. Perfect.

I got in the ambulance and... I'll tell you about a little ghost trick, here. You can't push through real solid things -- *I* can't anyway -- but you can put your ghost fingers right in someone's eyes, enough so it messes with their optic nerves. They don't feel it but they start to see things in flashes: on and off, on and off. Hard to drive that way. Even harder when someone is whispering, *"Look out look out look out you're gonna crash"* in your mind over and over, making them panicky. They didn't have their siren on; went right through a red light and a semi-truck plowed them over. Gave me some satisfaction to give Blondo's ghost a face-to-face earful about being a smartass over my body after the accident. He was too dazed to shout back and I left him to figure it out on his own. His partner drained away into himself, but Blondo just wandered off.

I walked in the opposite direction. We were only a few miles from The Holiday family house...

Franklin was up and around in a couple of days. He seemed pretty out of it and his dad said he must be overusing the pain meds but mostly he just forgot to take them. He had some pressure on his brain from the wreck, I think, probably a minor operation would have fixed it. Good thing for me I was able to get his dad to take him out of the hospital.

There was suspense in the Holiday house while the DA decided whether to charge Franklin with the manslaughter of his pal Justin. The cops pushed for it, but Rema got Franklin a good lawyer -- costing the family even more money, so they had to take out a second mortgage -- and it was looking like the lawyer was going to get him off...

So I waited, bided my time. Making suggestions along the way, guiding Franklin to search for certain kinds of websites. And making sure he saw an interview on that YouTube thing with some kid who'd almost died at one of those boot camps for problem teenagers. Just lucked onto that one. He happened to be on YouTube and I saw it there, scrolling by, as I watched over his shoulder. I made certain he watched it.

I'm not sure exactly how I got so caught up in this process. How it got to be so *important* to me. Felt kind of pushed, myself. Funny to think that now. But one thing is, ol' Boyd reminded me of my old man. That'd be a good reason right there.

One night, when Boyd was working on his third Tequila Sunrise, Rema broke it to him that a summons had come: they were being sued by Justin's family.

A nice rage from Boyd. "Franklin has ruined us! Lawyers, lawsuits!" It was handy, how he yelled that loud enough for Franklin to hear, clear upstairs. I went up and whispered to Franklin that he better go down and listen in, see what his parents were planning. Franklin came and sat on the bottom steps of the stairs, eavesdropping. Then I went back in the living room and whispered to Boyd with my mind, *"What about putting him in one of those boot camps for troubled teens? Hell, he stole your car, was getting high on drugs, got his friend killed... Oughta go to jail anyway..."*

And Boyd said it right on cue: "Kid ought to go in one of those boot camps for problem teens..."

Franklin was already feeling scared and sick. This was too much. Which was what I figured. He raced upstairs before he could hear his dad reassuring Rema,"Oh hell, you know I'd never do that to the boy, I wouldn't send him away. Maybe you're right, maybe he needs therapy..."

Later that night when his parents had gone to bed, Franklin took a handful of codeine and, at my suggestion, drank a tumbler of his dad's tequila. I remembered having heard you mix hard alcohol and codeine, it puts you in a *real* bad mood, sometimes a killing mood. And the kid was primed already, when I told him, *"They're gonna put you in that boot camp. To get rid of you. Just lock you up in that boot camp for bad teens..."*

Lucille was out with "Droppy". Coast was clear in the room with the gun cabinet.

So I made some more suggestions and a little later Franklin got into the tool box in the garage, found a hammer and chisel, went to Lucille's room, Boyd's old den, and busted the lock on the gun rack. He picked out the pump shotgun, which his dad had shown him how to shoot, loaded it up good, and went marching through the house, swept along on the red wave of rage I could see in the air around him. His dad was sitting up in bed arguing with Rema when in came Franklin. There was a moment of hesitation. The kid almost got a grip on himself.

I told him, *"The old man thinks you're disgusting! Look at him! He's disgusting! He's disgusting! It's him!"*

I felt almost like *I* had the gun, as Franklin brought the butt up against his shoulder and aimed at his dad, but his mother jumped up and shouted *"No!"* and got in the way. The shot intended for Dad caught her right in the neck, blowing most of her head all over the pillows; she fell like a little rag doll. That really made Franklin mad and I told him it was his dad's fault and he pumped two rounds at pointblank range into his old man, right up under the sternum, blew his chest bones up into his head, and he heard someone yelling behind him and he turned and fired without even looking. He didn't quite hit the girl, Lindy, directly. Mostly she caught splinters from the doorframe and a few pieces of buckshot, but it put her down on her back and then he was yelling at himself that he was disgusting, "I totally suck, I'm totally fucked!" and he did suck; he sucked on the gun barrel and *blooey*, his addled little brains were all over the ceiling.

I tell you what, it was a good night's work.

That's what I thought, looking around. But I wasn't alone in the room. There was Franklin and his mother and his dad.

Their ghosts. Franklin's ghost was walking in circles, clutching himself, calling for his mom, and his dad was just melting away, like there was so little soul to him it just couldn't sustain itself without his body. And his mom's ghost was looking sadly at Franklin and reaching for him but then she drained away into her own heart...

Lindy was alive, though. She was lying on her back, looking at me. Right at me.

Seems like being close to death made it possible for her to see me, her being sensitive anyway. "You're a ghost," she said. "You're the one. You and that other."

"Whatever, kid," I said. "All I did was make suggestions. They didn't have to take them." Then I wandered off to the living room, to look at the Tequila and wish I could have some.

Lucille came home pretty soon after and found the mess. Called the cops, and Lindy was taken to the hospital.

She told Lucille what she saw and she called the fake ghostbuster and here I am, talking on his gear. One thing about this jerk is he's totally --

Sorry -- we cut out there. He tried listening back to see if anything was on the tape and couldn't hear me. Ended up recording over some of what I said about him just now. Okay: we're back. Almost out of tape though. I think my story is there, but it's super faint: probably need some kind of special gear to hear it. I think somebody might, one of these days.

I've got a new project. That airline pilot, Burford, across the street. I think I can talk him into getting blitzed out of his gourd before he flies the plane. Then I use my other little tricks and get him to crash that 747. It'll be full of people, of course. Going to start work on it tomorrow.

People probably see things in the papers, like what happened to the Holidays, and they ask themselves, "Why did that happen?" Well, now you know. Because I can't be the only one up to this.

I wonder if I should feel bad about it. I can't feel much, you know.

Anyway I try not to.

Hey, all I did was make suggestions. Not counting Blondo. Him I flat out killed. But mostly -- just suggestions.

Sometimes I think there's a voice I've heard, myself. From somewhere. Making suggestions. To me. Only, not exactly in words. But still... whispering to me. Pushing me into all this stuff. Wouldn't that be funny.

But same deal: I don't have to listen to it, just like Franklin didn't have to listen to me...

That's the bottom line, man. It's all just a suggestion. You know?

John Shirley is the author of numerous novels, books of short stories and one non-fiction book. He has also written television and movie scripts, e.g., *The Crow*. His story collection *Black Butterflies* (Leisure Books) won the Bram Stoker Award. His newest books are *Bleak History* (Simon and Schuster), *Black Glass: The Lost Cyberpunk Novel* (Elder Signs Press), *Demons* (Del Rey Books), and *Living Shadows* (Prime Books). He is also a songwriter, having written lyrics for the *Blue Oyster Cult* and for himself. His blog is at *www.johnshirley.net*

What the author writes about this story:
"Some time back I found myself in a Costco store, and had an uncanny sense that the people around me in the giant discount store were sleepwalkers, drowsing along, easy prey to suggestion. We usually picture ghosts in graveyards or haunted houses, but how would a ghost, I wondered, end up in Costco, and what depraved advantage would he take of the sleepwalkers in this suburban limbo? It was also my desire -- just trimming on this story -- to make fun of *Ghost Hunter* types."

LOVE & MAGICK

by James Robert Smith

A nervous giggle crept out. "I'm in trouble," he said.

Outside, there were thirty deaths waiting for him. For now, they were not in the house where he intended to remain. But they would come. Nothing he thought of could stop them.

"How much trouble?" Teresa asked, arching her back as she stretched, her breasts breaking from the starched sheet like a couple of glorious beasts breaching foam. It was just moments ago -- during that bit of sex magick -- that he had divined what was up. His lips had been firmly clamped around one of those great nipples (leaving tiny dark bruises where he'd bitten down). He couldn't help it; it was quite a shock to know you were going to die at midnight.

"Someone's after me. Someone's got nasty surprises waiting outside my door." He peeked under the sheet, making sure there were no spiders or such in the bed.

"Who?" Teresa looked, too, but only because she did everything Vance did. He was her teacher; she his apprentice. His wife suspected nothing.

"I don't know." He speared her with that look. "If I knew precisely, perhaps I could do something about it."

"Who have you angered?"

He thought. Truly, he didn't quite know what he was messing with. He read the books and consulted the odd practitioners here and there; but mainly he was doing things on his own. Magick. Black. White. Indifferent. It worked, and he was good at it and Life was now his in a big way. Money, new friends and possessions; lo and behold there were followers. And there was Teresa. He admired her beauty, and even knowing he was probably going to die in a few hours, he felt himself stirring with lusty ambitions so soon after satisfaction. *Magick*.

"I don't know who I've alarmed. I didn't think anyone else dabbled in the areas that I did." He sat up. "I'm going to die here... You should leave."

Teresa knew better than to disbelieve Vance. He didn't mind her questions -- in fact, he liked her inquisitive and challenging nature, so different from that of his wife -- but she'd learned that his word was true. "Can I hang around? Maybe help?"

"You've already done all you can." He reviewed the vision. Magick was like a puzzle, a maze: a strange equation that did not follow traditional logic. He had found a strand that led to him and, in the throes of their sex, had followed it. *Thirty: ten insects, ten animals, ten plants.*

The insects, of course, worried him the most. They could get in easily; at least they were outside, for now. *What kind were they?* He left the bed and went to the window. The house was secluded, down in the center of his five hundred-acre wood. The nearest neighbors were two miles away: Teresa and her husband, Phil, in fact.

Thousands of big trees loomed about the house, standing along the slopes of the steep hills sweeping up from the cove that he had built. There were oaks and hickories and poplars and pines and sycamores. He'd identified almost a hundred species just within the ten acres closest to the home site. *And shrubs? Jove! Grasses and ferns and vines and mosses and...* He was doomed.

"Can't you ward them off?" she asked, growing concern tightening her throat.

"No!" He was angry, but not at Teresa. It would be nice to know what practitioner was betraying him, killing him. *That, at least, would be a comfort.*

Teresa knew it would do no good to ask why; struggle was pointless, so she remained silent. Sunlight streamed into the room: gold, warm, wonderful; it glowed on her auburn hair, raising a blush. His own hair was close enough in color, his skin light enough, so that someone seeing them together would think them brother and sister.

Vance turned away from the window, looking small before the forest. The woods swallowed up the driveway, a mile away from the county road. "You need to leave," he blurted.

"Don't you want me to try to help? A Warding spell or something?"

"Forget it." He crossed the bedroom and opened the door to the shower. "Anyway, Annie and Lisa are due home in a couple of hours, and you need to be gone before they see you -- or even catch you driving down the county road for that matter. I don't shield your comings and goings from them, you know." She knew. He never used magick to influence the ones he loved. Except Teresa -- she was his exception.

As the sound of the shower seeped out of the bathroom, Teresa rose and dressed. She didn't worry about any telltale signs of the sex she'd had with Vance. They had seen to it that Phil never noticed anything; she figured they'd seen to it that no one did. *I'm leaving*, she thought, and Vance understood her. *See you later: remember what I've told you*, he replied soundlessly.

Vance was drying himself with a rough, white towel when he realized Teresa was making a Circle of Protection around the house. She had stopped her car about a half-mile up the road and set out on foot, making Signs to Protect *VANCE* and the *HOUSE*; even *ANNIE* and *LISA*.

Vance screamed: "No! Teresa, you fool, *no!*" Biting his lip till it bled, he sat down hard on the thick pile carpet, seeing Teresa's little Nissan there in the green wood, gravel pale and blue under those black tires as the Warding was turned back, the Magick sucked in like marrow from a shattered bone. It greedily ate up Teresa's pitiful attempt at conjuring.

Teresa was running then; Vance had to watch, unable to tear himself away. He never turned the cheek, feeling the cold breath of Death blowing down on his beautiful Teresa. A hundred yards from the car, still cloaked and hidden amidst all that cloying, growing green, *THEY* caught up with her: plants (grasping), chitinous little jaws (biting), animal teeth (slashing). Teresa was torn and torn until there wasn't a Teresa any longer. The screams faded away, although Vance knew he would have been able to hear them for hours if he hadn't blocked them out: souls persisted for quite a while, he had discovered.

"Jesus!" he muttered. *Yes, Jesus: and now there is fuel for sixty deaths...*

Around five-thirty in the afternoon, Annie and Lisa came home. Vance heard the crackling of gravel, as if it were being chewed beneath the wheels of the car. They came in. Vance stood inside the door waiting, watching to see if anything came in with them.

"Is that Phil and Teresa Perkins' car parked up the way?" She set the bags full of her purchases on the table in the foyer. The bags settled, crinkling and crumpling lightly with their contents. Vance only gave them a glance and wondered what could have sneaked in with them.

"Yes," he said, peering through the window in the front door.

Annie waited a moment for clarification, which never came.

"Why is it there? Is something the matter?"

Vance turned to his wife. Lisa had wandered off to find something interesting to do; her parents' conversations bored her. "You *do* understand where my success came from?" he asked.

"I do," his wife said, without hesitation.

"And you believe that there is truth in it? That it's what makes me successful?"

"You know I hate talking about it, Vance. It goes against everything I was raised to believe... But, yes. I accept it." She pretended to busy herself putting the groceries away.

He went to his wife and hugged her. He truly loved her; she had loved him before all of this. *Before the magick.* She had loved him when he was poor, earning a meager living with his hands. "Something bad is going to happen tonight, Annie."

"Something bad? What?" Her face was ashen as she pulled away from their embrace.

He smelled her hair, breathing in. "I'm going to die."

"What do you mean? You're not making any sense! *You're going to die?*"

"I'm the doctor, Annie. I made the diagnosis: I saw it, and there's no stopping it. Someone... someone who's a lot like me, but better at it... that someone has seen to it that I'll be dead by midnight."

"How do you know? How can you be sure?" Her voice was rising, and Lisa appeared at the top of the staircase, her steps muffled by the thick carpet.

"I just know," he said, thinking of Teresa.

Annie grasped Vance by the hand, squeezing. "Well, we'll just leave, then! We'll get in the car and get out now!"

Vance stiffened when she made to pull him toward the door. "No. There are sixty assassins waiting for me out there. As long as I stay in here, I'll be safe. They'll have to come inside to get me, and I mean to make them do it."

"*Who*, Vance? Who's going to do it? Sixty *men*? Where are they? Is Lisa safe?"

Vance peered up the stairs at his little girl, who peeked back at him from behind the banisters. Sometimes he thought she was afraid of him, which was a shame, because he loved her so. "No. The two of you are safe. Whoever wants me has made certain to specify that only I will die. Not you. Not Lisa -- so long as you don't interfere. Neither of you knows *how* to interfere in any way that would matter." He sighed. The tension was getting to him. The fear was coming as shadows lengthened in the forest.

"Why don't you and Lisa go into town? Pack a bag and stay until morning. That way, you don't have to be here at midnight, to see -- to see me..." He patted her soft shoulder, forcing a smile.

"What about the police, Vance?"

"Don't be ridiculous; what would you say? That your husband practices magick and someone's cursed him to die?" He paced away, going from window to window, making certain each was locked down tightly. He glanced up and down at the vents blowing air from the ceiling and floor.

He thought he saw something darting through the trees and bent to look through the picture window in the den. Whatever it had been was gone. His stomach knotted.

"What do you say, Annie? Will you please take Lisa and go into town to wait this out until morning?"

"And leave you here?" She was behind him, clutching the countertop. He could see her black hair reflected in the window. "I'm not leaving you."

Just before the sun hid below the rim of the hills, he looked out the kitchen window that faced upslope and saw a shape shuffling heavily from a stand of pines toward a poplar thicket. It might have been a great shaggy dog, its body misshapen, twisted. No dog moved that way, nor had a head so round. *This is very dark magick, indeed.*

In the guestroom upstairs, he had a gun cabinet: rifles and shotguns. He unlocked it. He loaded the best of the rifles: the 22.220. It felt good in his hands. He fed five slugs into the twelve-gauge shotgun. Annie knew how to use it. Surprisingly, it was her favorite. *She's a good shot...* During hunting season, he often kissed the bruises its potent kick left on her shoulder.

Downstairs, handing her the shotgun, he whispered: "When they try to come inside..."

He retreated up the stairs, to the guestroom where there was a grand view of the grounds surrounding the house. Turning on the floodlights before going up, the area about the house was now lit in golden, artificial light. A bulbous shadow oozed across the lawn and vanished into the trees. Wondering what it had been, he pondered, following one strand, then another. There *had* to be an answer. All paths led to void.

It was eight o'clock.

Too wound up to nod off, Vance sat on the bed, listening to the drone of the television downstairs, the one in the den. He'd told Annie to let Lisa watch it so she would be distracted and not upset by the tension he and Annie were showing. *Kids are perceptive.* The television leaked fake voices into the room. Then, he heard the odd, metallic ticking near his feet.

He looked down.

What was trying to come in through the narrow vent in the floor had probably once been some kind of beetle. *But that was before the magick had gotten to it.* Its carapace was a gorgeous fluorescent green. Its thickened limbs were asphalt black, spotted with a disturbing shade of crimson. Human eyes stared up, through the vent, where compound eyes should have been. By then, the vent had been pried free, and the creature was flexing its keratinous wings.

Vance stood, grabbing a metal bookend on the shelf near the bed. It was heavy in his hand, and he threw it. There was an almost womanly cry as metal crushed bugflesh, blood not unlike a man's squirting out.

He must have made some alarming noise, for he quickly saw Annie swinging the door wide. Immediately she saw the broken vent, the oblong bookend, and the target of Vance's attack. She crept over. "Sweet Jesus..."

"You and Lisa can still leave."

Annie looked out the window, searching for movement. "No. We'll stay."

"There are fifty-nine more."

"We're staying!"

He reached deep for personal calm, once more took up the magick paths and mentally followed them. They all still led to his death.

Ten o'clock.

Something that had been a small land tortoise jutted its long, yellow neck through the kitchen window, shattering the glass. It bared shark-like teeth, and Annie fired once, spraying its cold, reptilian blood back out the window. After that, they closed the door to the kitchen, locking it. Lisa whimpered, and Annie lied to her, consoling her. Annie took her to mommy and daddy's room.

"Lock yourselves in," Vance instructed.

Vance returned to the guestroom. He stared into the forest, which was still illuminated by the security lights. He covered the ruined vent with a thick rug, bracing it with a heavy end table. From time to time something prodded at the barrier, but he didn't want to see what it was.

A large pair of figures stalked out of the woods, jumping lithely to the covered porch below. They moved so quickly that he did not have time to fire. Now they were thumping at the front door. He knew that the windows would never hold. Vance crawled under the bed, trance-like and prone.

He found a faintly glowing pathway, reluctant to follow it.

How could something so black be illuminating? What good could come of such a thing? Could he follow it? He checked his watch.

Eleven thirty.

He found it.

There is a way, if I'm man enough...

He heard glass breaking, and sounds, as if the earth was heaving. He crawled from beneath the bed, where he'd been for long minutes, and looked out. An oak -- the one he and Annie shot mistletoe from during Christmas -- was writhing, as if some tornado had gotten hold of it and was spinning it free of the ground. *Only there* is *no wind.* He pushed away from the window, just as a branch shot through the glass, reaching, clawing for him. He opened the bedroom door, stepped out, and slammed it behind him. Living wood scrabbled against dead.

Creeping to the staircase, he saw a rattlesnake with an ape's smile lift itself above the top step. He shot it cleanly between the eyes. It sighed, tiny hands beneath its jaws flailing in slow motion. The scorpion on the railing would have leapt on him had he not seen it and demolished it with a single shot. Green poison dripped.

Downstairs:

A clinging vine reached toward the windows of the foyer, but had not built enough mass to gain entry. Beyond the front door, heavy, furred bodies were trying to tear through, all so eager to get at him that each was getting in the way of the others. Splinters fell as a great bulk smashed against it, again and again. There was howling. Something roared.

Vance was pounding on the bedroom door. "Annie, let me in!" Behind him, the front door gave. A stench of warm breath poured in.

The door angled and Vance fell in. He rose, pushing his body weight against the door. A mass walloped against it from the other side.

Annie had braced a mattress in front of the window; their dresser held it tight. Vance dropped his rifle and opened his arms. Eyes wide with fear, Annie moved toward him, bringing Lisa, whimpering into his arms.

Eleven fifty-five.

The great oak finally pulled free, taking a lumbering step toward the house. A hemlock cousin soon followed. The garage gave way with a crash of disintegrating wood, glass and wire.

It's not too late: there's still a path that can save me.

"Annie?" He screamed, voice nearly swallowed by the mayhem of destruction engulfing them.

"What?" She exclaimed, shielding the child.

The bedroom door cracked. He took a step toward her, hoping the lock would buy the time he needed.

"Do you love me? Truly?"

"Yes, of course!"

"Will you help me?" A second step.

"Yes! Anything! Just make it stop!"

"Lisa, will you help save Daddy? Would both of you do anything

to save me? Save us?"

In unison: *"Yes!" "Yes, Daddy! Anything!"*

Can I do this?

His chant was short and silent, unheard beneath the pounding and roaring. A simple spell before their entrance, of Transference. The door finally collapsed, the wall behind them coming down as they huddled together. Things that had been dogs, cats, spiders, ticks, trees and vines poured in. It required great, heartfelt love on everyone's part. And an act of will for Vance.

He averted his gaze as wife and child died in his place.

ᛑᛑᛑ

One a.m.

Vance went away from the house. He stalked through darkness, at home in it. It held no secrets from him. *Magick misdirected always makes the intended target that much more powerful.*

Now Vance was strong indeed: *Whatever doesn't kill you...* That went tenfold for him. The woods glowed for him, as they never had before. He could see every living thing, and within everything that was unliving. *Oh, but I am a great one now.*

Vance trudged up the hills where the pieces of Teresa lay, peering about, feeling power and magick flowing into him, seeing blue and green bits of it seeping up through the soles of his feet. Teresa's bloodied remains oozed at his toes.

He reached down and lifted her head, cradling it in his arm. He touched her brow.

Her eyes opened.

"Teresa," he hissed. His whisper made the mountain tremble. "You'd like to help me?"

"Yes." Her mouth soundlessly formed the word.

He knelt and began to assemble the parts of her, knowing she would be lithe and beautiful and inviting again. Necromancy was his now -- the last bastion. "We have things to do, Teresa. First, there's Annie and Lisa." His eyes glowed with a cold, red hatred that frightened even Teresa, who had been dead.

"Then we have others to attend." His voice steamed out. A damned few heard it. They shivered, far away though they were, and resigned themselves, even then grasping for a strand.

James Robert Smith was born in Brunswick, Georgia in June of 1957. He has never believed in the supernatural or in any god. He's  been married for 25 years to Carole, and has one adult son named Andy; he and his wife live with three cats in Charlotte, NC. When he's not writing, he works for the US Postal Service (many horror stories, yes). His first novel, *The Flock* appeared in August 2006 from Five Star Books. He also co-edited *Evermore*, a Poe-themed anthology for Arkham House in 2006. He sold the movie option to *The Flock* to producers Don Murphy and John Wells; the film is in development at Warner Brothers with a projected release date of 2011. His books *Hissmelina, The Living End: A Zombie Novel (With Dogs)*, and *Enchanted Boy* are currently making the rounds, and he's hard at work on his latest novel, *Family*. Smith no longer counts his short story sales, but has sold somewhere between 50 and 60. He's not sure anymore; he suspects his cat, Sophie, knows, but she ain't talkin'.

What the author writes about this story:

"I tackled the theme behind 'Love & Magick' for a couple of reasons. On the surface, I've always wanted to do a story based on the premise that, if there were such a thing as 'magic', then it would be whatever you made of it. That is, it would exist purely as your whims. You'd pretty much make it up as you went along.

Secondly, over the years of my dedication to reading horror fiction, it bothered me that so much of the stuff I'd read wasn't really horror. The stories were, mainly, moral fables wherein somebody bad got what was coming to them. This bugged the hell out of me. Where was the horror? Thus, I decided to storm into the temple and overturn those Judeo-Christian tables and put horror back in the fiction."

THE BLEEDING EDGE

MADRI-GALL

(A Short Skit for the Stage)

by

Richard Matheson

and

Richard Christian Matheson

SETTING:　　　　　THE STAGE IS DIMLY LIT AND EMPTY.

Scene One

AFTER SEVERAL MOMENTS, THE <u>CONDUCTOR ENTERS</u> FROM
THE AUDIENCE'S LEFT, PUSHING WHAT LOOKS LIKE A
LONG CLOTHES RACK ON WHEELS. WHATEVER IS HANGING
FROM ITS TOP BAR IS COVERED BY A CLOTH.

<u>HE</u> PARKS THE RACK MID-STAGE, GOES OFF-STAGE AND
RETURNS WITH A MUSIC STAND, MUSIC AND A BATON. <u>HE</u>
PUTS THE STAND IN FRONT OF THE RACK, SETS THE MU-
SIC AND BATON ON IT, THEN MOVES TO THE RACK AND
REMOVES THE CLOTH.

EIGHT MALE HEADS, CUT OFF AT THE NECK, DANGLE FROM
THE TOP BAR, THEIR EYES ALL CLOSED.

THE <u>CONDUCTOR</u> FOLDS THE CLOTH AND LAYS IT NEATLY
ON THE RACK PLATFORM. THIS ACCOMPLISHED, <u>HE</u> MOVES
TO THE STAND, PICKS UP THE BATON AND TAPS IT ON
THE STAND.

THE EYES OF THE EIGHT HEADS OPEN SIMULTANEOUSLY.

THE <u>CONDUCTOR</u> REMOVES A PITCH PIPE FROM HIS POCKET
AND BLOWS IT TWICE WITH SEVERAL SECONDS BETWEEN
THE FIRST AND SECOND BLOWING.

<u>HE</u> RETURNS THE PITCH PIPE TO HIS POCKET AND RAISES
THE BATON TO THE FIRST HEAD ON HIS LEFT.

<u>FIRST HEAD</u>

(On the downbeat)

Do.

THE <u>CONDUCTOR</u> POINTS HIS BATON TOWARD THE SECOND HEAD.

<u>SECOND HEAD</u>

Re.

THE <u>CONDUCTOR</u> POINTS HIS BATON TOWARD THE THIRD HEAD. THE <u>HEAD</u> ATTEMPTS TO SING "MI" BUT IS TAKEN BY A FIT OF COUGHING.

THE <u>CONDUCTOR</u> PUTS DOWN HIS BATON ON THE STAND, REMOVES A SMALL SPRAY BOTTLE FROM A POCKET, MOVES TO THE THIRD HEAD AND GESTURES FOR IT TO OPEN ITS MOUTH. THE <u>HEAD</u> DOES SO AND THE CONDUCTOR SPRAYS SOME OF THE BOTTLE'S CONTENTS INTO ITS MOUTH. (IF POSSIBLE, WE SEE IT DRIPPING OUT FROM THE BOTTOM OF ITS SEVERED NECK AND ONTO THE STAGE.)

THE <u>CONDUCTOR</u> RETURNS TO THE MUSIC STAND, PUTTING THE BOTTLE BACK IN HIS POCKET. <u>HE</u> PICKS UP HIS BATON AND POINTS IT AT HEADS ONE, TWO, THREE AND FOUR.

FIRST HEAD

>   Do.

SECOND HEAD

>   Re.

THIRD HEAD

>   Mi.

FOURTH HEAD

>   Fa.

THE CONDUCTOR POINTS AT THE FIFTH HEAD. IT HITS
THE PITCH CORRECTLY BUT THE SOUND IS GARBLED.
THE CONDUCTOR TRIES AGAIN WITH THE SAME RESULT.
HE STIFFENS. PUTTING HIS BATON DOWN ON THE MUSIC
STAND, HE MOVES TO THE FIFTH HEAD AND HOLDS HIS
PALM IN FRONT OF ITS MOUTH. THE HEAD LOOKS ASHAMED
AND CAREFULLY SPITS A WAD OF GUM INTO THE CONDUC-
TOR'S PALM. THE CONDUCTOR GIVES THE HEAD A DIRTY
LOOK AND, REMOVING A PIECE OF PAPER FROM HIS POCK-
ET, WRAPS THE GUM WAD INTO IT, FLINGING IT ASIDE
CONTEMPTUOUSLY. THE FIFTH HEAD LOOKS HUMILIATED.
THE OTHER HEADS GRIN SCORNFULLY.

THE <u>CONDUCTOR</u>, GETTING TESTY NOW, RETURNS TO THE
MUSIC STAND, PICKS UP HIS BATON AND QUICKLY POINTS
AT HEADS ONE, TWO AND THREE.

FIRST HEAD

Do.

SECOND HEAD

Re.

THE <u>THIRD HEAD</u> STARTS TO SING "MI", THEN LOSES IT
IN A WET, EXPLOSIVE SNEEZE. THE <u>CONDUCTOR</u> GROANS
IN FRUSTRATION AND MOVES TO THE HEAD, YANKING A
HANDKERCHIEF FROM HIS POCKET. <u>HE</u> HOLDS IT TO THE
NOSE OF THE <u>THIRD HEAD</u> WHICH BLOWS ITS NOSE OBE-
DIENTLY. THE <u>CONDUCTOR</u> MAKES A HARASSED SOUND AND
RETURNS TO THE MUSIC STAND. SNATCHING UP HIS BA-
TON, <u>HE</u> POINTS JABBINGLY AT HEADS ONE, TWO, THREE,
FOUR AND FIVE.

FIRST HEAD

Do.

THE BLEEDING EDGE

SECOND HEAD

Re.

THIRD HEAD

(a bit nasally)

Mi.

FOURTH HEAD

Fa.

FIFTH HEAD

So.

THE <u>CONDUCTOR</u> POINTS AT THE SIXTH HEAD. NO SOUND
EMERGES. THE <u>CONDUCTOR</u> POINTS HIS BATON AT THE
HEAD AGAIN. <u>IT</u> KEEPS ITS LIPS SEALED. THE <u>CONDUC-
TOR</u> MAKES THE SOUND OF "LA" HE WANTS. THE <u>HEAD</u> RE-
FUSES TO COOPERATE. THE <u>CONDUCTOR</u> BECOMES VISIBLY
ENRAGED. <u>HE</u> WALKS OVER TO THE HEAD.

CONDUCTOR

(in anger)

La!

NOTHING.

                    CONDUCTOR

                                        <u>La</u>!

NO RESPONSE.

                    CONDUCTOR
                (He raps the head with
            his baton as he sings the note.)
                                        <u>La</u>!

THE <u>HEAD</u> BLINKS ITS EYES BUT IS OBDURATE.

                    CONDUCTOR
            (The conductor raps it three times
                on the skull, accentuating
                each blow with a "La".)
                                    LA! LA! LA!

THE HEAD SPITS AT HIM. INCENSED, THE CONDUCTOR
SLAPS IT MIGHTILY, DISLODGING IT FROM ITS PLACE
SO THAT IT THUMPS DOWN ONTO THE STAGE AND ROLLS
ACROSS IT, CRYING OUT IN ALARM.

THE CONDUCTOR STALKS OVER TO IT AND PICKS IT UP
BY THE HAIR. IT WHIMPERS AS HE CARRIES IT BACK TO
ITS PLACE AND RE-HANGS IT. HE POINTS AT IT STERNLY
WITH THE INDEX FINGER OF HIS RIGHT HAND.

SIXTH HEAD

(meekly)

La.

SATISFIED BUT STILL EXCEEDINGLY VEXED, THE CONDUC-
TOR RETURNS TO THE STAND, GRABS UP HIS BATON AND
JABS IT FIERCELY AT EACH OF THE FIRST SEVEN HEADS.

FIRST HEAD

Do.

SECOND HEAD

Re.

THIRD HEAD

(still nasally)

Mi.

FOURTH HEAD

Fa.

FIFTH HEAD

So.

SIXTH HEAD

La.

SEVENTH HEAD

Ti.

THE <u>CONDUCTOR'S</u> BATON JABS TOWARD <u>HEAD NUMBER</u>
<u>EIGHT</u> WHICH EVOKES A NOTE NOWHERE NEAR WHAT HE IS
LOOKING FOR. <u>HE</u> FREEZES, GLARES AT HEAD NUMBER
EIGHT. JABS THE BATON AT IT AGAIN. <u>IT</u> SINGS THE

SAME NOTE AGAIN, TOTALLY SOUR, TOTALLY OFF-KEY.
THE <u>CONDUCTOR</u> SINGS THE NOTE HE WANTS. HE GETS
BACK THE SOUR ONE. <u>HE</u> SINGS THE CORRECT NOTE AGAIN
AND AGAIN, KEEPS GETTING THE CLINKER IN RETURN.

WITH A SUDDEN SNARL, <u>HE</u> FLINGS ASIDE THE BATON,
LUNGES AT THE OFFENDING HEAD, RIPS IT FROM ITS
PLACE AND HURLS IT OFF-STAGE WITH A CRY OF RAGE.
THEN <u>HE</u> STANDS, BREATHING HARD, COMPLETELY FRUS-
TRATED, THE <u>OTHER HEADS</u> LOOKING AT HIM APPREHEN-
SIVELY.

<u>HE</u> MAKES A DECISION NOW AND WALKS OFF STAGE. WE
HEAR A CHAIN SAW BEING STARTED. THE <u>SEVEN HEADS</u>
GRIMACE UNEASILY AS THERE IS A GHASTLY <u>SOUND</u> OF
CHAIN SAW BLADE CUTTING THROUGH FLESH AND BONE.
THE CHAIN SAW IS TURNED OFF. THE <u>CONDUCTOR</u> COMES
OUT CARRYING HIS OWN HEAD WHICH HE HANGS IN THE
EIGHTH SPOT. THE REST OF <u>HIM</u> MOVES TO PICK UP THE
FALLEN BATON, RETURNS TO THE MUSIC STAND AND RAPS
THE BATON LOUDLY ON IT. <u>HE</u> JABS THE BATON TOWARD
THE EIGHT HEADS, ONE AT A TIME.

<u>FIRST HEAD</u>

Do!

<u>SECOND HEAD</u>

Re!

THIRD HEAD

(nasally)

>Mi!

FOURTH HEAD

>Fa!

FIFTH HEAD

>So!

SIXTH HEAD

>La!

SEVENTH HEAD

>Ti!

CONDUCTOR'S HEAD

>Do-o-o-o!

PERFECT. THE <u>HEADLESS CONDUCTOR</u> OPENS THE MUSIC,
TAPS HIS BATON ON THE STAND, BEGINS TO CONDUCT.

<u>ALL EIGHT HEADS</u>

(in fine eight-part harmony)

<u>Put your head on my shoulder…</u>

BLACKOUT.

###

Richard Burton Matheson was one of the writers for the original *Twilight Zone* series, which set him on a career path that would encompass 50-plus years, establishing him as a towering force in dark fantasy and speculative fiction. Since that time, he has earned a well-deserved reputation as a master of suspense, science fiction and terror in the written (*Bid Time Return; I Am Legend; The Shrinking Man*) and cinematic worlds (*Dracula; Trilogy of Terror;* Roger Corman's *Poe* films). His penchant for comedy and musical composition are less acknowledged, but worthy of recognition, also.

Richard Christian Matheson is a novelist, short story writer and screenwriter/ producer. His fiction has been published in award-winning anthologies (*Year's Best Horror; Year's Best Fantasy*)as well as *Penthouse* and *Omni* magazines. His stories are collected in *Dystopia* and *SCARS and Other Distinguishing Marks*, as introduced by Stephen King. His novel *Created By* was a Bram Stoker Award nominee. He has written and co-written feature film and television projects for Richard Donner, Joel Silver, Steven Spielberg, Bryan Singer and many others, as well as taught college creative writing and screenwriting classes. An expert on the occult (having worked with the UCLA Parapsychology Labs investigating haunted houses, and paranormal phenomenon), Matheson has also been a professional drummer for over thirty years, (one of his instructors was legendary *Cream* drummer Ginger Baker) and worked as a studio musician. He plays drums with *SMASH-CUT* a rock band which includes fellow author Craig Spector, and Preston Sturges, Jr. Their debut album, *Dharma Rain*, was released in June '09.

The author (Richard B. Matheson) writes about this play:
"Richard (my son) and I wrote this for the *Grand Guignol* a number of years ago... To my knowledge, they never used it. I think it's funny -- ghastly enough for this anthology."

Hope and the Maiden

by Nancy Kilpatrick

*L*ife didn't seem as good as it once had been, but still, it wasn't hopeless, was it? Faith had had dreams, shattered now, but that didn't mean new dreams couldn't take the place of old ones. At least she'd been trying to convince herself of this -- a daily mantra -- and it was something Sherry told her too, again and again.

"Sweetie, you've got to get *out!* You're not gonna meet Mr. Right Goth Boi couch-potatoing it. Come with me Saturday to *Requiem*. It'll be cool. We'll get drunk, maybe get laid, have fun, like we used to."

Faith had last been to a goth club five years before, when she was trolling. When she met Jerold. She'd been a regular at this one -- it used to be called *The Sanctuary* -- one of the two clubs in the city back then. The other club, *Bella Donna*, crashed and burned. Now, *Requiem* served the entire goth community, mainly a younger clientele, and Faith, five years older, several lifetimes wiser, wondered if at pushing forty she had outgrown goth, or it had outgrown her.

The building looked the same, red brick, matte black door, up a couple of crumbly steps. The little brass gargoyle had been replaced by a small bat or dark moth or something, stencilled about eye level. Inside, the tiny coat check was still on the right, and a young thing with anorexic arms lifted a long velvet cape over the counter and handed the Marilyn Manson look-alike a ticket. Faith decided to keep her black leather jacket on. The club, if she remembered correctly, would be hot as hell -- no windows, little ventilation, lots of cigarette smoke and sweaty bodies -- all of which she needed protection from, even if she ended up perspiring like the proverbial Miss Piggy. Protection from what, she didn't know. Maybe from the vulnerability screaming at the edges of her consciousness. Soul-piercing screams that, as the night wore on, and the alcohol rolled down her throat, with any luck would dissipate to a blunt-edged roar.

Sherry checked her faux leopard coat, and they paid the cover and had the insides of their wrists stamped with a 'Fuck You' in black by a large red-headed guy wearing at least thirty rings in each ear, and one in his nose. Faith wondered if, like Jerold, he had one in his dick.

Jerold had pierced himself at the front of his cock. "Prince Albert," he told her proudly, "had this done to enhance sensation. Queen Victoria loved it!" Jerold wore a thick stainless steel ring for a couple of months, and then decided too late that he didn't like the piercing. He ended up peeing out of both holes. Faith had wondered many times if he ejaculated out of both too, but he'd always been inside one of her orifices when he came, so she didn't know for sure.

Of course, she could have checked with the others, his long stream of bimbos, female and male. Jerold had an insatiable lust for young bodies, the more androgynous-looking the better. He liked them stick-thin, hairless, and bald if possible. Basically babies in Doc Martens with wide eyes and ready smiles formed on full, receptive lips. His lure had been drawings -- come up and see my etchings! She'd always thought that was sooooo lame, but to paraphrase P. T. Barnum, there's a goth sucker slithering out of a womb every minute, and god knows, that line had worked on her. At first.

Then the kindergoths began to stream, in endless numbers, to his warehouse studio. And at the beginning she believed him -- nothing sexual was happening -- even though she herself had gone there initially to be sketched, which had led to a sweet spring evening, with one of the huge multi-paned warehouse windows tilted open, and the glow from neon outside and a dozen fat black candles inside bathing their glistening bodies, while *Sisters of Mercy* sang "Lucretia", and they danced the ghost until dawn.

Now Faith had to face herself. Jerold had been a mega-perv. A pedophile even though his desirable ones were usually over the legal limit. Faith figured she'd been too old for Jerold's tastes. She knew she was no longer young, and maybe too decayed for this goth club, judging by the frail-looking, made-up-as-impending-death faces crowding the doorway.

She and Sherry stepped into darkness, down the dozen steps she could not see well but instinctively remembered. Bar still on the right, tables left, dance floor taking up most of the room. The decor had altered -- odd-looking machine and computer parts welded together replaced the coffin-shaped light fixtures and crosses, and reflective silver metallic curtains hung where lush red velvet once had reigned.

"Friday's 80s music and Dark Wave," Sherry had assured her, but nothing recognizable came from the DJ's booth. The beat was closer to techno than to industrial, and definitely not 80s goth. She hated the hard pounding of techno, and what assaulted her ears felt nearly unbearable. Just as Faith was about to tell Sherry this wasn't the best idea of the century and she was outta here, the music changed. *Rammstein.* Industrial, at least. Sound ground from the speakers, people rushed the dance floor, and Faith stood watching the classic goth dance movements that had not, thank god, changed in five years. Women in PVC mini-skirts and leather bustiers, guys with more hardware than velvet -- the current vogue it seemed -- over black pants and shirts, all doing the forward/backward lean thing, feet planted in the earth, waving their arms in symbolic movements, making air pictures that spoke of their lives, their hopes and despairs, their joys and frustrations, and -- if you could read the signs -- their fate.

Sherry tugged her elbow and Faith followed to a cafe-sized table in the far corner. They shoved empty beer bottles aside just as a busboy came to pick them up and place them in the empty carton he carried.

"Want a beer?" Sherry asked.

"Why not?"

"What?"

"Anything."

Faith sat resting her chin on her folded hands, staring at the crowd, trying to will herself to want to be here. Everything had changed, and nothing had. Five years ago she had sat, if not at this very table at one close by, watching people dance, watching Jerold, his six foot frame sturdy, powerful, yet at the same time somehow achingly graceful and fluid. The soul of the sensitive artist shone through in his every gesture. Slightly older than her, he wore his decades like wisdom, and they often joked about being the grandparents of the then current crop of goth babies, although that didn't stop granddaddy from diddling them.

Jerold had noticed her from across the room. He was not a game player at all, but focused all his attention on her, letting her know he knew she was looking, and he was too, his eyes mesmerizing.

She had wondered then if he would be a good lover. Later that night she found out. Aggressive and directed, unlike half of the goth boys she'd gone home with, he'd had no trouble getting and keeping a hard-on.

That night they fucked endless times at his studio, until the silver dawn faded the ebony sky, and she heard happy birds, and early Sunday morning traffic cranking up. They slept for a few hours, had sex some more, ate leftover cheese and drank the dregs of the wine, and spent that day and the next and the next together. Jerold, who couldn't believe her age because in his eyes she looked twenty-five and not thirty-five, insisted on sketching her over and over, until he had littered his studio floor with full and partial drawings of her naked body, legs spread lustfully, nipples taut, innocent blue eyes peering through the strands of black hair he'd artfully arranged as a veil over her face, a sly, vixen grin upon her lips.

One thing led to another, and they were a dynamic duo. *A great team*, she thought. They had a life, together, and he promised her it would grow and change, leading to marriage and children and "An Addams Family house of our own," which gave her a giggle. These were all the things she wanted and, until she met Jerold, hadn't really known she'd needed to fulfill her. And she hadn't known she'd needed him either, until he was gone.

Her flare-ups at his suspected indiscretions brought rebuke from him that made her feel silly and petty and paranoid. She was ruining everything, he said, their dreams. As an artist, he needed models, all the time, he reminded her. He couldn't just draw her, could he? "Did Rossetti only paint Lizzie?" She needed to know that, and respect his ways. And she did, despite some obvious looks between him and his model *du jour*, and even in the face of hurtful rumors that found their way to her ears, overt and covert.

And then, inexplicably, one day, everything morphed. She awoke and felt differently. It was almost as though the betrayals had built to an Everest of disappointment, and she had silently and gradually and imperceptibly slipped down an invisible crevice until her heart felt bruised to within an inch of its life. She no longer wanted to be with him. She still loved Jerold, but now, instead of "Lucretia", "This Corrosion" felt like the only way to describe what was left. She'd had enough, and told him so, hoping he would say or do something to soothe her pain, to make things right. But he hadn't cared, which created amidst the bruising a wound that felt as if her heart had been severed.

"This Corrosion" was the next song in the line-up, synchronizing her inner and outer reality, not surprising at all to Faith. Synchronicity had tailed her all her life, for good or ill, and now it appeared like an old friend you're sometimes glad to see and at other times, well, you wish it was something else consuming your energy.

Everybody loved *Sisters'* classic music, even these young things that would have been lucky to have been in black diapers when the band began recording. The dance floor crammed further, to overflowing.

Faith perused the crowd, searching for something interesting of legal age. There wasn't much. Somehow, goths had gotten younger, while she'd gotten older. Here and there she thought she saw a face she recognized from half a decade ago, but the looks in this scene were reinvented constantly. She saw one guy she did not recognize, but who seemed interesting, black hair tied back in a ponytail, fishnet shirt with the sleeves ripped out to reveal upper arms with sculpted muscles painted with black swirly tribal tattoos.

A couple of size-zero girls danced so close to the seating area they bumped into Sherry's chair. One of them scowled at the chair, as if it were somehow responsible for being in her path.

Faith laughed suddenly. *Youth,* she thought, *never changes.* And then she felt horrified that she had placed herself into the 'adult' category. She squelched the vomit rising from her gut, a sense of being unable to digest such awareness here, now, ever.

Gradually *Sisters* worked their magic, and she felt the urge to dance, but couldn't overcome her hyper self-awareness without help.

Help arrived when Sherry plunked down two bottles of Black Label. "All they had," she said, elbowing past the dancing-virgins duo, "except for the imported stuff." The minute she was seated, Sherry took a big swallow of beer, and Faith joined her.

The beer tasted sharp and salty; Faith was already suffering from the accelerated temperature created by the tightly-packed crowd, but she refused to remove her jacket. Another deep swallow to slake her thirst and she set the half empty bottle onto the table. The alcohol couldn't have reached her bloodstream yet, but the act of drinking it allowed her to relax into the state she knew would come.

"War" played next, intense, driving, aggressive. One of Jerold's favorite bands. Long defunct. Like Jerold in her life.

"So, listen," Sherry said suddenly, "there's this booze can everybody goes to; we can check it out later, okay? They don't let the babies in, because it's, well, kind of illegal, you know, selling drinks after hours, and it's usually cool. It's not just goth, but everybody is okay."

Faith did not feel much like checking out another club. She glanced at her watch -- they'd come late, always the smart thing to do, and the bar would close soon. Then, suddenly she panicked about the immediate future which created a mental picture where she saw herself in her bed alone, again, in her too-quiet apartment. *We'll see about the booze can*, she thought, but said, "Sure, why not," wishing a second later that she hadn't committed herself.

Two beers down the road and she found herself on the dance floor. Beneath her well-worn Fluevog Angels, the slightly bouncy tiles let her feel as if she could ascend into the air, as if the earth beneath her vibrated, but she knew she was just loose, ready to release a shit-load of frustration. The music rode her backbone, up and down, settling every few minutes in her pelvis, then reverberated deep within her organs, a reliable lover, rocking her body in a wave of passion divorced from thinking. She'd forgotten how much she loved dancing. Almost as good as sex. But she'd forgotten about sex, too.

When *Requiem* closed and the Children of This Particular Night began flowing out onto the street like a dark mist, and while she and Sherry waited in a line at the coat check for Sherry to get her leopard spots, Faith took a step back to make room for the crowd and bumped into someone behind her.

She gasped at the contact and spun around. The guy with the ponytail gave her face the instant once-over, apparently liked what he saw, and then grinned at her. She focused for a second on his lipring, and then smiled back. "Sorry."

As she looked away he said confidently, "I'm not."

She flashed him a quick smile, finally turning back for good. Flirting was fun, always. But she had no intention of picking up somebody at the end of a night, when desperation fueled action, and regret was about the only thing you could expect to wake up to. Hell, she hadn't drunk enough beer for that! Besides, he couldn't be older than twenty-five.

Outside in the cool air, Sherry said, "Let's cab it. Maybe six blocks. You okay with that?"

Now Faith remembered the booze can they were supposed to go to, and wondered how she could get out of it. She began a protest, but Sherry said, "Oh, come on! Look, tomorrow is Sunday, nothing happens Sunday, then Monday we both go back to work, so at least give yourself something to *not* talk about this week over the water cooler!"

Faith was just about to begin a reasonable protest when she stopped talking to stare at the most unusual girl she'd ever seen -- how the hell had she missed her? Must be at least six feet tall. Prerequisite thin. More industrial than goth, wearing midnight PVC that covered her neck to wrists and ankles. Pale bald head, big pouty lips, labret through her left eyebrow, a barbell in her tongue that glinted under the streetlight, large luminous eyes that met Faith's, blinked once, continued to stare, until the ponytailed guy moved left and blocked Faith's view.

Sherry was busy hailing a taxi. One pulled to the curb, Sherry opened the door, yanked on Faith's jacket sleeve, and the next thing Faith knew she was inside the cab speeding away, watching ponytail trying a tête-à-tête with the bald gurrrl, while another goth babe who had her arm around the girl's waist looked pissed.

Faith turned to face the front in time to hear Sherry say, "Don't worry, he comes every weekend. His name's Maurice, or Bernie or Frank or something like that, and no, I haven't slept with him." But it wasn't only ponytail that Faith was thinking about.

She woke to a buzzing noise. Once her eyelids pried themselves apart, Faith realized it was the damned alarm clock, which she'd forgotten to unset. She tried to glare at it, but the hangover precluded too much facial action and diluted evil feelings.

Then the baby in the apartment next door began to shriek. *Great! Just great!* she thought, covering her head with the pillow. *Another perfect Sunday morning.*

The booze can had been boring. Sleazy guys, stupid blond bimbos, expensive beer that Faith had had too much of, and yet another taxi ride home at God-knows-when and now here it was nearly time for Sunday dinner at her mom's where she would get the usual 'When are you getting married and giving me grandchildren' speech, and her head hurt and she felt like puking. At least she hadn't been so wasted she'd dragged some perv home and screwed a guy without a condom because she was so out of it and would end up with a disease or two or having to take the nausea-producing morning-after pill, plus having to entertain some moron who might rip off her stuff.

God, wasn't clubbing fun? She'd forgotten about it. Gee, she'd have to go again next weekend! "Never fucking again!" she snarled, throwing the alarm clock against the wall.

But that's exactly what she did. Friday night, at *Requiem*, much to her amazement, at the same table, with Sherry. "I guess I'm a regular again," she yelled grimly at her friend, who took a big swallow of beer, pointed the head of the bottle at and nodded towards the door, and Faith looked that way and saw the guy with the ponytail.

He's still cute, she thought. *But do I need cute?* She downed the rest of her beer, lifted the empty bottle into the air; Sherry nodded, and Faith got up and moved towards the bar. She and ponytail arrived at the same moment, colliding again.

They turned simultaneously. His pale eyes seemed to emit light in the glow of the bar's candles. Heat swirled around her body, starting at her genitals, ending at her genitals, forcing her to breathe rapidly through her nose. *He's hot,* she realized, really *hot! And so am I!* She felt embarrassed. A little. But didn't shy away from his blatant 'fuck me' stare.

"Wicked cross," she said, picking up the ankh adorned with Celtic scrawls that hung around his neck. Her knuckles brushed his chest, and she quivered. She just wanted to touch him, even his shirt. Something. Anything! And why couldn't she think clearly right now?

"Is it just the cross you like?" he said brazenly.

"Want to fuck me?" she blurted out. *Oh my god, what did I say?*

He didn't answer, just grinned, took her hand and led her to the washroom area. *What the hell?* she thought, then thought, *I'm not drunk enough for this. Or am I? I don't have a condom, he must.* How long had it been since she'd had sex? She couldn't remember now, but what she knew for sure was that the sensations were a tidal wave, building in intensity moment by moment, and she found herself trembling. Thoughts vanished as if she'd never had a brain.

They arrived at the three unisex cubicles, two with opaque glass lighted doors you couldn't see through, the third one with a glass door that worked with the light inside to allow those waiting to see the silhouette of the occupant or occupants. Through that door a shadow entertained the small group of waiters, a guy peeing into a urinal, and she was glad ponytail pulled her into the next available, since Faith had never liked putting on a show for strangers, even if it was her shadow starring.

He bolted the door, and instantly they were at each other, lips sucking lips -- the ball of his lipring warm sensuous metal mixed with slippery fleshy mouth. They pulled at one another's clothing like two rapists. His hard cock stabbed at her stomach. Her hand stroked the hot flesh and she grinned, remembering what all this was about.

His lips discovered her nipples, and nipped at one, then the other, in quick succession, forcing little gaspy cries out of her mouth. He tugged on her nipple rings, twisting, turning, making the flesh burn, driving her crazy with the ecstasy of pain. Moisture seeped between her legs, coating her thighs, and he discovered that wetness when his fingers slid up inside her.

God, she wanted to taste that cock! She shoved him back hard, pulling his fingers away from her nipples and out of her vag, forcing him against the sink. She squatted before him, still wearing her boots and skirt but no underwear, her legs spread, butt bare, and took his flesh into her mouth like a woman starving. Hot lava flowed out of her as she sucked on him and her vagina spasmed in anticipation. Her little moans surrounded his cock. She licked and sucked, her eyes closed, her naked butt inches from the cement floor, all that hot moisture dripping, dripping, waiting to ignite.

Suddenly he lifted her up by the waist and slammed her down onto his cock with perfect marksmanship. She felt staked, desired. Heat rushed in on her in waves. She wrapped her legs tight around his hips. Hands gripped her buttocks, sending more sensations through her. He lifted her up a little, then down, again and again. She grabbed his head and her head fell back as she cried out an orgasm that rocked her for so long she felt it would tear her apart. It would never end, it could never end...

But it did.

She came.

He came.

They washed up, dressed -- all the while Faith swamped by worries about having unprotected sex, about AIDS, about pregnancy, about what a slut Jerold had turned her into -- then they opened the bathroom door to find a stony-faced Robert Smith clone, just past the age of majority, black jeans, spiky dog collar around his throat, t-shirt with *The Cure* silk-screened on the front in Gothic lettering, looking every which way but at them.

But Faith felt good. Really good. She'd forgotten how great sex was. As they reached the table, Sherry's eyes grew round and large and her mouth threatened to drop open. Faith sat, and ponytail whispered in her ear, his steamy breath getting her excited all over again, "Want a beer?"

She nodded.

He didn't ask what kind, just turned and headed towards the

bar.

Sherry leaned over and shrieked, "You fucked him in the bathroom?"

"Yeah," Faith said, stretching out the word, grinning, being playful, and trying not to feel guilty.

Sherry laughed and shook her head. "Way to go, my hungry friend. Get 'em early in the night so you can get it a couple more times, right?"

"That's the plan!" Faith chirped. *Yeah,* she thought, *I could fuck this guy all night and all day and still be horny.* She laughed at herself. Despite the guilt, she felt *really* awesome.

Trisome 21 played that light song she never knew the name of, the one that brought every woman in the room to the dance floor. She couldn't help herself. She leapt to her feet, rocking and swaying, moving her arms and creating air pictures that spoke of love and faith and renewal. She felt the oh-so-ungoth smile on her lips, but what could she do? In moments, life had gone from dismal to glorious, and nothing could bring her down.

Except what she saw.

Ponytail. At the bar. With the tall, lean bald gurrrl from the week before -- at least she thought it was her. Faith stopped dancing and just stared as the two kissed and groped as if they were alone in the room.

Her body turned to lead. Feeling unloved, unlovable, she stomped back to the table. She grabbed her jacket off the back of the chair, and as Sherry looked up she said, "I'm outta here."

Before Sherry could say or do anything, Faith turned and raced to the stairs, taking them two at a time, as if she were on fire and only the cool night air could put out the flames.

She walked quickly without being aware of the direction, seeing nothing, feeling betrayed all over again, and she didn't even know this guy's name! Hadn't even had time to offer her heart on a Victorian silver platter like she did with Jerold. *Life is fucked!* she thought, *and men really are the most fucked!*

Her rage got her home, into a shower of cold water that poured over her head, along her teary face, down the length of her slumped body and washed all traces of him and the immediate sadness down the drain. Now she just had the usual despair to contend with. And a worry about HIV or some other STD, and getting knocked up. And she hated herself for being so cheap as to screw a total stranger in a bathroom!

Over the following week, her psyche returned to a semblance

of normality. Faith got her period, so at least one worry vanished, yet somehow that left her feeling disappointed. *Stupid,* she thought, *the biological clock thing...* and she forced herself to not dwell on it.

Sherry phoned, talked about the rest of the night at *Requiem,* finally got bits and pieces out of Faith about ponytail, claimed she didn't see the bald gurrrl and him -- "They probably left together," Faith assured her -- then Sherry changed the subject to what she was dying to talk about, the Oriental boy she took home and had been fucking all week. *Great,* Faith thought bitterly, *at least somebody's lucky in love.* But the moment she felt that icy, barbed wire snake around her damaged heart, she was horrified at how bitter she'd become. So much so that she couldn't even take delight in her friend's happiness.

When Sherry wanted her to go to *Requiem* again on the weekend, Faith felt guilty and said yes, although it was the last place she wanted to be. Still, she knew she had nothing better to do. Except go for an HIV test, which she did after work on Thursday night. They told her to come back next week for the results, and assured her she was low risk. But she'd have to return in three months and take the test again before she'd know for sure. And, they reminded her, next time, wear a condom! *Next time? There wouldn't be a next time!* Tonight, Faith would keep a handle on her brain!

Friday night. Same club, same table. Same beer. Like an episodic TV show, the plot had moved along but the set and characters never changed. Tonight, ponytail was absent, but the bald gurrrl, who seemed to be so-damned-attractive-to-everybody-and-their-iguana, was present. Stirring it up on the dance floor. Faith could only see her head again, but this time she got a closer look. A skull a craniologist would die for, round and smooth, depressions in the right spots, perfectly symmetrical. Large, waif eyes, as if they were liquid and would drip down her face at any moment. Cheekbones carved by some pre-Raphaelite artist. Huge lips that made her look starved and sorrowful, and as if she would suck on anything. *But then,* Faith thought, *so will I, apparently!*

The bald gurrrl seemed to float, her head never jerking or bobbing, just smoothly rocking, as if she picked up the most subtle undercurrents of the music and plugged in. Most of the time she kept her eyes closed, but once Faith saw her stare at a small guy wearing stainless steel shin- and armguards and within seconds he was dancing in front of her -- not with her, since that just didn't happen in a goth club -- but staring, and it was fucking obvious what he wanted. Faith watched them hook up, talk for a while, then leave the bar, well, she saw the head of the bald gurrrl, and caught the flash of metal as the little industrial guy trailing after her frantically passed beneath a red spotlight near the stairs, struggling to keep up with those long legs.

Later, ponytail entered, scanning the room. He spotted Faith

-- Sherry took time away from her fragile-looking Oriental boi-toi to report that -- but it wasn't her he wanted, that was obvious. Faith, totally disinterested in games with this guy, tracked his movements without trying to disguise what she was doing. She caught him checking out shadowy corners, knew who he was searching for and, when he couldn't find the gurrrl, only then did he give Faith a second glance. She laughed loudly and bitterly, causing Sherry and the boi to jerk their heads in her direction. The emitted fury, or desperation, or whatever, must have sprayed across the room, because he didn't waste a second pretending to ignore her after that, he ignored her for real.

Somehow, the fact that the bald gurrrl had departed with metal man made Faith feel vindicated, though she couldn't have said why. Guys were pigs. No morals. She knew it, felt it, believed it. Maybe it was time for a female. It wouldn't be her first, but it had been quite a while. She finished off the beer in her bottle and headed to the bar to buy a round for the table.

As time danced on, Faith hit despair. Everything around her turned acidic. Fearful of touching anything or anyone, of being burned, she crawled inside a rock-hard bubble. Her life, it seemed to her, had been wasted on a planet where pretence was the norm, and honesty, love, caring and commitment were too frequently manufactured and only useful as a means of controlling the person who still lived out such obsolete emotions. Jerold, if not the final nail in her coffin, had likely been next to the last. Now she was fucking guys in bathrooms of bars, guys who then dumped her for someone else within minutes. And she might -- *oh please God, no!* -- have contracted a disease out of it because her passion got away from her. A passion borne of starvation, for sex, for love, warmth, intimacy, caring. God, she was a mess!

Nobody's fool, Faith wouldn't open up again. Part of her wanted to go home to safety, but the emptiness waiting there terrified her. She would hang on here, not wanting anyone or anything, not waiting even, just being, assured of disappointment in advance, so what was the use of caring? The barbed wire around her heart now had a lock affixed, and she would place one around her vagina as well. Maybe she could learn to live vicariously.

She glanced at Sherry from time to time, wrapped around the boi with blue hair and almond eyes, lips touching lips and ears and necks, hands groping, faces smiling, bodies alive with sexual tension. *Save it for the bedroom!* Faith wanted to snarl, but had she been any better? *Where do you go when you're forty?* She didn't know, and it didn't seem like anybody else did either.

Sometime later, she watched ponytail make a move on a little moth wearing black feathered wings on her back, wings that people kept accidentally bumping into, which brought a scowl to her pixie face and turned her momentarily into a flying screw. The girl was thirtyish, both too old and too young for instant sex in the can with a stranger, her hormones rock solidly in the middle of womanhood and power. Faith enjoyed ponytail's multiple rejections, payback for her own missed multiple orgasms. But in the end it gave her no real joy, just a quick jolt to her embittered self like a hit of coke that wore off before it had even been paid for.

"You're depressed," Sherry said, when the boi went outside to smoke a joint.

"Oh, you're a psychiatrist?" Faith said coldly.

"Look, go dance or something. Mingle. Forgive the guy with the tail or fuck him again so at least you get laid. *Do* something!"

"I'm not interested in getting fucked by an asshole. And don't psycho babble at me, Sher. I don't need it, and you're lousy at it."

Sherry, too happy with new-found romance to be put off by Faith's pain-in-the-ass cynicism, said cheerfully, "Well, you need *something*. Go check yourself in a mirror. You look like somebody died, and maybe it was you. Life's short, you know."

"Not short enough! And if I'm raining on your lovers' parade, just say so and I'll leave."

"Come on, Faith, I'm worried, okay? You been sitting there snapping at me and scowling at everybody for hours. You can't be having fun. And nothing's gonna come your way with that attitude. Lighten up. Forget all the stuff you're worried about; it'll be there tomorrow."

Faith stood and picked up her jacket.

"What? Now I've like insulted you or something?"

"No. Don't worry about it, Sher. I just need air. I'm going for a walk. I'll be back."

"The bar's closing in an hour."

"Well, if I'm not back, I'll call you. Don't worry, okay. I'm alright. I just need to get out of here."

Before Sherry could say anything more, Faith dragged her dismal self towards the door, breezing past ponytail, alone at the bar, who started to say something, but she kept walking. She didn't want to worry Sherry, but she'd been down so long tonight she was beginning to feel if not up at least less in pain, in a perverse way. She was drunk by two too many beers. *This can't go on,* she thought, and she knew she would have to struggle to remember that thought tomorrow when she awoke with a hangover, alone.

Outside, the air revived her spirits in a real way. She took a deep breath, inhaled exhaust, exhaled it fast, then another breath and got something cleaner. Above, a bright full moon lit the sky like a night sun. That, plus all the high-rise lights meant no stars could be seen, shooting or otherwise, but she wasn't into wishing on a star anyway -- she'd probably used up her quota. Suddenly, she didn't feel half bad, and began walking north, towards the water, instead of south towards her apartment. She fired up the joint Sherry had passed her earlier, smoking as she wandered the quiet streets.

It's people, she thought, *that make me crazy. Maybe I'm better off alone. I don't need their shit. I can entertain myself. And I can masturbate and get myself off better than most guys.*

Her pace picked up and she snapped her jacket closed against the cool air. This time of night, the bars hadn't let out yet, so the streets were emptier than they would be in a little while. It was a great time for a walk. Just her and her thoughts and none of the murky madness to distract her from reality.

Jerold was a monster, in his own way. He'd used her, abused her, and love was what clouded her vision and kept her from seeing him clearly. Love, always the problem, made her do things that benefited him and not her. And what was love but need. Pure loneliness. Maybe, if she caught that loneliness, tried to nip it in the bud instead of letting it flower and then rot inside her, maybe she could make some better choices, so she wouldn't end up in despair, emotionally black and blue all the time. It was a plan worth trying out.

Down by the water, the lights from this shore and the shore on the opposite side glittered on the lake's surface, mirroring everything around. Mirroring her as well. She gazed into the dark liquid, rippling gently, and saw herself clearly. She wasn't half bad. Not by half. Still young enough, still hot, she had a lot going for her. She just needed to think a bit before she acted, and think good things about herself, not just that she suffered loneliness all the time. Think about what she wanted, and how to get it. And cut the love crap, because that was the thing that did her in every fucking time. It was too late for love. Maybe it always had been.

A clock in the city hall tower struck the half hour. The bar would close in thirty minutes. Renewed, she hurried back. She wanted to give Sherry a hug, tell her how much she appreciated her friendship, and let her know that things would be different from now on.

Inside, the place was still alive with sound and people. She made her way to the table, but it was empty. Apparently Sherry and her boi had left. Well, that was okay. Faith glanced around, noting she didn't see ponytail either. *Who needs them?* she thought. *Who needs anybody?* Not her, not tonight.

She found Sherry's half empty bottle of beer on the table and drained it. The song changed, and that song about God having a sick sense of humor came on. She *loved* that one! Faith leapt to her feet and ran to the dance floor, feeling pretty good about herself, about life, about everything.

She danced that song, and the next two, eyes closed, rocking, grabbing the fastest part of the beat, letting energy flow through her. How could you feel this good and survive? She didn't know, but it didn't matter, she just wanted it to last forever, or at least the rest of the night.

And then, suddenly, there was the bald gurrrl, in front of her, smiling. Luscious lips, liquid fire eyes. Oh, what a beauty! They stared at one another, invisible ley lines binding them, and smiled and laughed together, dancing song after song, until last call, and then the music died and they were left alone together on the dance floor, touching through Faith's leather jacket, and the gurrrl's latex shirt. They walked to the door, the gurrrl got her coat, and outside, without a thought or a question, they grabbed a cab and Faith brought her home, the only conversation when she said, "My name is Faith."

"I'm Hope."

They looked at one another and said simultaneously, "Where's Charity?" and laughed.

The booze, the dope, the night, those eyes ready to melt her, all of it made Faith act. They stripped inside the door, without turning on the lights, and Faith led this tall gurrrl to her bed. They fell onto it, touching, sliding hands over soft flesh and the taut muscle beneath. The gurrrl found her breasts, first with her fingers, then with her tongue, sucking and lifting as only a woman can. Delicious wet heat coated Faith's nipples and the aureoles and her head fell back and she thrust her chest out wantonly, wanting more, wanting everything this gurrrl had to offer.

Fingers slid inside moist vaginas, then tongues, acting like fingers, acting like penises, licking in a way that made knowledge of the anatomy evident. Faith moaned shamelessly, luxuriating in the pleasure of this encounter that already fulfilled her. Then an unexpected orgasm rocked her to her roots, but the bald gurrrl did not stop, she brought Faith higher, licking her clitoris until it burned, then exploded in flame and Faith fell into glorious exhaustion. Still, she pulled herself together to crawl the length of that long lean body investigating crevices and curves, licking at the hairless crotch, sliding her tongue between the sweet wet vaginal folds, happy for every elicited twitch and shiver and tremble she produced, licking and sucking harder, clutching the gurrrls small hard nipples and twisting them, grabbing her bottom and kneading the flesh and sliding a finger into that small nether hole, delighting in the out-of-control response her efforts produced. And then a searing cry, a pain/pleasure scream, while flesh writhed and spasmed, and Faith didn't let up until everything reduced to silence and stillness.

They lay side by side, holding one another for the longest time, until Faith stretched over and lit the three candles in the holder by the bed, and the gurrrl reached for a pack of cigarettes in her purse and lit two, old-French-movie style, and they both laughed at that unspoken allusion.

Somehow Faith felt no need for words, and Hope didn't either, it seemed. They lay smoking until Faith smashed her cigarette butt in the ashtray and turned towards this Hope gurrrl, seeing her clearly for the first time in the candleglow.

Tattoos stained flesh, every inch, from neck to ankles and wrists. Most were black tats, but a few had been shaded grey, or were inked in with color. They swirled from her wrists, up her arms, along her shoulders, cascading down her chest and around the swell of breasts, across the soft roundness of belly, over hips, snaking legs, and back again. Only the hands and feet were clean, and her neck from the shoulders up. Everywhere else her skin came alive with fleshy artwork that at first glance seemed chaotic. Faith sat up and studied the torso, the gurrrl lying still as a canvas. With concentration, she could see some tats formed identifiable and common images: bat, crow, wolf, the Medusa, a gargoyle, a vampire face, all dark yet familiar. Others swept up and around with no pattern, conveying feelings of comfort as her eye followed the graceful curves. Faith traced one movement with her fingertip and soon realized that all the lines intersected like an Escher and transformed from one image or pattern to another like Picasso's artwork, blending to abandon what they had been as they evolved into what they would become, on and on. Stories formed, of lives lived, love found and lost, fortunes created and destroyed. Babies birthed, and a dead infant asleep forever in a coffin like a Victorian death daguerreotype; Faith watched the box sink into the ground then transform into a woman in widow's weeds, weeping as if her heart had been torn from her chest. Faith looked closer. The heart was still there, in the center of the chest! Beating weakly. Bound with barbed wire that cut into it until it bled like the sacred heart, tears of blood spreading across the universe, a red haze blurring everything, leaving nothing untainted, and there the story ended with Faith sobbing.

The gurrrl of Hope with the moist eyes pulled her close, and whispered in her ear, hot breath swirling like a mist inside her, "Everybody has a story. And they're all sad. People find me when they need me and their broken lives impress themselves on me and through me they finally see their fate." She paused. "Life is endless disappointments."

Faith suddenly understood the bald head, the cadaverous body, the dark smudges of despair beneath those eyes that spoke of impending demise. The truth jolted her. She pulled back to examine this gurrrl named Hope, so alluring in too many ways. Hope. The one thing Pandora kept forever, hidden in her box.

No one, she realized, *has a corner on sorrow, or loss, or on the loss of what has never been.* Comfort manifests in strange forms: a fading rose, an eroded tombstone, a chilly slivered moon slicing through the dead black sky, and all the other swirling mournful images that define humanity as it blindly stumbles towards oblivion.

It isn't good, Faith thought, *not at all.* She looked at the gurrrl.

She had Hope, at least for tonight. And for that small gift from the universe that assuaged the agony of existence, she breathed a silent prayer of gratitude. But even as the breath left her body, Faith recognized the stark truth: tomorrow, and for all the tomorrows to come, Hope would be gone.

Award-winning author **Nancy Kilpatrick** has published 18 novels, around 200 short stories, one non-fiction book and has edited several anthologies. She writes

mainly horror, dark fantasy, mysteries and erotica and has been working on two new novels over the last year. Her most recent short fiction has appeared in: *Blood Lite* (Pocket Books); *Bits of the Dead* (Coscom Entertainment); *The Living Dead* (Nightshade Books); and *Traps* (DarkHart Press). Look for upcoming stories in: *Darkness on the Edge* (PS Publishing); *The Moonstone Book of Zombies; The Moonstone Book of Vampires* (both from Moonstone Books); *By Blood We Live* (Night Shade Books) and *Don Juan and Men* (MLR Press). She has just finished co-editing, with David Morrell, *Tesseracts 13*, an all horror/dark fantasy anthology for Edge Publishing. Currently she is editing her 10th anthology, the all-vampire *Evolve*, to be launched at the *WHC 2010,* Brighton. You can check out Nancy's latest at her website:

www.nancykilpatrick.com

What the author writes about this story:

"On one level, this story clearly is about the goth world. But it's also about the world in general, and growing older. Most people, whether or not they are artistic and/or counter-culture types, hit a time in their lives when they can no longer romp comfortably in the realms they once played in so freely, yet they don't exactly mesh with the so-called status quo. Add to that the fact that when you're twenty and single, everyone else is single too; when you're single at forty (or fifty plus) -- let's just say that the number of solos dwindles as your personal years increase. I wanted to show what that state feels like and especially the effects on women in our youth-oriented culture. I think anyone pushing forty feels at least a wee bit awkward. Things aren't what they were, and usually there's not much of a sense of where to go from here. This is what the French have deemed 'little deaths' that we all experience throughout our lives as we head towards the Big D. I hope I've captured some of that in 'Hope and the Maiden'."

The Death and Life of Caesar LaRue

by Earl Hamner, Jr.

Max Gehrig was seated at his porcelain-covered dissecting table late that afternoon. He was absorbed in the work at hand. A customer had brought in a sixty-pound Chinook salmon to be mounted, and Max had already removed the skin and had it soaking in the embalming fluid. He was in the process of carving the balsawood frame for the finished mount when she entered.

"Do you do snakes?"

"What did you say?" called Max. He set aside his carving and gazed at the vision that was approaching.

Her walk was a miracle of motion through space and time. Her pelvis was thrust slightly forward and the swivel of her hips caused Max to catch his breath. Her hair was long and blonde and flowed gracefully across her shoulders. She was dressed in a black leather jacket. Below the jacket appeared a band of bare abdomen graced with a two-carat diamond adroitly embedded in the navel. Continuing downward her leather pants clung so tightly to her torso that it might have passed as skin itself.

Max had only seen such women in films or pictured in magazines, and it was with a feeling of awe and wonder that he rose to meet her.

"Candy LaRue," she said and held out her hand.

There was a warm open sweetness about the woman, and Max felt a surge of longing and excitement he had not known in years.

Max accepted the outstretched hand. It was a warm, moist, strong hand, and as if hypnotized he held it until she gently and with an understanding smile withdrew it.

"I sure hope you do snakes," she announced and hauled up what appeared to be a large pet carrier.

"I never have, but I'm sure I could," said Max.

He watched in astonishment as she began extracting the limp body of a seven-foot-long boa constrictor from the pet carrier.

"His name is Caesar. Like the Palace in Vegas, you know," the woman explained. "I use him in my act down at *The Male Call*. You've probably been there?"

"I can't say I have," replied Max.

"Well, you've just got to come by and say hello. I'm the featured dancer, Caesar and me. Or was."

Max gazed at the body of the reptile. The worktable was six feet long. The body of the snake filled it completely, but even so a section of the tail drooped limply off one end.

"What was the cause of death?" he asked.

"I think he caught pneumonia or something," said Candy. "I'm going to have a little service for him, but I'll wait until he's all stuffed and everything. What's your name?"

Max told her his name and asked, "Do you have any special requirements?"

"Like what?" she asked.

"After I finish my work, I can display him in a special setting. A woodland setting, for instance, with some natural stones and grass, or coiled on a log with some autumn leaves around it, or resting on a rock, or however you like."

"He loved grass, just loved to go to the park. I think he'd like some grass."

"I'll come up with something," said Max.

"Just put a little plaque on it that says: Caesar   LaRue. He was all the family I had."

"How could that be?" inquired Max, his heart going out to the woman not only for the loss of her friend, but also for how deeply she must be experiencing that loss.

"Do you want me to pay you now, Max?" she asked, ignoring his question with a shrug.

"After I'm finished will be fine," he said.

"Just call me down at the club, and I'll come pick him up."

She touched the snake's head affectionately, and then with a catch in her throat she said, "He was my boy."

Max watched as she swiveled her way to the door. Just before she made her exit, she turned back and blew him a kiss and a smile. Max crossed to the door and watched in amazement until she was out of sight down the street.

Back at the table Max examined the snake. Its marbled skin was dull, but even in its lifeless state it was oddly beautiful. Max resolved to start working on it first thing the following morning. He considered storing the snake in the refrigerator overnight with the other specimens waiting for his attention, but then he reasoned that it would be easier to remove the skin at room temperature. He rearranged it so that its full length rested on the table and covered it with an old blanket.

Max closed the door to his workroom and entered the downstairs hallway. As he did so, he came face-to-face with his brother Tony and a woman. They had just entered the front door. Tony was still in his security guard uniform from the uptown bank where he worked, and the woman was also in a uniform that read "Street Services." Max guessed that she might be a meter maid.

As they started up the stairway, Max scowled at them.

When his lady companion shied away, Tony put his arm around her reassuringly and said, "It's just my dumb brother."

"You keep it quiet up there tonight," warned Max.

"Screw you," said Tony and mounted the stairs with his companion, who gave Max a sheepish smile.

Max could feel the anger that always surfaced when he encountered his younger brother. They had inherited the old brownstone jointly when their parents died. Tony had harassed his brother incessantly since the death of their parents. Tony was determined to sell the building. He tried every way possible to force Max to go along. Max so far had refused. He loved the neighborhood. He had grown up here, had friends here, and his business was here. Besides, if he sold the building, where would he move?

Tony devised one ploy after another to get Max out of the building. There was an apartment overhead. Tony had moved into it and stomped around night and day. Usually the noise did not bother Max. He enjoyed his work and frequently became so engrossed in what he was doing that he hardly heard the noise.

Tonight Max could not sleep. Visions of Candy LaRue floated through his mind, and he imagined what wonders were concealed underneath all that black leather. It did not help that his brother and his date were having sex in the room above. Max was certain his brother was what he thought of as a sex addict. Night after night he arrived home with some woman. At first the sounds of people walking around overhead would waken Max, then the booming of alarmingly loud music, and finally the screeching bedsprings and the moaning voices would jolt Max out of his sleep.

On this night he had endured all he could and just when the music of the bedsprings had become rhythmic and more frequent he found a broom and with the handle began beating on the ceiling.

In a moment silence fell in the room above, but then the phone on Max's bedside table began to ring.

Max picked up the receiver knowing it would be his brother.

"I'm going to break your damn neck, you son of a bitch!" shouted Tony.

"You keep it quiet up there," said Max. "I don't know about you people, but I need my sleep."

"You need your damn head examined," said his brother and slammed down the receiver.

It was well after midnight before the noise subsided and Max was finally able to sleep.

In the morning Max looked in the refrigerator at the work that lay ahead. There was a dog that had died of old age and his owners wanted stuffed, a pigeon an eccentric woman had fed in the park for several years that she had found dead on her morning rounds, a wild white squirrel someone fed until it had become a pet. But somehow the idea of mounting the boa constrictor seemed more interesting and challenging.

At his worktable he removed the blanket from the snake's body. Since he had never mounted a snake before he was not quite sure where to begin, but then he decided the principle was no different. So he felt along the body of the snake to get a general idea of its structure. When he reached the head of the creature and examined it, there was just the faint flicker of its forked tongue. At first Max reasoned that the flickering tongue might have been an involuntary reflex action, but when he cautiously touched the snake's head again the snake flicked its tongue a second time.

He certainly did not want to take a chance and stuff a live animal, so he called young Warren Berks who owned a small independent pet store several doors down the street. Their mutual interest in animals had brought about several collaborative events in the past and Warren promised to come by as soon as he could.

When he had finished examining the boa, Warren announced that it was definitely alive: "Starvation more than likely. Most of these people who keep them have no idea what their needs are."

Warren went back to his shop and returned with a concoction, which he said contained food and vitamins and injected it into the snake's mouth with an instrument that looked like a turkey baster.

"Keep it warm, and one more thing," Warren advised. "These guys are wild animals."

"This one's a pet," replied Max. "Woman uses it in her dance act."

"I don't care how many people use them in their acts. It's the boa's nature to suffocate other animals. I've got a really young one at the shop and it shut down on my arm once so strong I had to fight to get it unwound."

"So far it hasn't shown any signs of aggression," said Max.

"I'm just telling you to be careful. Keep your distance. And check with me in a day or two, and if it's still alive I can bring you some food."

The snake had so improved within four days that it showed interest in the white rat Warren delivered to the shop. Max and Warren watched as the boa cornered the rat and then somehow encircled it and then slowly began squeezing it tighter and tighter. When the snake released its grip, the rat fell to the floor. Caesar opened his mouth wide and began the gradual process of engorging the rat.

Before he left, Warren issued one last bit of information. "Don't ever try to handle this guy alone. They're strong as hell and can do the same thing to you he just did to that rat. And never turn your back on him."

Mindful of Warren's advice Max closed all the doors and windows to his workroom before he went to bed. The next morning when he entered the room the boa was nowhere to be seen. He searched everywhere without success. His anxiety had reached near to panic when he passed the pet carrier in which the snake had been delivered; and there, coiled and comfortable and very much alive, was Caesar. Max guessed it was a familiar place to the snake, it felt at home there, so that is where he kept it in the days that followed. Max resolved that as soon as he was absolutely sure that the snake was in good health again he would call Candy LaRue and share the good news.

But another matter drew his attention away from the snake. In the weeks that followed, Tony became so abusive that Max became suspicious that his brother was trying to kill him. A bomb designed to kill insects exploded inexplicably in Max's studio and he had difficulty getting outside. A shot was fired through the window of the basement room where Max worked, and it barely missed him. Max had his suspicions but no proof that it was his brother who was trying to do him in.

Another reason Max did not want to move was for the health of the snake. It was doing well, gaining weight, and seemed more and more alert. Each day brought it closer to the day when Max felt the boa was ready to be returned to its owner.

He telephoned Candy at *The Male Call* and invited her to come to the shop.

"How does he look?" she asked.

"You'll be surprised," he replied.

She was more than surprised. Max had ignored Warren's admonition and arranged Caesar on the same table where Candy had laid him out on that first visit.

She approached the table almost tearfully. "He looks wonderful," she cooed. "He looks just like he did when he was alive."

"He *is* alive," announced Max.

"What did you do? Are you some kind of miracle worker? Caesar, it's your mom!" she said and began stroking the snake, who flicked his tongue appreciatively.

And then to his surprise and delight, Candy threw her arms around Max. He was engulfed with the aroma of a good perfume and the warmth of that spectacular body.

It was then that Tony entered the room without even a knock or a how-do-you-do. Startled, Candy released Max from her embrace.

"My God," said Tony. "It's Candy LaRue!"

"Do I know you?" asked Candy as she adjusted her blouse over one of the breasts that appeared about to escape.

"Last Thursday night at *The Male Call!*" exclaimed Tony.

"Was that *you?*" she cried.

"Hundred-dollar bill -- right in the valley there," said Tony and pointed to the spot between her breasts.

"Oh," said Candy. "Wasn't that the nicest thing of you to do!"

Max observed this scene with a sinking heart. His brother had a way with women that he did not; and before he could demonstrate his own adoration of her, Tony had maneuvered Candy toward the door.

"This calls for a celebration!" Tony said.

"Come with us," Candy called to Max.

"Can't," said Tony. "He's got other plans."

"I'll be back for Caesar!" called Candy to Max, and then they were gone.

When he heard his brother arrive home later that night, Max phoned him and told him that he was ready to make some kind of arrangement about selling the brownstone.

"I'll be right down," said Tony.

Before his brother arrived, Max carried the pet carrier into the closet, opened the door to the cage, and closed the closet door behind him.

When Tony arrived, Max ushered him into his workroom and took a seat.

"Let's get right down to business," said Tony.

"That's exactly what I was hoping for," said Max. "There's some beer in the mini fridge there in the closet. Help yourself if you're thirsty."

"Since when did you start drinking beer?" demanded Tony.

"It's a surprise for you," answered Max.

Just as Tony entered the closet Max crossed the room, slammed the door shut, and turned the key in the lock.

"What the hell are you doing?" he heard his brother say. Max did not answer.

"Let me out of here, you bastard!" called Tony. "What's going on?"

And then his brother's voice took on a high shrill cry of urgency.

"Jesus Christ, Max, there's something moving around in here! For God's sake *open the door!*"

Max did not open the door until after the screams had subsided and all was quiet again. After a while he rose and checked his wallet. The hundred-dollar bill he had collected earlier at the bank was safely there. He could hardly wait to get to *The Male Call* and place it in the sweet and lovely valley of Candy LaRue.

Earl Hamner, Jr., television writer and producer, is probably best known
for his work in the 1970s and 1980s on
the long-running series *The Waltons* and
Falcon Crest.

The novel *Spencer's Mountain,* inspired
by his childhood in the South, formed the
basis for both the film of the same name
and *The Waltons*, which he created/nar-
rated. Hamner, a friend of Rod Serling,
also wrote eight episodes for the original
Twilight Zone. His first script acceptance
for the series was his big break in Hollywood.

What the author writes about this story:

"The model for Caesar Larue was not a boa, but a gopher snake. My neph-
ew, Nay Hankins, had been a counselor at a Boy Scout camp in Nevada.
When I picked him up at the airport he carried something large and writhing in a pillowcase. When we reached home he opened the pillowcase and
there on the floor of our living room was a five-foot long gopher snake.
Nay's fascination with snakes led me to learn more about them and to the
writing of this story."

A Certain Disquieting Darkness

by Gary A. Braunbeck

You should see the expression on your face right now -- all the trouble you've been through in order to get the clearance to interview me, and I start off by talking about household appliances and math instead of those twelve people I killed. Not that anyone gives more of a damn about them now than they did ten years ago -- after all, what'd the world lose? A dozen mental patients who were a drain on society's pocketbook. None of them were ever going to be released, they were lifers, and as far as I ever knew none of them had any living family.

Huh? Do I feel *bad* about it? What the fuck kind of Journalism 101 question is that? No, I don't feel bad -- I feel *horrible* about it. You weren't there, you didn't see those faces, those eyes... Christ. Those lonely, isolated, frightened eyes.

You want to know something that the news reports back then never mentioned? *Not a one of them tried to run away*, to get to safety. It was like shooting tin ducks at a carnival booth. Hell, some of them seemed to *welcome* it.

I tried to explain everything to the authorities at the time but I was pretty... out of control. No, wait, scratch that -- I was so fucking *scared* it was like I wasn't even *me* any longer, I was trapped somewhere inside myself just watching it all happen and... ah, never mind. But I'll tell you the same thing I told my lawyer and the court -- I was *not* insane. Not for one second.

As you can tell from our posh surroundings and this lovely canvas jacket with the wraparound arms that I'm sporting, they didn't believe me.

Look, it all started because Steve and I got this idea about using entrainment to visually illustrate how the human body can --

-- excuse me? Oh, sorry.

It's been proven that externally-imposed sound vibrations can have a profound influence on our physiology. We've all experienced this phenomenon -- it's called entrainment. Say you're sitting in your kitchen trying to balance your checkbook and you begin to notice that your shoulders are hunched up and your back is tighter than normal.

Suddenly the refrigerator snaps off and you heave a sigh of relief. Your shoulders drop, your back loosens up, and your whole breathing pattern changes. What do you think just happened? Certain biological rhythms have unconsciously "entrained" themselves to the 60 cycle hum of the refrigerator's motor.

Right -- *sound* caused your body to temporarily alter itself from within.

Think you can bear with me for a minute or two while I bore you with some specifics?

No, *Steve* was the Music major. I'm the Physics dude.

I was doing some research into the work of Hans Jenny. He was a Swiss doctor, artist, and researcher who helped pioneer the field of Cymatics -- which is basically a very specified and intensely focused form of entrainment, geared toward using sound and vibrational waves to heal the human body. He followed the work of a German physicist and acoustician named Ernst Chladni who, toward the end of the 18th Century, created intricate sand patterns by vibrating a steel plate with a violin bow. Jenny employed the modern technology of the day to carry out more precisely replicable experiments. He used a sine wave generator and a speaker to vibrate various powders, pastes, and liquids, and succeeded in making visible the subtle power through which sound *physically structures* matter.

Now, imagine hearing a tone, and watching as sound waves involute an inert blob of kaolin paste, animating it through various phases in a nearly perfect replica of cellular division -- or watching as a pile of sand is transformed into life-like flowing patterns, mirroring fractals -- the symmetrical geometric forms found in nature -- simply by *audible vibration*.

Jenny described our bodies as being "nested hierarchies of vibrational frequencies" which appear as discreet systems functioning within larger, more complicated systems, which themselves are contained within even larger and more complex vibrational structures, right? *All physical existence* is determined by vibrational frequencies and their formative effects on matter.

You can view the whole universe in this way, from sub-atomic particles to the most intricate life forms, to the nebulae and galaxies themselves -- all are resonating fields of pulsating energy in constant interaction with one another. The science of it all aside, I find it profoundly moving to think that sound in all its forms might very well be the glue that holds our consensual reality together.

I was really excited about this when I was explaining it to Steve, and I didn't want to bore him, so I started putting it in musical terms. The universe exists -- beneath all or most other layers of perception -- as essentially a vibrating-string note among a wild symphony of equally vibrating harmonic or non-harmonic quantum notes being played on similar strings --

-- *yes*, like an orchestra. Exactly like an orchestra.

Steve asked me if it were possible to show him how this process worked, so he and I repeated one of Jenny's early experiments. We placed a small wooden ring containing about 20ccs. of kaolin paste on top of a magnifying lens, then attached a crystal to the lens and applied a small sound current, creating a specific vibration... which can vary, depending upon the frequency or the current if you apply electricity directly. Just as a speaker vibrates, displacing air and creating specific sound waves according to the frequencies it's subjected to, the vibrating crystal transmitted its oscillations from the sound current frequencies, through the lens, and directly into the paste sample. Light was projected up from beneath the lens, through the paste, and into a camera lens looking down from above. I was able to photograph the disturbances -- the standing wave patterns -- created in the paste as it vibrated in response to the sine waves -- the music -- to which it was subjected. Steve played some of his recent composition on the cello, which was attached to the lens by a string of piano wire. A bit on the primitive side, I admit, but effective nonetheless. The moment was captured, then it was just a simple matter of instantly freezing the shape the paste assumed and encasing it in amber.

No, we *didn't* freeze sound, we froze a specific instance of sound physically altering matter.

The next thing we did was even simpler. We ran the music through a basic computer visualizing program -- you know, one of those extras that come bundled in with music playing software? Right. We decided to use the Fractal Pattern option, and I gotta tell you, the flow of images that accompanied the music was quite lovely. So now we had both the music and the fractal visualization for sensory input.

This really got us both going.

Steve had just finished a new composition -- he hadn't given it a title yet, he always sucked at titles, anyway -- but he was stressing over it because something was missing. He kept lamenting how it was impossible to gauge a person's emotional reaction to music, aside from what they themselves would tell you after hearing it.

I thought of Jenny and Chladni.

I thought of all the Cymatic equipment gathering dust in the Bioacoustics Department.

And I thought about how both Steve and I were in danger of losing our scholarships if we didn't come up with a term-end project that would floor everyone.

Have you heard the piece of music that Steve composed for the initial phase of the experiment? No? Too bad -- it's a beautiful piece of work.

It begins with an acoustic guitar rhythmically picking out four simple notes, the sound of raindrops pinging against a cold autumn window, four austere notes that remain constant and never change, then builds in musical and emotional intensity, culminating in a three-minute finale where the guitar is joined and then *replaced* by an orchestra whose individual instruments compliment the underlying four-note foundation in the same way that wind, thunder, and lightning accompany a sudden spring downpour. The music is both glorious and sad, tinged at the edges with a certain disquieting darkness -- an unnamable fear that we all experience during strong storms. As this section nears its end, the four-note foundation suddenly stops, leaving only the melancholy musings of the other instruments, which mix into one another like the stray thoughts of one for whom the rhythm of the rain brings a sense of peace, but when robbed of that rhythm, when finding there is no longer the hypnotic pinging of those raindrops against the cold autumn window, is left to their own devices: slowly succumbing to the sadness and unsettling fear that the sound of the rain had helped them avoid facing. In these final moments, one could close one's eyes and easily picture the drab grey sky and the cheerless, soaked, bleak world.

Initially, we decided to use individuals, people we knew. They'd come into one of the acoustically-tiled rehearsal rooms and sit in a chair, I'd hook them up to the EKG and EEG machines, and then Steve would play a recording of the piece for them while the fractal program was projected through an LCD screen. The EKG and EEG machines would measure their physiological reactions during the music while watching the LCD, and that was the extent of their participation.

After three or four people had done this, both Steve and I realized that, well, most of our friends had high blood pressure, for one thing, but more than that, there was no way to holistically quantify the results -- at least, not the way we were doing it. All we had was a series of readouts to show how these people's bodies reacted to the music, nothing to prove that Cymatic theory was even applicable.

Then Steve got this bright idea about incorporating synthesizers into the experiment. I had to do a lot of begging and fast talking to the Bioacoustics Department heads, and I have *no* idea what Steve said to the bigwigs of the Music Department, but we were both given access to the equipment we needed.

I got the use of an EEG- and EKG-measurement/interpreter that served as a conduit between the EEG and EKG machines and the synthesizer bank. The M/I had once been used for Cymatic experimentation -- specifically the direct estimations of the main parameters of neurons -- time constant of integration, level of internal noise, etc. -- received by the cells, or for our purposes, the auditory reactions located on different levels -- or in this case, the subjects -- hooked up to the system.

I'm sorry, I'm getting off on a technical tangent. I'll try to put it in simpler terms, but I make no promises. After all, I'm crazy, aren't I?

The basic experiment remained unchanged. A subject would come into one of the rooms and we'd hook them up to the EEG and EKG machines and then have them listen to the music and watch the fractal program, only instead of just getting a simple readout of their physiological reactions during the music, those reactions were filtered through the M/I into the synthesizer's computer where they were interpreted as an actual auditory event.

The computer then took all of this catalogued information and fed it into the output ports of the synthesizer banks, which -- employing the information received from the M/I -- assigned each set of recorded physiological reactions a specific musical scale, as well as a virtual instrument to play the individual notes within that scale.

This took all of maybe forty minutes -- the piece was short, otherwise we'd've been looking at days, even weeks, of data processing. Anyway, the person was asked to come back in an hour, and when they did, they got to listen to a musical interpretation of their physiological reaction to the original piece of music, as well as watch a visual representation *of* those physiological reactions.

Steve and I were both stunned that it worked.

So we took it a step further. After we'd done this with half a dozen test subjects, we decided, just for shits and giggles, to play all six reaction pieces simultaneously. Now, all of them were in the same key -- the computer had been programmed to make certain of that -- but that's where any similarities in the pieces should have ended. But that wasn't the case.

Incredible as it sounds, when all six of those reaction recordings were played back simultaneously, they *fit together*. It was as if someone had taken a pre-existing piece of music and broken it up into six isolated parts. Individually, these six reaction recordings were pleasant enough, okay? No real melody to speak of, but not discordant, either. Each one was like a musical tone poem.

But when we combined them, they created an almost *complete* piece of music.

Are you getting this, Miss Reporter? Think about everything I've told you up to this point and apply it to those results.

All consciousness is connected as a primary wavefront phenomenon that allows us not only to resonate to such notes, but to play a few of our own back here where we sit among the other quantum woodwinds!

Which means, like it or not, that there exists some *base* wavefront to which all others are connected. I wouldn't go so far as to call it God, but... it gave me pause, that's for certain.

But it didn't stop there. We noticed there were sounds on the periphery of the music, soft chattering noises, so Steve made a master recording and started to isolate the sounds. It never occurred to us to play it with the visualization program -- we were too excited about the music and the sounds. Maybe if it *had* occurred to us to run it with the fractal program, thing would've... never mind. Shoulda-woulda-coulda. You could make yourself crazy cataloguing all the what-ifs.

So we started concentrating on the Cymatic side of the experiment. If these wavefronts, these vibrational frequencies, could also be employed to heal the body, then why not go for it? We'd proven -- at least to ourselves -- that there was a definite *structure* underneath all of this, so the question became, how do we *apply* it?

We didn't have to wait too long for our answer. Of the six people who participated in the original phase of the experiment, *four* of them reported that they'd been feeling better since doing so. One girl who suffered from migraine headaches -- she told us she got at least one every two weeks, on average -- told us that she hadn't gotten a headache in almost a month. Another guy, a halfback on the university football team, had been having severe problems with his back and was on the verge of being cut. *He* came back to tell us that whatever was wrong with his back, it had cleared up since he'd helped us out. Another person who'd been having problems with insomnia started sleeping like a baby, and the fourth person, who'd been on anti-depressants for years, suddenly started feeling *fine*. She stopped taking her medication, and hadn't suffered any setbacks.

Word of this got to the head of the Psychology Department, and he requested to see all our data. We were more than happy to show him -- hell, we'd documented everything from the first minute we began -- and he was impressed, so much so that he suggested we take the experiment to the next level.

One of the things Jenny had attempted was to use Cymatics as a way to treat mental illness -- entraining misfired synapses in the brain to fall into a steady, predictable pattern. So what effect might genuine madness might have on the structure of things, and vice-versa?

The Psychology Director made arrangements for us to conduct the experiment on a handful of schizophrenics at the state mental hospital. I was amazed he was able to arrange all of this so quickly, but he pointed out that there was nothing about the experiment that put anyone in danger; it was a simple measurement of physiological reactions to auditory and visual data.

The only difference was that, this time, we'd be doing it with a dozen people simultaneously. The hospital had more than enough EKG and EEG machines to supply us.

So everything was arranged, and off we went.

The first part of the experiment went beautifully. The patients sat there and watched the screen and listened to the music -- Steve's original composition, not the reaction recording -- and then we made arrangements to come back in two days and play the results.

There was no deviation. Each of the twelve reaction pieces were the same kinds of tone poems that we'd gotten before, and just like the original batch of recordings, these twelve pieces, when played simultaneously, created a single melody. And just like the first series, there was that *chattering* on the periphery.

Steve had isolated the original chattering, but it was gibberish -- a bunch of monosyllabic noises, like grunts or hums. This new series of noises was just more of the same, but then we overlapped the two sets of noises...and I suppose that was the moment we damned ourselves, because when combined, the two sets of noises formed a *chant*, some sort of... I don't know... incantation -- Steve was the one who called that one. He said something about the rhythms and tonal phrasings matching those of Gregorian religious music led him to believe it was chant of some kind. Neither one of us recognized the language -- assuming it *was* an actual language. We thought about taking it to the Language Department, but that would have delayed the second part of the experiment at the state hospital, so we just added that to our To Do list for afterward.

By this time, the two of us were the talk of the university. Even though the term wasn't over, we received notification that not only would we remain on scholarship, but would be receiving a small stipend to help continue our work -- hell, the Bioacoustics Department even decided to resurrect the Cymatics program for the next term. We were stars.

A week later we went back to the state hospital to perform the second half of the experiment. Besides the original twelve patients, the state hospital director was present, as were two armed security guards and the head of the university's Psychology Department.

The patients' chairs were arranged in a half-circle in front of the large LCD screen. The hospital director and Psychology Department head sat in chairs a few feet off to the left of the group, and one security guard stood at each end of the half-circle of chairs. Steve and I were hunched over the equipment in a far corner of the room, a good ten feet away from everyone.

The lights were lowered, and we began the playback. Steve had made two master recordings; one of the patients' reactions, and one wherein their reactions were combined with those of the original test subjects. We'd programmed the system to play these back to back.

During the playback of the patients' reaction recording, Steve and I began to notice that the Fractal Visualization program wasn't behaving normally; instead of showing a cascading series of images, it was showing bits and pieces of the same image over and over, sometimes combining pieces, but more often just displaying a flash here, a section there. The patients themselves seemed utterly transfixed by it all, so we made a note and sat back to watch what would happen during the next playback.

The patients' reaction recording segued seamlessly into the combined recording, but this time, even though Steve had done nothing to amplify the chanting, the words could be clearly heard: *Iä-R'lyeh! Cthulhu fhtagn! Iä! Iä!*

We looked at one another. The chanting was the same volume as the music itself, and we had done nothing to alter the recording.

Iä-R'lyeh! Cthulhu fhtagn! Iä! Iä!

It didn't take long to figure out why. Many of the patients were moving in their chairs, rocking back and forth, and repeating the chant over and over.

Iä-R'lyeh! Cthulhu fhtagn! Iä! Iä!

I was watching the reactions of the hospital director and the head of the Psychology Department when I felt Steve's hand grip my forearm and squeeze. I looked at him, and he pointed toward the screen.

I don't know if I can find the words to describe the image I saw displayed there. It looked at first like some kind of huge squid with its writhing feelers whipping and curling all over the screen, but the more the music played and the louder the patients' chanting became, the image began to solidify.

It wasn't a squid, not exactly -- whatever this thing was, it had the *head* of a squid. Its shoulders were dark and massive, and it was *reacting* to the chant and music. I saw something like a clawed hand press against the screen and almost laughed, it seemed so absurd.

But then the screen itself began to... and I know how this is going to sound... the screen began to bend and expand, almost as if it were melting outward.

Iä-R'lyeh! Cthulhu fhtagn! Iä! Iä!

And then it happened: a tentacle moved forward from the screen and out toward the patients. The air was suddenly filled with the stench of dampness and rot. Both Steve and I started choking as soon as the stink hit us, and I saw, for one brief moment, the tip of another tentacle push outward as the screen continued to expand.

Both security guards unholstered their weapons and began firing at the tentacle, but by then the second one was fully free and they... Christ, they never had a chance. Each of them was grabbed by a tentacle that wound around their torsos, lifted them from the ground, and began crushing them. They dropped their weapons as blood began spouting from their mouths; by this time the hospital director was running for the alarm and the head of the Psychology Department was screaming for us to turn everything of, turn it off now. And we did: we yanked the cords and hit the switches *but the music continued*, it grew in volume and intensity as the screen kept expanding and more tentacles began slithering through, only now I could see the first few clawed fingers tearing through the scrim, and I realized that whatever this *thing* was, it was the size of a small mountain on its side of the screen, but when it emerged into our world, it easily tripled in mass and if it somehow managed to get all the way through...

I started to move -- where I was going or what I was going to do, I had no idea, it just seemed to me that it was important that I *do something, anything* to ground myself, to get a hold on matters, to somehow come to grips with this... this *nightmare* that was unfolding before my eyes, so I began to move and my foot kicked against something solid... and when I looked down, I saw one of the security guards' guns and grabbed it up, firing into the nearest tentacle, but it slammed me aside and grabbed the Psychology Department head while another took care of the hospital director... Within seconds there were four crushed, thrashing, bleeding bodies bouncing around in the air above our heads like marionettes; I couldn't move without having blood rained down on my face and in my eyes, and that's when I realized that the music and the chanting were coming from the patients themselves, many of whom had risen from their chairs and fallen to their knees, arms reaching upward, imploring, giving me my answer, telling me that, yes, all consciousness is connected as a primary wavefront phenomenon that allows us not only to resonate to such notes, but to play a few of our own back here and that there *was* a base wavefront to which all of them are connected, and I would have been wrong calling that base God but not *a* god, because right here, right now, that god was pushing through the boundaries of perception to reclaim some part of the world over which it once must have ruled and, oh God, God, *God*, there was no way to stop it, no way to send it back because the nested hierarchies of vibrational frequencies that had opened this doorway were no longer under the control of our machines, they were in the control of those kneeling before this god and howling *Iä-R'lyeh! Cthulhu fhtagn! Iä! Iä!* For a moment I was paralyzed with this knowledge, then I saw Steve's broken, bleeding body dance across the air over my head and I did the only thing I *could* do, I scrambled on hands and knees to find the gun that I had dropped, and I not only found it, but the other guard's gun as well. I ran to the front of the room and I began firing at each and every one of their heads. Some of them looked at me before I killed them, and their eyes... oh god, their confused, frightened eyes... they were in the grips of some form of rapture that was both euphoric and terrifying; they couldn't choose, they couldn't fight against it -- maybe they didn't *want* to fight it, I'll never know -- but I killed them, I killed all of them, and with the death of each one some part of this thing, this god, this monster, this creature of rot and death and putrescence, recoiled back into the screen until it was done, until they all lay dead at my feet, and I faced the screen and I saw it *looking* at me, sitting very still, and I *felt* as much as heard its voice vibrate through my body.

You have shown me the way back, and here I will wait, for I will not have to wait long. Thank you for this music of bleak entrainment, this song that will very soon call me home.

I was in the process of removing the discs when the authorities arrived.

And that, as the saying goes, is that.

What? Yes, I know I was charged in all seventeen deaths, but I'm telling you for the record -- for all the good it will do -- that I only *purposefully* killed twelve people. Though I suppose, in a way, I did kill them all.

Now let me ask you something – *why* are you here? I mean, I've been locked up in here for one-third of my life and you're the first reporter to show up here since the initial circus right after it happened. What's going on that's made me the focus of interest all of a sudden?

They *what?*

Oh, dear God... who's got them? When were they found? Have they been played yet?

Listen to me -- *they must never be played again*, do you understand? *Never.* Because that's what it's waiting for, what it's been listening for ever since that night. Please, *please*, tell whoever has them that those discs must *not* be --

-- why are you calling for the doctors? There's no need to --

-- hello, folks, look, yes, I got a little excited, but she's got to be made to understand that -- oh, Christ, not with the needle again, wait, wait one second, *just give me ten fucking seconds and I'll* --

-- ohgod --

-- please tell them, *please*, I beg you... don't play the discs... never   play them... because... if you do...   he'll   come   home...

...feeling so tired now... so tired...

...he's still listening...   he'll   always be   listening...
        ...sing him no songs, or   the world will   never

sing   again...

Gary A. Braunbeck has published over 200 short stories in the horror, science fiction, fantasy, mystery, romance, and western fields. He is the author 10 novels, including several in the acclaimed Cedar Hill Cycle such as *In Silent Graves; Coffin County*, and *Far Dark Fields*. He has also published 10 short story collections, including *Things Left Behind, Graveyard People: The Collected Cedar Stories, volume 1*, and *Home Before Dark: The Collected Cedar Hill Stories, Volume 2*. His work has thus far garnered five Bram Stoker Awards, three Shocklines "Shocker" Awards, an International Horror Guild Award, and a World Fantasy Award nomination. He lives in Columbus, OH, with his wife, author Lucy Snyder *(Installing Linux on a Dead Badger; Spellbent)* and five cats who will not hesitate to draw blood if he forgets to feed them on time. You can find out more about Gary and his work at *www.garybraunbeck.com*

The author writes about this story:

"The idea behind 'A Certain Disquieting Darkness' came to me several years ago during the writing of the story 'Small Song' (*F&SF*, April 1999). At that time, I was researching an arguably obscure area of physics called 'bioacoustics' -- the study of/search for sound existing on a sub-atomic level. Several of the theories advanced the idea that sound -- and specifically music -- can and does have a direct effect on human physiology, and can even affect physiology to the extent it can *alter* that physiology. Since physics -- especially quantum physics -- is an area of intense interest to me, and because, as a storyteller, I couldn't fully explore this idea in one short story, I have written to date 5 other stories that deal with different theories presented in the bioacoustics field; the subject is simply too rich and complex to limit the possible number of stories that can be inspired. When the opportunity to present a (admittedly) dark twist on the subject came my way, I couldn't resist. The result was 'A Certain Disquieting Darkness'."

The Boy Who Became Invisible

by Joe R. Lansdale

The place where I grew up was a little town called Marvel Creek. Not much happened there that is well remembered by anyone outside of the town. But things went on, and what I'm aware of now is how much things really don't change. We just know more than we used to because there are more of us, and we have easier ways to communicate excitement and misery than in the old days.

Marvel Creek was nestled along the edge of the Sabine River, which is not a wide river, and as rivers go, not that deep, except in rare spots, but it is a long river, and it winds all through East Texas. Back then there were more trees than now, and where wild animals ran, concrete and houses shine bright in the sunlight.

Our little school wasn't much, and I hated going. I liked staying home and reading books I wanted to read, and running the then considerable woods and fishing the creeks for crawdads. Summers and afternoons and weekends I did that with my friend Jesse. I knew Jesse's parents lived differently than we did, and though we didn't have money, and would probably have been called poor by the standards of the early sixties, Jesse's family still lived out on a farm where they used an outhouse and plowed with mules, raised most of the food they ate, drew water from a well, but curiously, had electricity and a big tall TV antennae that sprouted beside their house and could be adjusted for better reception by reaching through the living room window and turning it with a twist of the hands. Jesse's dad was quick to use the razor strop on Jesse's butt and back for things my parents would have thought unimportant, or at worse, an offense that required words, not blows.

Jesse and I liked to play Tarzan, and we took turns at it until we finally both decided to be Tarzan, and ended up being Tarzan twins. It was a great mythology we created and we ran the woods and climbed trees, and on Saturday we watched Jungle Theater at my house, which showed, if we were lucky, Tarzan or Jungle Jim movies, and if not so lucky, Bomba movies.

About fifth grade there was a shift in dynamics. Jesse's poverty began to be an issue for some of the kids at school. He brought his lunch in a sack, since he couldn't afford the cafeteria, and all his clothes came from the Salvation Army. He arrived at history class one morning wearing socks with big S's on them, which stood for nothing related to him, and they immediately became the target of James Willeford and Ronnie

Kenn. They made a remark about how the S stood for sardines, which would account for how Jesse smelled, and sadly, I remember thinking at that age that was a pretty funny crack until I looked at Jesse's slack, white face and saw him tremble beneath that patched Salvation Army shirt.

Our teacher came in then, Mr. Waters, and he caught part of the conversation. He said, "Those are nice socks, you got there, Jesse. Not many people can have monogrammed socks. It's a sign of sophistication, something a few around here lack."

It was a nice try, but I think it only made Jesse feel all the more miserable, and he put his head down on his desk and didn't lift it the entire class, and Mr. Waters didn't say another word to him. When class was over, Jesse was up and out, and as I was leaving, Mr. Waters caught me by the arm. "I saw you laughing when I came in. You been that boy's friend since the two of you were knee high to a legless grasshopper."

"I didn't mean to," I said. "I didn't think."

"Yeah, well, you ought to."

That hit me pretty hard, but I'm ashamed to say not hard enough.

I don't know when it happened, but it got so when Jesse came over I found things to do. Homework, or some chore around the house, which was silly, because unlike Jesse, I didn't really have any chores. In time he quit stopping by, and I would see him in the halls at school, and we'd nod at each other, but seldom speak.

The relentless picking and nagging from James and Ronnie continued, and as they became interested in girls, it increased. And Marilyn Townsend didn't help either. She was a lovely young thing and as cruel as they were.

One day, Jesse surprised us by coming to the cafeteria with his sack lunch. He usually ate outside on one of the stoops, but he came in this day and sat at a table by himself, and when Marilyn went by, he watched her, and when she came back with her tray, he stood up and smiled, politely asked if she would like to sit with him.

She laughed. I remember that laugh to this day. It was as cold as a knife blade in the back, and easily as sharp. I saw Jesse's face drain until it was white, and she went on by laughing, not even saying a word, just laughing, and pretty soon everyone in the place was laughing, and Marilyn came by me, and she looked at me, and heaven help me, I saw those eyes of hers and those lips, and whatever made all the other boys jump did the same to me... and I laughed.

Jesse gathered up his sack and went out.

It was at this point that James and Ronnie came up with a new approach. They decided to treat Jesse as if he were a ghost, as if he were invisible. We were expected to do the same. So as not to be mean to Jesse, but being careful not to burn my bridges with the in-crowd, I avoided him altogether. But there were times, here and there, when I would see him walking down the hall, and on the rare occasions when he spoke, students pretended not to hear him, or James would respond with some remark like, "Do you hear a duck quacking?"

When Jesse spoke to me, if no one was looking, I would nod.

This went on into the ninth grade, and it became such a habit, it was as if Jesse didn't exist, as if he really were invisible. I almost forgot about him, though I did note in math class one day there were stripes of blood across his back, seeping through his old worn shirt. His father and the razor strop. Jesse had nowhere to turn.

One afternoon I was in the cafeteria, just about to get in line, when Jesse came in carrying his sack. It was the first time he'd been there since the incident with Marilyn some years before. I saw him come in, his head slightly down, walking as if on a mission. As he came near me, for the first time in a long time, for no reason I can explain, I said, "Hi, Jesse."

He looked up at me surprised, and nodded, the way I did to him in the hall, and kept walking.

There was a table in the center of the cafeteria, and that was the table James and Ronnie and Marilyn had claimed, and as Jesse came closer, for the first time in a long time, they really saw him. Maybe it was because they were surprised to see him and his paper sack in a place he hadn't been in ages. Or maybe they sensed something. Jesse pulled a small revolver from his sack and before anyone knew what was happening, he fired three times, knocking all three of them to the floor. The place went nuts, people running in all directions. Me, I froze.

Then, like a soldier, he wheeled and marched back my way. As he passed me, he turned his head, smiled, said, "Hey, Hap," then he was out the door. I wasn't thinking clearly, because I turned and went out in the hall behind him, and the history teacher, Mr. Waters, saw him with the gun, said something, and the gun snapped again, and Waters went down. Jesse walked all the way to the double front door, which was flung wide open at that time of day, stepped out into the light and lifted the revolver. I heard it pop and saw his head jump and he went down. My knees went out from under me and I sat down right there in the floor, unable to move.

When they went out to tell Jesse's parents what had happened to him, that Marilyn was disfigured, Ronnie wounded, and James and Mr. Waters were dead, they discovered them in bed where Jesse had shot them in their sleep.

The razor strop lay across them like a dead snake.

Joe R. Lansdale is the multi-award winning author of thirty novels and over two hundred short stories, articles and essays. He has written screenplays, teleplays, comic book scripts, and teaches creative writing and screenplay writing occasionally at Stephen F. Austin State University. He has received The Edgar Award, The Grinzani Prize For Literature, seven Bram Stoker Awards, and many others. His stories, "Bubba Hotep", and "Incident On And Off A Mountain Road", were both filmed. He is the founder of the martial arts system *Shen Chuan,* and has been in the International Martial Arts Hall of Fame four times. He lives in East Texas with his wife, Karen.

The author writes about this story:
"The story was inspired by a real event. A kid I went to school with killed his family and came to school the next day. The events didn't go down from there like in the story, but that was the stimulus behind it."

Getting Along Just Fine

by William F. Nolan

*E*aster morning in Bend, Oregon, almost four weeks into spring. It was snowing outside his apartment again.

November, December, January, February, March, and now mid-April. Five and a half months of rain, wind and snow.

Frank hated rain, wind and snow. He felt sorry for himself, secluded here -- trapped in his living room -- with his wife, Elizabeth, back in California; they had been married over thirty years -- still on fine terms, still cared about each other, would never get divorced -- but would never live together again, either. Success as an artist (which he excelled in) hadn't been enough; they found out the hard way that quality did not necessarily translate into riches, especially once one grew older, and the opportunities dried up like a puddle in the desert. Twelve consecutive years of heavy debt had stressed her to the point of near collapse. She needed her personal space.

So, he had volunteered to get out of her life; he left sunny California and moved to this dark two-bedroom apartment in the Pacific Northwest because he had a good friend here -- Bill Singer -- who collected his work. Bill had over a thousand pieces. Soon, however, he discovered that Singer was almost always on the road, and they saw each other only infrequently. True, he'd been over to Bill's house for dinner a couple of times over the last year and a half (his wife was sweet) but their interaction was far less than Frank had originally hoped for. *Not Bill's fault. Just the way the cookie crumbled.*

At his age, it wasn't easy making new friends. Frank had lived in various parts of Greater Los Angeles for more than fifty years, and, although he wasn't a native, he felt that it was his true home. Not Missouri where he'd been born and raised, and certainly not Oregon where people liked to ski and hike and fish and climb mountains. He did none of these things. In Bend, he passed the time reading (classics he'd missed when younger, plus a hundred Max Brand Westerns), painting, watching television (reality shows, mainly) and sleeping -- a *lot*: nine hours a night, plus another hour each afternoon.

Sure, he'd made a couple of new friends (both much younger) during his exile in Oregon, but they lived in Vancouver, Washington, a good distance from lonely, cold Bend. *There are always the pen pals*, he supposed. Sometimes he just liked to whine; truth be known, the complaining made the solitude more bearable.

Although Central Oregon was beautiful -- ringed by the white-capped Cascade mountain range and thicketed with endless conifer trees -- the beauty of nature didn't raise excitement in him; Frank preferred the agitation of a metropolis, with plenty of bookstores, theaters, all-night diners -- even its car-choked freeways. Fired with a sense of constant motion, of existence lived at a heightened level, cities made him feel *more* connected to the world, while -- paradoxically -- the "great outdoors" made him withdrawn, sad, isolated; as though smothered in the bosom of its grandeur.

Bend was quiet; the silence was staggering. Tranquil to a fault. He was a latter-day Robinson Crusoe, except for the numbing cold. He planned a move to Tucson, Arizona next spring, for the heat if for no other reason. *I'd rather deal with the dry desert heat over the penetrating Oregon cold any day.* The gusty winds in Bend cut into his skin no matter what coat he wore. Even with the sun out, the winds were fierce. Now it was late afternoon. *Still snowing. How long have I been standing here, daydreaming?* Frank moved to his bedroom, watching the snow feather down into the slushy street beyond the frosted glass of his window, flocking the trees. He was warming himself in front of the paltry wall heater when the phone rang. He walked into the second bedroom (converted into his studio) and picked up the receiver.

"Hello?"

"Hello, Frank. It's Charles."

"Oh, hi," said Frank. Charles was a frustrated producer living in California who was attempting to get a TV series off the ground. He wanted Frank to design the show's logo. *If and when...*

"I just talked to Eddie's wife, Shirley," he told Frank. "She asked about you, about how you were doing."

"I'm fine. Getting along just fine."

"Eddie is still very shaky after the stroke."

"Stroke! My God, when did that happen?"

"Couple of months ago. Eddie was driving in the San Fernando Valley when the stroke hit him; got into a minor accident, but nobody was hurt. Shirley says he's doing okay now. Can't drive anymore of course... The two of them, they just stay home in their apartment. Eddie never answers the phone. Doesn't want to talk to anybody. It's sad, really..."

"Well, I can understand that." There was a pause. Frank felt out of the loop; captivated by the snow in his view from the studio window as it hissed into the trees at the edge of the small apartment complex. It swallowed reality in a mantle of bluish-white, adding inches by the hour to an already deep accumulation. *Why did I ever come to Bend? Bend sucks!*

Frank's reflections and what his mother said when she was in her late seventies (as he now was) tumbled through his mind like the snow cascading to the frozen earth: *"If you live long enough you outlast your family and all of your friends -- and unless you've had children you end up all alone in the world."*

He had never been a father.

As for his mother: she'd been right.

Indeed, he had outlasted his family (except for a first cousin -- in his nineties -- who resided in Santa Barbara) and a few of his old friends. Brilliant Chuck, his best pal for over a decade, had aged seemingly overnight, a victim of early Alzheimer's disease. He died looking like an old man of ninety while still in his thirties... *Chuck's lovely wife, Helen, followed him to the grave four years later, of cancer (was it the stress of watching Chuck disintegrate that brought it on?)... Chad, my Texas friend, succumbed to melanoma... Paul died of acute diabetes in New York... Wendl suffered a fatal heart attack in Arizona... Pipes drowned inside the cabin of a commercial airliner after a crash out of Washington, DC... Bruce hanged himself somewhere in Oklahoma, following a severe bout of depression...*

Then there was Rod: he hadn't survived the open heart surgery undertaken to save his life, and Relling ended his life in a garage full of carbon monoxide... Squires lost his battle with lymphoma... Bob in Santa Barbara -- bedridden after back surgery -- never recovered... Dan (a real powerhouse of energy) and his wife Elaine both died of brain tumors... Dan's daughter, Linda, had preceded them in death: stoned on Angel Dust, she believed she could fly and jumped from the top of a ten-story building -- she had been only twenty (I sense Dan never got over this, though we never spoke of the incident after the funeral)...

So many...

"Frank? Are you okay?" Charles asked, interrupting his thoughts.

"I- I'm fine Charles... Sorry, what else is going on? How is the show coming along?"

"Glad you asked: there's been a little news..."

Frank listened, but really couldn't focus on Charles... his voice droned from the earpiece, blending into the wind gusts outside as the snow swirled like ash from Mt. St. Helens. He could feel the frigid air on his skin as it permeated the thin glass of the old apartment window. *McKnight was hit by a car in Kansas City just after high school... my old school buddy, Bill Hennessey, survived a colon operation only to die five weeks later -- ironically -- of peritonitis, the same thing that killed my beloved father... Maggie -- a chain smoker who was never without a cigarette -- died of lung cancer, the same way my old friend Stan lost his wife... Steve was unable to beat mesothelioma... Ken died in a fiery racing crash at Riverside and Arthur cut his throat after shooting his wife, Adele, back in Missouri (they had been like a second set of parents to me when I was a boy)... Jerry passed away after a series of strokes... OCee had some kind of deadly back problem... Phil died of Parkinson's... Back in K.C., Mary Kay's heart gave out... Forry withered away, drooling from the mouth... And Peter died suddenly in the U.K. while playing outside with his kids...*

Gone... All of them... Gone...

Well, it's like they say about life: nobody gets out alive. Frank's thoughts flashed suddenly to the vast multitude of soldiers -- blue and gray -- who perished in the Civil War. *The irony is, they'd all be dead by now even if there had never been a war!*

Friends, lovers, strangers -- each as individual as a snowflake, each equally fragile, equally ephemeral. Here, then gone...

So many gone.

Even the old friends I have left are in poor shape: Ray is a shadow of his former self -- rendered half-blind and half-deaf (plus crippled in one leg) after his stroke at age 79... Dick is incredibly frail after those two spinal operations... Dennis, another chain smoker, with his tic and cigarette cough... Ada Beth, unable to walk, languishing in some rest home... and Herb, wracked with a variety of ills...

"Well, I can tell you're busy, Frank... How 'bout we chat next week, okay?" Charles offered at last, nervous as ever. Frank smiled, eyes rimmed in tears, brimming with remembrance and lament. *Where have all the years gone?*

"Sorry, Charles; I'm not much company right now! Next week will be fine; 'bye, 'bye." He hung the phone up without looking, still transfixed by the snowflakes' suicidal dance in the icy twilight, their lives at an end. *Where did all the time go?*

Overall, though, Frank had to admit that he had great family genetics: his father was close to eighty-eight when he died, his mother nearly eighty-five. His grandparents had both lived into their nineties, as did several aunts and uncles. Still, he couldn't depend on genetics alone for a longer life. He worked out with weights, exercised on a trampoline, and took several vitamins and food supplements (zinc, pine bark, grape seed, and magnesium among others). He had never smoked, and had given up meat and coffee many years ago. Beyond a glass of wine now and then he never drank alcohol. Soy products formed the basis of his vegetarian diet.

Result: I look, act and feel much younger than my calendar years.

Thinking about all of his dead family and friends as he watched the snow come down in the early evening chill, Frank was suddenly ashamed of feeling sorry for himself. *Dammit, I'm as healthy as a horse!*

That was a great blessing. A rare gift, especially at his age. *Like a beautiful snowfall, and the time and patience to enjoy it.* He smiled, now at ease with his thoughts, his memories, his apparitions: *To hell with self-pity.* He picked up his paintbrush, studying the snow-draped landscape beyond the window.

"By God, *I'm* alive...

and getting along just fine..."

William F. Nolan writes mostly in the science fiction, fantasy and horror genres. He is best known for co-authoring the novel *Logan's Run*, with George Clayton Johnson. He is the author of more than 2000 pieces (fiction, non-fiction, articles and books), and has edited 26 anthologies in his 50+ year career. Adept at poetry and screenwriting as well as fiction, he was also co-writer of the screenplay for the 1976 horror film *Burnt Offerings,* and co-wrote *Trilogy of Terror* with his friend Richard Matheson, both for Dan Curtis. An artist, Nolan was born in Kansas City, Missouri, and worked at Hallmark Cards, Inc. before becoming an author. Of his numerous awards, there are three of which he is most proud: being voted a Living Legend in Dark Fantasy by the International Horror Guild in 2002; twice winning the Edgar Allan Poe Award from the Mystery Writers of America; and, in 2006, being bestowed with the honorary title of Author Emeritus by the Science Fiction and Fantasy Writers of America, Inc.

What the author writes about this story:
"I wrote this story as an exercise in personal therapy, with no market in mind. As with my protagonist, I was "isolated" in Bend, Oregon with just one friend in town (who was on the road most of the time).

I had no family, with both of my parents deceased. My friends had died exactly as described in the story. (I even used their real names.) I was alone, cut off from society. The constant snow added to my depressed state.[*]

Then, suddenly one afternoon, I realized that I had no valid reason for self-pity, that actually, I was getting along just fine. The depression lifted. I was back to normal, and my creative life resumed.

I had made an important change, and 'Getting Along Just Fine' celebrates that change."

[*]A nod of gratitude to my dear pal and fellow editor, Jason V Brock, for his vital "snow contributions" to this story.

The Twilight Zone

THE GRANDFATHER CLOCK

(A Teleplay)

Written by

George Clayton Johnson

"The Grandfather Clock"

FADE IN:

INT. GRANDFATHER'S BEDROOM - DAY

CAMERA BEGINS on a CLOSE SHOT of a massive Grandfather clock, heavily carved and ornamented. Through a glass window in the lower body of the clock we see a large brass pendulum swinging to and fro. There is a loud, deep tick-tock as the clock keeps time.

CAMERA PULLS BACK as CONNIE enters the room. She is pregnant and from the look of her figure, the baby is about due. Her face creases in a worried frown as she looks about the room at the huge four-poster bed, the rococo night tables, the ancient chest-of-drawers -- the odds and ends of furniture treasured by an old man. FOSTER enters. He is Connie's husband and as we shall discover, not a bad sort.

                    CONNIE
          Foster, it doesn't seem right somehow.

                    FOSTER
          Don't worry, Connie. It will
            work out all right. If he
          isn't complaining why should
          you? This is the ideal room
         for the nursery. The baby will
          have a room to itself and if
            it cries we can hear it.

                    CONNIE
              This has always been
              Grandfather's room.

> GRANDFATHER'S VOICE (O.S.)
> (gently)
> Foster's right, of course.

ANOTHER ANGLE

They react as GRANDFATHER enters room. He is stitched and weathered by the years.

> GRANDFATHER (CONT'D)
> I really don't mind moving into the den.

> CONNIE
> What about your things? There isn't any room for them down-stairs. The den is already furnished modern.

ANGLE ON GRANDFATHER

> GRANDFATHER
> (with a twinkle)
> I'll tell you something I've never told anyone. I've always hated that bed. It's too proud. No mere human is good enough to sleep in that bed.
> (expansively)
> Sell it. Sell everything.

GROUP SHOT

Connie relaxes a bit and looks tremulously from one to the other.

> CONNIE
> It will work out all right, won't it?

> GRANDFATHER
> Of course. Of course. Now don't you worry about a thing.

FOSTER
I know a guy who deals in antiques.
He'd go for the bed and the dresser.

GRANDFATHER
And the end-tables. I paid a
price for them. Genuine hand-carved walnut.

ANOTHER ANGLE - CLOCK IN B.G.

FOSTER
And as for the clock -- I'll bet some
museum would like to get a hold of
that.

FACE CLOSEUP - GRANDFATHER

At the mention of the clock, a sudden, fearful look comes over
him.

GRANDFATHER
(bewildered)
What was that? The clock?

FOSTER puzzled.

FOSTER
Yeah, the Grandfather clock

GRANDFATHER sudden fear.

GRANDFATHER
(harsh)
No!

TWO SHOT - CONNIE AND FOSTER

                CONNIE
What is it Grandpa? Is something wrong?

They look curiously at GRANDFATHER.

His entire aspect has changed. Now he backs away from them toward the clock as though to shield it with his body. There is an almost hysterical note in his voice when he speaks.

               GRANDFATHER
     You can't do that! There's been some
kind of a mistake! Sell the clock? I won't let you!

GROUP SHOT

They are shocked by his reaction.

               CONNIE
             (surprised)
             Grandpa?

               FOSTER
             (irritably)
    What is this? I thought we had
     everything settled? You said
  yourself that we should sell the
           stuff.

             GRANDFATHER
    Everything else, yes, but not
    the clock. I didn't know you
    were talking about that. It's
    mine. I couldn't live without
            it.

              CONNIE
  In that case we don't have
      any right...

                    FOSTER
    Wait a minute. He knows there
    isn't any room for it. If you
     two think I'm going to drag
    that thing downstairs to the living
    room, you're wrong. There are other
    clocks in the house. He can use one
     of those. It isn't as though it's
     something he actually needs. Let
     the clock go with everything else.

                  GRANDFATHER
    What if something happened to it?
    It's too big a risk! You can't ask
    me to do it! What if someone were
                  careless?

INTERCUT CLOSEUPS OF CONNIE AND FOSTER reacting.
They are stunned and puzzled by his strange out-
burst.

                GRANDFATHER (CONT'D)
                    (wildly)
        Yes! Don't you see? What if
      someone forgot to wind it and it
          ran down? It would stop!

CONNIE reacting. Apprehensive. She looks at: FOSTER

FOSTER returns her look. He has never seen Grandfather be-
have like this and it worries the hell out of him.

                    FOSTER
                   (puzzled)
     So it would run down. I don't get it...

GRANDFATHER a look of immense terror.

GRANDFATHER
Don't you see? It would stop ticking!
(sees they don't understand)
It would stop ticking!
The minute that happens I'll die!

He stares wildly from face to face as:

ANGLE ON SERLING leaning against the clock.

SERLING
A Grandfather clock. A cumbersome and
noisy relic of a vanished era. (Taps the
clock lightly with his knuckles.) But
this particular clock is unique. It
keeps time in The Twilight Zone.

FADE OUT

BILLBOARD

(FIRST COMMERCIAL)

ACT ONE

FADE IN:

INT. GRANDFATHER'S ROOM - DAY

The scene is much as before. Connie and Foster stare at
Grandfather. He tries to pull himself together.

GRANDFATHER
I know what you're thinking. If
I were you I'd think the same thing.

Connie's face softens.

> CONNIE
> I understand, Grandpa. I've said
> things like that myself. If some-
> thing or other doesn't happen
> I'll simply die. It's just an ex-
> pression.
> Grandfather shakes his head miser-
> ably. In silence, he moves halt-
> ingly to the bed and sits on the
> edge of it, a hangdog expression
> on his face.

> GRANDFATHER
> No, Connie. I wish that's
> all there was to it.

He pauses.

ANGLE FEATURING GRANDFATHER

> GRANDFATHER (CONT'D)
> In some way I can't explain my
> life is connected to that clock.
> If it stops -- if the pendulum
> stops swinging -- I'll be dead.
> You've seen me. I take special
> care of it. Every day I oil it,
> and before going to bed I wind it
> by resetting the counterweights. I
> never miss a night.
> (a beat)
> I don't dare.

> FOSTER
> That's absurd.

> CONNIE
> (warningly)
> Foster!

                    FOSTER
        Well it is. It's crazy talk and
        not like him at all. You know
                      that.
        (to Grandfather, in a softer tone)
        I mean -- if you want to be philo-
          sophical about it, every man's
        life is connected to a clock. Each
          time a second ticks it's gone
          forever and we're all that much
        closer to the end -- but a specif-
        ic clock? I can see how you could
        get attached to something and try
        to make it more than it is. When
        I was in school, I had a fountain
        pen. For a while, I began to think
        there was something special about
        it. I began to think I wouldn't be
        able to pass a test unless I used
        that pen, but it wasn't true… and
          deep down I knew it wasn't.

                  GRANDFATHER
                  (a whisper)
          I wish I could believe that.

                    FOSTER
          Look, you've had that clock
              a long time, right?

                  GRANDFATHER
                      Yes.

                    FOSTER
            When did you get it?

                  GRANDFATHER
            The day I was born.

Foster looks sharply at Grandfather.

                    GRANDFATHER (CONT'D)
                        It's true.
                It belonged to my Grandfather be-
                fore me. He died the day I came
                into the world. He left the clock
                            to me.

Grandfather's face smoothes out, softens. He goes to the
clock and touches it affectionately.

                    GRANDFATHER (CONT'D)
                I don't suppose you know what it's
                like to own something all your
                life. No. Not the way they build
                        things these days.
                    (a reflective pause)
                It becomes a part of you. It takes
                on your moods. This clock now --
                when I'm feeling poor it ticks
                            slower.
                When things go well it has a brisk
                    and happy sound.

                          FOSTER
                Being sentimental is one thing,
                but to believe -- to really
                believe that your life...

Foster is so exasperated by the idea he can't continue.

                        GRANDFATHER
                          (a cry)
                        But it's true!

And now, abruptly, Foster is blazing angry.

                          FOSTER
                You know how I licked that busi-
                ness with the fountain pen? I lost
                it just before final exams. I went
                in and took those tests without
                        it. I got an "A".

Foster strides briskly to the Grandfather clock and flips open the glass door on the front of it. The pendulum is exposed.

> FOSTER (CONT'D)
> It took something big like that
> to show me the truth about that
> pen. When I got back to the dormi-
> tory, I found it in my other coat.
> I never felt that way about it
> again.

> GRANDFATHER
> (apprehensive)
> What are you going to do?

> FOSTER
> I'm going to prove that what you've
> been telling us is nonsense.

> GRANDFATHER
> Wait...

> FOSTER
> You said if the pendulum stops swinging
> you'll be dead. I'm going to
> show you it isn't so.

ANOTHER ANGLE FEATURING FOSTER

He has his hand poised inches from the swinging pendulum.

> FOSTER (CONT'D)
> (grimly)
> All I have to do is reach out
> -- grab the pendulum -- stop the clock.

> GRANDFATHER
> Don't! You mustn't!

                    FOSTER
        When I stop the pendulum you'll see
            how ridiculous you've been!

TIGHT SHOT - GRANDFATHER

His eyes go wide with shock as he realizes that Foster
really intends to stop the clock. He throws himself at
Foster with a cry.

                  GRANDFATHER
                    Don't!

ANGLE ON PENDULUM

Foster's fingers close on empty air an inch from the pendulum as Grandfather's hands enter SHOT and grab his
wrist. The hands tremble as Foster tries to pull free and
Grandfather tugs at him.

                GRANDFATHER (O.S.)
                   (pleading)
                  No! Please!

With frantic strength, Grandfather's hands pull Foster's
reaching fingers away from the pendulum.

ANGLE ON CONNIE

The excitement is too much for her. With a gasp, she sags
back onto the bed.

WIDER ANGLE

As Foster and Grandfather react to Connie's faint.

                    FOSTER
                   Connie!

Followed by Grandfather he rushes to her side. He begins
to pat her wrist.

TWO SHOT - CONNIE - FOSTER

With a flutter, her eyes blink open. She moans.

> FOSTER
> Are you all right?

> CONNIE
> I think so. It was just
> all the excitement.

> FOSTER
> The baby?

She shakes her head.

> CONNIE
> Not yet.

Foster helps her to her feet.

> FOSTER
> I think you'd better lie down for a while...

CAMERA PANS THEM to the door as Foster assists her.

ANGLE ON GRANDFATHER

He looks after them until they are out of sight down the
hall. He is still shaken from his recent ordeal. He takes
out a key and locks the glass door on the front of the
clock. He goes to the bed and sits down. After a few moments, he looks up as Foster re-enters the room.

TWO SHOT

It is evident that Foster regrets the recent contretemps.
He shrugs sheepishly.

> FOSTER
> I'm sorry. I didn't mean for it to be like that.

                    GRANDFATHER
                    I know.

                      FOSTER
        It is your clock and I didn't have
        any right -- I mean -- I was sim-
        ply trying to show you that it's
        only a machine -- a mechanical
        device inside of a slightly fool-
        ish wooden box. It's made of le-
        vers and wheels and weights. It's
        a tool to measure the passage of
                      time...

Grandfather understands. He simply nods.

                  FOSTER(CONT'D)
        It's just a rough patch is all.
        Connie about to have the baby. Ev-
        erything upset; then you with that
                  clock business.

                    GRANDFATHER
        I'm sorry for the trouble I've caused.

Foster nods.

                      FOSTER
        We're not trying to be mean about
        the clock. You can see that it's
        simply out of place here. We'll
        get you a new clock. An electric
                      one.

He looks expectantly at Grandfather.

Grandfather shakes his head.

                    GRANDFATHER
                    Listen!

Puzzled, Foster becomes quiet.

                    GRANDFATHER (CONT'D)
                  Do you hear it?

In the stillness, we hear:

TIGHT SHOT - THE CLOCK
as the pendulum swings back and forth with a deep, reso-
nant tick-tock.

ANGLE ON GRANDFATHER

His face has become serene as he listens to the music of
pawl and ratchet.

                    GRANDFATHER (CONT'D)
                      (remembering)
             I've listened to that sound all
               my life. I hear it everywhere:
             downtown on crowded streets -- in
             the park -- on buses. It's got so
             I don't even have to be near the
               clock to hear it plain. When I
             was a boy I had a bad dream -- a
             nightmare. I woke terrified. I lay
               there in the dark afraid to move
               I was so scared. Then I heard a
             sound. That sound. I knew instant-
             ly where I was, everything was all
               right. I was safe. I was home.
             Hearing that sound what do I re-
             member? A lifetime. In the morn-
             ing, the chimes woke me for break-
               fast and sent me off to school.
               Evenings it called me in from
             games of hide and seek. At night,
             the ticking soothed me to sleep.
               Listening to it ticking in the
             darkness gave me strength to face
             whatever had to be: bad times --

GRANDFATHER (CONT'D)
sitting up with sick children, or
when Grandmother passed away. Good
times -- marriage, parenthood.
Oh, I can tell you that clock has
a voice, a personality. It's a
friend, a companion and you want
to replace it with a dinky, silent
electric model?

INTERCUT FACE CLOSEUPS - FOSTER reacting.

ANGLE FEATURING FOSTER

FOSTER
Look at it. The clock is an eyesore.
It doesn't even keep accurate time!

GRANDFATHER
It's just old. Everything gets old.

FOSTER
And, when things are old and
worn out it's time to
get rid of them.

CLOSE SHOT - GRANDFATHER

Foster's statement has cut deep. He might as easily be
talking about Grandfather himself. He too is old, worn
out.

CLOSE SHOT - FOSTER

Realizing how Grandfather has taken it. He wishes he
could call back the sharp and hasty words.

TWO SHOT

FOSTER
(faltering)
Grandfather, we shouldn't be shouting at each other.

                    GRANDFATHER
                     (subdued)
                  No, we shouldn't.

                      FOSTER
             We don't have to make a decision
                  this moment. I'll talk to
                     Connie about it...

Grandfather nods without looking at him. He has withdrawn
into himself.

ANGLE ON FOSTER

He looks at Grandfather as though he is about to say
something else, then shrugs helplessly and leaves the
room.

ANGLE ON GRANDFATHER AT CLOCK

He raises his eyes to look up at the clock face. His expression one of deep inward pain.

                                              CUT TO:

INT. LIVING ROOM DAY

Connie lies on the sofa. Foster enters and goes to her
side.

                      FOSTER
             Is it time to go to the hospital?

                      CONNIE
          (looking off toward Grandfather's room)
                   What happened?

                      FOSTER
         It's nothing to be concerned about. Right now
          young lady you've got your hands full.

                      CONNIE
                 (not to be put off)
                      Tell me.

                    FOSTER
    When you get down to it, I guess
      it's simple enough. Grandfather
      has identified himself with the
      old clock. Grandfather -- Grandfa-
      ther clock -- it fits.(sighs)
        I don't suppose it's ever easy
        to live in someone else's house.
      With the baby due and things being
      shifted around, he feels insecure.
      I suppose he feels that if we can
        get rid of the clock we can also
              get rid of him.

                    CONNIE
                  (horrified)
    But we wouldn't do anything like that.

                    FOSTER
      Of course not, but look at it from
        his standpoint. He's seen too many
          things change in this world to
        ever be certain of anything. He's
            old and he's frightened.

ANOTHER ANGLE - TO INCLUDE GRANDFATHER

He has come down the stairs and stands in the hall concealed from view. He cannot help overhearing.

                    CONNIE
        That's terrible. Someone should
      tell him he can live with us as long as
        he cares to. This is his home, too.

                    FOSTER
I'm afraid the only way he'll really believe that is if
        we let him keep the clock.

                    CONNIE
                  (sharp)
            Then let him.

FOSTER
We've gone through that. Where will we put it?

CONNIE
I don't know but we'll find a place if we have to
throw some other piece of furniture out.
Grandpa's more important than the furnishings!

FOSTER
What about the noise? The
chimes will keep the baby awake.

CONNIE
They didn't keep Grandfather
awake when he was a baby.
No. If he wants the clock, he can keep it.
Go tell him.

Suddenly Connie reacts to an inward pain. The labor has
begun.

FOSTER
The baby?

Connie nods through gritted teeth.

At this moment, Grandfather enters the room. Connie sees
him. Foster goes to get the car started.

CONNIE
Grandpa, we have something to tell you.

GRANDFATHER
No need. I was in the hall.

CONNIE
Then you know you can keep the
clock if you want to?

GRANDFATHER
I know.
(pause)

GRANDFATHER (CONT'D)
Foster is right. The clock is an
eyesore. It clashes with everything else in the house.

CONNIE
But that doesn't matter --

GRANDFATHER
I've behaved foolishly. The old must
make room for the new.

CONNIE
What are you going to do?

GRANDFATHER
Call the man to come get the furniture.

CONNIE
The clock too?

GRANDFATHER
(after a pause)
The clock too.

Foster re-enters the room with Connie's coat and bag. He
helps her to her feet.

CONNIE
Maybe you should wait, Grandpa.

He doesn't answer.

Clinging together, Connie and Foster go to the door. She
pauses and looks back at Grandfather.

CONNIE
Grandfather?

Before he can answer, another pain hits her. She stiffens and goes out with Foster.

When they are gone Grandfather goes to the telephone. He dials.

                    GRANDFATHER
          Is this the Antique Shop?

                                        DISSOLVE TO:

EXT. DRIVEWAY - MOVING VAN - DAY

As two men in coveralls come out of the house carrying the clock.

                    FIRST MAN
          Careful! These babies are fragile...

TIGHT SHOT - THE CLOCK

They are carrying it upright, the pendulum swinging back and forth as the clock continues to loudly tick.

ANGLE AT WINDOW

A look of doom in Grandfather's eyes as he watches them load the clock on the truck.

INT. GRANDFATHER'S ROOM DAY

He turns away from the window and looks about the empty room. He stares miserably at the faded outline of the great clock where the sun has etched the image onto the wallpaper. Grandfather sadly shakes his head.

EXT. AT TRUCK - DAY

As the two men set the clock into place on the truck tailgate.

                    FIRST MAN
          Hold it while I get a better grip.
          This thing is killing my fingers.

                    SECOND MAN
               Look out! It's slipping!

TIGHT ON CLOCK

It slips from the man's fingers, drops an inch, thuds
against the tailgate.

CAMERA ZOOMS INTO SHOT OF PENDULUM

it falters in mid-swing. The rhythm of the ticking
breaks.

                    FIRST MAN (O.S.)
                    Hold it!

                                        CUT TO:

INT. GRANDFATHER'S ROOM

Caught in mid-stride, Grandfather suddenly freezes. His
face goes gray as he clutches at his chest. He cries out
and crumples to the floor.

EXT. AT TRUCK

                    FIRST MAN
                    Listen!

                    SECOND MAN
          What? You can let go now. I think I've got it.

The two men settle the clock into place.

ANGLE FEATURING THE CLOCK

The pendulum slowly begins to move again. The clock
starts ticking.

The two men stand there, listening.

                    SECOND MAN
          How about that? After that beating,
             the clock is still ticking!

FIRST MAN
No, not that: I didn't mean the clock.
Did you -- did you hear something? A yell?

SECOND MAN
Naw. Come on. We've done all the damage we can here.

They hop down off the tailgate and swing it up into
place. As we:

FADE OUT

BILLBOARD

(SECOND COMMERCIAL)

ACT TWO

FADE IN

INT. HOSPITAL ROOM - DAY

Connie is in bed dressed in a hospital gown. Foster
stands beside the bed. He lovingly gazes down at her.

CONNIE
I'm worried about Grandfather.

FOSTER
Oh, he'll be all right --

CONNIE
I'm not so sure. I don't like to think of him
home all alone.
(a long pause) Foster...

FOSTER
Don't you think I ought be here with you?

CONNIE
I'm in good hands. There's nothing
for you to do anyway except get nervous!

FOSTER
OK, OK: Will you try to
get some rest if I go?

She nods.

FOSTER (CONT'D)
Will you have them call me?

She nods again.

FOSTER (CONT'D)
You're sure it will be all right?

CONNIE
I'm sure.

Still Foster hesitates. He is disinclined to leave her.

CONNIE (CONT'D)
Go on! Neither of you should be alone.

He kisses her and reluctantly goes. She looks after him.
A tight look as her labor continues.

DISSOLVE TO:

INT. GRANDFATHER'S ROOM

He lies crumpled by the door. OVER SCENE, we HEAR the
SOUND of the clock ticking. The SOUND grows louder as
Grandfather stirs. His eyes open as the ticking crescen-
dos. Comprehension comes into Grandfather's face as he
looks off at the faded image of the clock on the wall.

GRANDFATHER
(a fearful whisper)
The clock.

With this, the SOUND of the CLOCK fades OUT and UNDER.
Grandfather rises painfully and goes to the window. Disappointment creases his features as he sees the truck has
gone. He goes weakly to the door and exits.

INT. LIVING ROOM - DAY

Grandfather enters and goes to the telephone, fumbles for
a number among some papers, dials.

> GRANDFATHER (CONT'D)
> (painfully)
> I'm calling about the clock --
> the Grandfather clock. Yes. I've
> changed my mind about selling.
> I've got to have it back.
> (listens)
> Can't you just send it back in the
> truck?
> (listens)
> I'll come down then. Yes. Immedi-
> ately. Will you wait?

He hangs up, sways drunkenly. Grandfather is not well
and has no business leaving the house. He does not bother
getting his coat. He goes out in his shirtsleeves.

EXT STREET DAY

Grandfather makes his way along the sidewalk pausing frequently to catch his breath.

CLOSER ANGLE

He leans against a building breathing heavily.

We see a small boy pulling a wagon enter scene. He sees
Grandfather.

> BOY
> (tentatively)
> Hey, mister, you look kinda funny.
> Are you sick or somethin'?

Grandfather doesn't seem to hear. TIGHT SHOT - BOY
puzzled.

> BOY
> Mister?

LARGER ANGLE TO INCLUDE GRANDFATHER

As he continues along the street, weaving slightly. Curious, the boy follows.

                                              CUT TO:

INT. LIVING ROOM

Foster enters and tosses his hat on the hall tree.

                    FOSTER
              Hey, Grandfather?
              (a pause) Grandpa?

With a puzzled frown, he starts up the stairs.

INT. GRANDFATHER'S ROOM

Foster sticks his head through the door and looks about.

                    FOSTER
              Grandfather...?

He sees the furniture is gone. His eyes widen.

INT. LIVING ROOM - DAY

As Foster paws through the papers on the telephone table. He finds the receipt from the antique store. Immediately he knows where to start looking for grandfather. As he heads for the door we:

                                              CUT TO:

EXT. STREET - DAY

ANGLE AT INTERSECTION

Traffic comes and goes as Grandfather dazedly crosses against the light.

ANGLE ON POLICEMAN

He sees Grandfather and blows his whistle.

                         COP
             What's the matter with you?
            You wanna get yourself killed?!

When the light changes, the boy crosses the street, following Grandfather.

                                    DISSOLVE TO:

EXT. ANTIQUE STORE - DAY

It is a "treasures and trivia" kind of shop. Grandfather
comes into scene and enters.

INT. ANTIQUE STORE

Grandfather sees his clock immediately. It stands beside
the glass case that serves as a desk and counter. He goes
to it and gives it a cursory examination with an expression of relief. The dealer comes to greet him.

                       DEALER
            I'm sorry I couldn't return
                  it this evening,
          but the driver is off for the day.
                 If you don't mind
       waiting until tomorrow I'll have it delivered...

Grandfather stubbornly shakes his head.

                     GRANDFATHER
              I've got to have it now.

                       DEALER
        I'm awfully sorry you changed your mind.
            It's a lovely piece of mid-century
         craftsmanship. Is your truck outside?

Grandfather looks at him blankly.

                     GRANDFATHER
                       Truck?

                    DEALER
        Transportation -- for the clock.
             It's very heavy.

                  GRANDFATHER
    I suppose I could call a taxi or something.

                    DEALER
      Not likely. I doubt there's a cabbie in the
      city would take something as big as this
        clock! (peers closely at Grandfather)
            Are you sure you're well?

                  GRANDFATHER
     Maybe someone has a truck I could rent?

                    DEALER
      At this hour? Maybe you'd better wait until
      tomorrow. I could have it at your house first
               thing in the morning.

                  GRANDFATHER
                   (abrupt)
             No! That's impossible.

He looks about, frustrated, trying to figure this thing
out. He glances out the plate-glass window to see:

GRANDFATHER'S POV - The boy with the wagon.

ANGLE ON GRANDFATHER as his face lights up. He goes to
the door and waves the boy toward him.

                 DEALER (O.S.)
        It's your clock. If you change your mind
            about selling it, let me know.

But Grandfather isn't listening. ANOTHER ANGLE as the boy
comes into the shop.

                     BOY
            Did you call me, mister?

> GRANDFATHER
> How would you like to earn a dollar?
> I'd like to use your wagon for a few minutes.

> BOY
> Gee... sure.

The dealer has been looking on, puzzled.

Now, realizing what Grandfather intends he shakes his head dubiously.

> DEALER
> I don't recommend trying to
> move the clock in that.
> You might hurt yourself.

Grandfather ignores the advice.

> GRANDFATHER
> Give me a hand. Mind the pendulum;
> it's a delicate machine.
> I couldn't bear it if it
> stopped ticking...

The dealer shrugs, baffled. Together they lift the massive clock into the wagon, being careful to keep it upright, lest the pendulum stop. Grandfather is panting with the effort. They maneuver the wagon onto the sidewalk.

EXT. ANTIQUE STORE

> GRANDFATHER
> (to the boy)
> You get in back. I'll take the handle.

> DEALER
> (worried for him)
> Are you sure you want to do this?

Grandfather starts pulling the wagon as the boy pushes from behind. It is obviously a tough go for the old man. He is puffing before he has gone a dozen yards. The dealer shakes his head at the foolishness of old men and steps back inside his shop.

ANGLE AT CORNER as Grandfather pauses for breath.

> BOY
> How far, mister?

> GRANDFATHER
> Just a few blocks.
> Easy does it.
> There's no hurry now.

After a few moments, Grandfather takes the tongue of the wagon again.

> GRANDFATHER (CONT'D)
> Here we go.

EXT. STREET - DAY (SILENT)

From across the street we see Foster asking several people questions. One of them points off down the street. Foster hurries off.

ANGLE AT CURB

As Grandfather pauses again. He looks at the curb and then at the wagon. He had not considered the vicissitudes of street edges. He looks about, undecided what to do next.

> BOY
> What are you gonna do now, mister?

The sight of the old man wheeling the clock in the wagon has attracted several onlookers. One of them steps forward.

> FIRST ONLOOKER
> Hey, Pops! Why don't you carry a watch like everybody else? (He chuckles at his own wit.)

SECOND ONLOOKER
You need a hand with that?

Signaling that he needs help, Grandfather and the Second
Onlooker carefully lift the wagon onto the street.

GRANDFATHER
Careful! Please don't tip it!

SECOND ONLOOKER
Here's some advice: keep it
in the road till you get where
you're going... That way you won't
have to fight the curbs.
(He watches Grandfather as he
pulls the wagon off, shaking his
head.)

SERIES OF ANGLES

As Grandfather pulls the wagon along the streets, aided
by the boy. The volume of traffic has increased. Horns.
Brakes. Cars swerve aside. The journey is rapidly becoming a nightmare as Grandfather pauses more frequently to
rest his aching muscles.

INTERCUT WITH SCENES of Foster searching for grandfather.
We see the Second Onlooker from the previous scene giving
him directions. We see Foster's concern and apprehension
as he learns what Grandfather is doing.

ANGLE AT INTERSECTION as Grandfather prepares to cross.

GRANDFATHER
(panting with fatigue)
Almost there! Across the street...
down the block.

BOY
You gonna be all right, mister?

CLOSE SHOT — TRAFFIC SIGNAL

The light blinks red.

ANGLE AT INTERSECTION

As cross traffic comes to a halt. The street is clear.
Grandfather pulling, and the boy pushing, the wagon. They
start across. A laborious progress; the clock wobbles
precariously.

TIGHT SHOT GRANDFATHER struggling. The cords stand out on
his neck.

THE BOY looks up at Grandfather, worried.

> GRANDFATHER
> Push! Push! We're almost there!

They are in the center of the street as the light changes.

THE TRAFFIC SIGNAL turns green.

ANGLE ON GRANDFATHER VEHICLES — THE BOY The autos and
trucks race their engines as they prepare to get under-
way. Grandfather is squarely in the way. Horns begin to
honk!

> THE BOY
> The light!

> GRANDFATHER
> (with realization;
> intensely, to himself)
> Pull! Pull!

The boy stops pushing the wagon and grabs Grandfather's
hand.

> THE BOY
> Come on, mister! We're gonna get run over!

                         GRANDFATHER
                    No! (to Boy) Push! Push!

Grandfather shrugs off the Boy's hand, blindly, furious-
ly.

ANGLE AT CURB

As Foster arrives and sees:

FOSTER'S POV - GRANDFATHER struggling with the wagon.

FOSTER darts forward.

ANGLE AT INTERSECTION - FEATURING GRANDFATHER

The street is a bedlam of noise and confusion -- horns
honking! Drivers shouting. A police whistle shrills. Foster runs to Grandfather and attempts to tug him to the
safety of the sidewalk.

GRANDFATHER'S FACE wild, Frustrated. Fearful.

HIS POV - SERIES OF SHOTS

The cars. He is ringed by a menacing circle of honking
machines.

BACK TO SCENE and now Grandfather panics. Tugged at by
Foster, trapped by the cars, betrayed by age, he seeks a
haven in a hostile world.

                         GRANDFATHER
                  (almost incoherent; a wild, rush-
                         ing babble)
                  Foster! No matter what happens to
                   the clock I won't die will I?

Foster manages to get the old man to the curb.

                    GRANDFATHER (CONT'D)
                         (crazily)
                  That wouldn't be fair! Would it?
                         Would it?

                    FOSTER
         Easy Grandfather. It's all right!
           Everything is all right!

ANOTHER ANGLE

The Policeman from earlier has arrived on the scene and
is busy unsnarling the traffic. He stands near the wagon,
directing the cars around it, frequently blasting on his
whistle.

                    COP
         All right, pull ahead slowly.
         Watch the wagon there! Pull
         around it. That's right! Keep
            moving! Keep moving!
         (angry aside to characters)
         Get that thing out of here!
           You're causing a ruckus!

ANGLE AT CURB

As Foster tries to soothe Grandfather.

                    FOSTER
           It's all right Grandfather.
              You're safe. Easy!

But Grandfather can't take his eyes off the clock in the
wagon, standing high in the center of the moving traffic.
Now his eyes go wide as his view is obscured by a huge
truck that moves between him and the clock. From his angle, it looks as though the truck has run over the clock!

Grandfather tries to shake free! He feels a desperate
need to go save the clock from destruction.

                    FOSTER
                  Grandfather!

Grandfather is loose.

                    GRANDFATHER
                    (desperate)
                  No! It's true!
              I know it is! I don't
                  want to die!

Before Foster can stop him he rushes forward into the
street - into the moving traffic.

TIGHT SHOT - A DRIVER'S FACE

Sees Grandfather appear in front of him. Stomps the
brakes and swings the wheel.

ANGLE AT WAGON

The cars skid, trying to avoid grandfather, but brush the
wagon; it lurches forward. The clock teeters, tips!

TIGHT SHOT - GRANDFATHER

Eyes wide with horror. He throws himself at the clock!
Too late!

THE CLOCK falls as the wagon overturns. It smashes to the
unyielding pavement: wood splinters, glass shatters...

GRANDFATHER throws up his hands, screaming. He staggers,
then falls to the ground.

FOSTER - Horrified! He rushes to Grandfather.

ANOTHER ANGLE

Foster cradles Grandfather in his lap as the old man's
eyes open.

Nearby lies the nearly demolished clock; there is a sickly whirring sound as though of springs unwinding. As the
clock dies, we hear various ticks, clicks and scraping
sounds.

                    GRANDFATHER
                    (weakly)
                  Foster? Foster?

FOSTER
(brokenly)
Yes, Grandfather. Lie still.

GRANDFATHER
(in pain)
The... the clock? I saved... the clock?

FOSTER
Hush. You need your strength.

GRANDFATHER
You... you won't sell it, will you?
I don't need it anymore.
It... it's the baby's now.

His eyes close. His breathing stills, his body relaxes in Foster's arms.

TIGHT SHOT - FOSTER realizing that Grandfather is gone.

FOSTER
(softly)
No Grandfather: we won't sell your clock.

His face is determined as:

DISSOLVE TO:

EXT INTERSECTION DAY

The street is empty except for the Policeman, Foster, Grandfather and the overturned clock. There is a CROWD in the B.G. The SOUND of an ambulance dies in the distance.

COP
Funny. (crouching over Grandfather)
The car didn't touch him...
Did he have a bad heart?

CLOSE SHOT FOSTER - Thoughtful.

                              FOSTER
                    No. Nobody would say that
                       about Grandfather...
                    No, he had a good heart...
                    A really good heart...

TWO SHOT

The Policeman reacts to Foster's tone.

                               COP
                    I'm sorry... Let's get the
                    clock out of the street.

Together they move the damaged clock to the sidewalk.
They sit it upright.

CLOSE SHOT - FOSTER reacting to:

THE CLOCK - though the glass is broken, the edifice
gouged and crooked, the pendulum begins to swing. Halt-
ingly, the clock starts to tick. The rhythm becomes
strong and steady. It chimes once, mournfully.

                                                    CUT TO:

THE MATERNITY WARD OF THE HOSPITAL - A NURSE

Holding a tiny human bundle that begins to cry lustily.

Over the sound of the infant wail, we bring up the SOUND
of the CLOCK ticking time like a massive heartbeat.

                                                DISSOLVE TO:

INT. BABY'S ROOM - DAY

We see a crib, bassinet, etc. We see Foster and Connie
standing tightly together, peering at the baby sleeping
in the crib.

CAMERA PULLS BACK

and we see one very incongruous note in the room. Against
the wall is the Grandfather clock, its pendulum counting

time.

OVER THE SHOT, we hear SERLING'S VOICE

                    SERLING
          All men's lives are measured by
          clocks ticking, both the good man
          and the bad... But this we take as
          an article of faith: when one door
          closes, another opens -- in this
          world, and in The Twilight Zone.

And we:

                              SLOWLY GO TO BLACK:

                    THE END

                      ###

George Clayton Johnson was born in Cheyenne, WY in 1929. He served in the military and worked a variety of jobs until he discovered his talent for writing. Later, living in Los Angeles, he fell in with a pack of writers who called themselves "The Group". Johnson had written *Ocean's Eleven* with a partner, and was embraced by this coterie of young men, among them Richard Matheson, Charles Beaumont, John Tomerlin and William F. Nolan. It was as one of the go-to writers for Rod Serling's *The Twilight Zone* that Johnson made his name, followed by credits on *Star Trek, Kung Fu* and other shows. He also co-wrote the science fiction classic *Logan's Run* with William F. Nolan, and the animated short *Icarus Montgolfier Wright* with Ray Bradbury (mentor to "The Group"), which was later nominated for an Academy Award.

What the author writes about this teleplay:

" 'The Grandfather Clock' is simply my take on the familiar story-song 'But it stopped, short/Never to run again when the old man died…'.

'The Grandfather Clock' was the last script I wrote for that masterful producer Buck Houghton (*The Twilight Zone*), who left the show abruptly while the script was in work. I had wanted Buck to hire a coffeehouse folksinger that I knew to sing the beautiful and touching song to underscore 'The Grandfather Clock', but he told me that the job of Narrator was already taken…

To my dismay, the new producer used the paid-for story outline to construct his 'Ninety Years Without Slumbering', which starred Ed Wynn as the old man."

Triptych: Three Bon-Bons

I: The Part in Question
II: The Numbers
III: The Town Elders

by Christopher Conlon

1: The Part in Question

♦

They couldn't afford to resurrect all of Uncle Charlie, so they held a family meeting to decide exactly what part of him might be brought back from the dead. Initially there appeared to be a nearly unanimous vote for the head, but the nieces reminded all assembled there just how unpleasant Uncle Charlie could really be: his vulgarity, his prejudices, his insulting names for Aunt Madeleine. Did they really want the disembodied head of Uncle Charlie bellowing at them from the mantle day and night?

Well, then, what? The chest made no sense. What good would a living, breathing chest disconnected from any other part of the body be to anyone? Or the legs, for that matter -- they might run away, and it would be quite an embarrassment to the family to have the neighbors see Uncle Charlie's legs running around the block, especially if they had no pants on, and after all, how does one keep pants on a pair of bodiless legs?

When Aunt Madeleine was out of the room someone playfully suggested that the resurrected portion of Uncle Charlie should be his progenitive instrument, and this caused great giggles and guffaws all around the table. But once Aunt Madeleine had returned to her seat no one was willing to tell her what all the hilarity had been about.

The family was stumped. What no one wanted to say was that, really, Uncle Charlie had been an old cuss and no one actually wanted him back anyway. But resurrection, at least single-part resurrection, was relatively inexpensive, and virtually all their neighbors had had some part of someone brought back from the dead. It would look positively unChristian not to follow likewise with Uncle Charlie, who had not died nearly fast enough to suit anyone's taste at that table, including, though she would never admit it publicly, Aunt Madeleine's.

In the end it was agreed that the most inoffensive portion of Uncle Charlie they could think of was his left hand. This was the hand that wore his wedding ring, and it was not the hand he generally used to slap, pinch, or punch his wife. It was decided that the portion of Uncle Charlie that would be resurrected would be his left hand.

And so it was done. The hand was mounted on an old trophy base someone found in a thrift shop for twenty-five cents, and it looked handsome enough on the mantle, though the family quickly learned to stay away from its still-powerful grasp. Indeed, the hand was as strong as it had been when it had been attached to Uncle Charlie, and possibly even stronger. As a result they gave the hand a wide berth, which is why, when neighbors came to visit, what they would see mounted on an old trophy stand on the mantle far from anything else was a strong old male hand, its middle finger raised high.

♦

II: The Numbers

⌘

*O*ne morning every woman awoke to find a number imprinted upon her forehead. The numbers were wildly varying among different women, though the most common were in single digits. The numbers were approximately two inches high and something like the color of dried blood. They could not be removed, despite the endlessly innovative ways women tried to get rid of them. Cleansers were useless. Makeup only dulled them slightly. Harsh scrubbing pads designed for dirty pots and pans caused significant damage to many a woman's skin, but merely succeeded in forming a bloody patina around the ever-present, seemingly permanent number. Only young girls appeared exempt from these inexplicable intaglios.

The question of what the numbers meant was widely discussed, but it was left to a twelve-year-old girl with the undistinguished name of Ginny Brown to accidentally happen upon the answer. Ginny had begun to feel strange cramps one day, and since she had an extremely devoted mother who had prepared her exceptionally well for what in some other time would be known as "becoming a woman," Ginny knew how to prepare herself, and she did so. Later that afternoon she sensed the process beginning, and with the curiosity typical of a girl of that age she raised her hand in class to be allowed to visit the bathroom. Once there, she investigated what was happening down below and, satisfied and not feeling too uncomfortable, she put her clothing back together again and was about to leave the bathroom when she happened to glance in the mirror, discovering that one of the glowing two-inch-high numbers had appeared on her heretofore pristine forehead. The number was 0. Now, Ginny's extremely devoted mother was also an unusually honest and open one, and morally upstanding, as well. As a result Ginny's mind compared the 0 on her own forehead to the 1 she knew was on her mother's, and, knowing what she did about her mother's history, Ginny understood.

"I know what it is!" she cried into the school hallway, the bathroom door swinging shut behind her. "It's the number of people you've had sex with!"

Ginny was correct, though for many women the fact was not an entirely stunning revelation. Some -- those with highly organized and mathematically-oriented minds -- had suspected the ghastly truth almost immediately, and others who shared uncommonly close and frank friendships with other women already knew it almost for a certainty. This was, however, the first time that *men* heard the notion.

The repercussions were, alas, dire. Heated discussions occurred before many a family hearth during which epithets of a distinctly indelicate nature were hurled at wives and fiancées and sisters and daughters who had believed, naively as it turned out, that their private lives were destined to always remain private and inviolate. It was a disturbing fact that at times a man might go off to work, leaving his wife with her comfortingly low

2 or 3 on her forehead, only to return in the evening to find that her 2 had become a 3 or her 3 a 4. Unpleasant scenes were enacted in which men who had been led to believe that they were marrying virgins only once or twice or thrice removed found themselves staring at two-inch high scarlet numbers with unbelievable, even dizzying totals: 22, 49, 74. In one memorable case a man hacked his wife to death with a cleaver upon beholding a number rumored to have been 841.

In the midst of this frenzied activity, certain facts were nonetheless apparent. "Sex," for instance, was defined by the numbers as any erotic activity involving penetration by a penis of any of the obvious female orifices, none of which need be listed or described here. Penetration by foreign objects did not appear to count in the tallies; nor did sexual acts which occurred exclusively among females, no matter what instruments might have been utilized in the acts. Mutual masturbation was similarly irrelevant to the point totals. The duration of the act mattered not a whit -- two seconds or two hours, it was all counted the same in the total.

Rape presented an interesting aspect for study, for it appeared that it represented an exception. Women who had been violently gang-raped, for instance, but who were otherwise sexually inexperienced, found themselves displaying 0's on their foreheads. On the other hand, there were many women who had made various claims about how certain activities in their lives had unfolded, yet despite these claims, these women found the point totals on their foreheads to be alarmingly high.

In the ensuing weeks after the numbers had made their first unexpected appearance and Ginny Brown had deduced the terrible truth about them, hat-buying reached an all-time high among women. They would wear these hats low to their foreheads in an obvious but mostly futile attempt to disguise their numbers. Men found this practice unacceptable, and hats were routinely ripped from women's heads in the street. Some women attempted to take on the female headgear of faraway lands, long and black and face-hiding, but this too tended toward failure. Men seemingly would not allow it, and if the headgear was pulled away to reveal an exceptionally high number, the woman would often be attacked there in the street, stoned or shot or run over by motorized vehicles.

Indeed, as a result of the violence perpetrated by these aggressive and enraged men, laws were passed to protect the hapless women. Women were not to leave their homes even to go to work out to water their azaleas. It was recommended that houses with women have their windows covered over with brick or steel as a security measure, and that women arm themselves with handguns and, if possible, light artillery.

What good these laws and recommendations did is unclear at this late date, since the society in which these events occurred disappeared long ago and what records remain are sparse and fragmentary. Some historians have suggested that the whole civilization destroyed itself in a sudden and massive conflagration which wiped out its entire populace, female and male, in a matter of hours. This is mere speculation, of course, and should not be accepted as fact by any student of this quaint if unfortunate period of history.

○

III: The Town Elders

In their wisdom the town elders decreed that an ice skating rink would be built, and it was. Hundreds of happy skaters, loving couples, single men and women, teenagers, families with small wobble-walking children, came from miles around bundled in their snow clothes to enjoy gliding about on the ice under blue and white winter skies. Unfortunately the rink had been built, for reasons only the town elders might have been able to explain, on the top of a small lake, and as the weather turned from winter to spring skaters began to notice cracks which were at first no more than tiny pencil-scratches in the ice but which soon expanded to highly dangerous crevices and chasms. Skaters began to disappear under the ice into the lake, at first occasionally, and then on an alarmingly regular basis.

When blossoms opened all over town and the weather turned the warm of sandals and shorts, the ice rink was dismantled entirely and the same persons who had enjoyed the winter skating -- that is, those who still survived -- came to the lake, disrobing almost completely and allowing the sun to bronze their skin for hours on end. They ate from picnic baskets and cooked hamburgers on small barbeques. Many of them swam delightedly in the lake, paddling this way and that and playfully splashing each other. One problem, which the town elders failed entirely to solve, was that at times corpses left over from the fiasco of the skating rink would suddenly surface, and at the most inopportune times. It became an embarrassment and something of a public relations problem, never more so than when a young woman dragged a male corpse to shore, proclaiming it to be what remained of her first and indeed only true love, thereupon carrying the disintegrating thing over her shoulders to the local courthouse where she demanded that the town elders allow her to marry it. She was informed that the law did not allow for the marriage of woman to corpse, and this created a small but similarly embarrassing civil rights kerfuffle. The woman ultimately decided to cohabitate with her dearly beloved without benefit of wedlock, a decision which generated some controversy in itself -- but not, the town elders were certain, on the level that would have occurred had they allowed the two of them to enter an officially-sanctioned state of matrimony.

One odd aspect to this entire problem of the corpses in the lake was that the lake never seemed to tire of disgorging bodies onto the shore. After a time it became embarrassingly apparent that far more deceased persons were washing up onto the sands than had vanished from the ice rink during the winter. The town elders formed a committee to study this highly unlikely problem, but no final report from this committee is known to have been issued, or if issued, it appears to have been lost.

In the meantime winter came again and the lake was once more crusted over with smooth, inviting ice. Again came the young lovers and the men and women and the families with their small wobble-walking children. But now some noticed odd round bumps appearing on the surface of the ice, bumps which slowly split the ice in places and through which strange things, at first unrecognizable, began to grow. Some persons believed that the growths might be some new strain of cauliflower or tomato, but soon enough it became apparent that the growths were in fact human beings. One would see the clear ice-encrusted outlines of a forehead, a temple, a set of ears, frost-filled strands of hair. This for the town elders was the ultimate humiliation, and it was quickly decided that something would have to be done. Fortunately there was a course of action readily and even obviously available to them.

The town elders began to cultivate this unprecedented winter crop. One would see them late at night in their heavy coats tilling the ice rink with shovels and hoes, always careful to smooth the ice again after pulling nature's peculiar yield from the ice. Eventually the story, which was true, went around that the crops were in fact delicious to eat when prepared properly, and soon the townspeople themselves were tending what was now less a skating rink than a glorious winter garden.

If you ever decide to go to the town, by all means do so in the depths of winter. Buy one of the readily-available cookbooks for sale at various shops near the garden, then go and collect some winter crops for your own dinner. There's more than enough for everyone. Indeed, the supply is ample and even, at times, overwhelming. The heads of teenaged girls are said to be especially succulent when stewed for several hours in chicken stock with carrot, onion, and celery. Or snap off some baby fingers, which are simple to gather and requite no preparation at all. The town elders assure us that they are delicious straight from the ice, sweet and unexpectedly tangy.

Christopher Conlon is the author of the novel *Midnight on Mourn Street* (Earthling Publications, 2008) along with several collections of stories and poems. He has also edited a number of books, including *He Is Legend: An Anthology Celebrating Richard Matheson* (Gauntlet Press, 2009), *Poe's Lighthouse* (Cemetery Dance, 2006), and *The Twilight Zone Scripts of Jerry Sohl* (Bear Manor Media, 2004). He lives in Silver Spring, Maryland. Visit him online at *http://christopherconlon.com*.

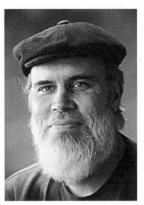

What the author writes about these stories:

"The little stories I call my 'bon-bons' (after the ice cream treats as well as Poe's comedic tale) might be thought of as finger-exercises in fantasy and/or surrealism. These vignettes are free from the usual straitjackets of logic and reason -- in them, as in dreams, anything can happen. Often the writing of these pieces is immediate, spontaneous, almost free-associative, as with 'The Part in Question' and 'The Town Elders'; others take years, like 'The Numbers,' whose basic plot germ tugged at my sleeve for a decade before I finally discovered its proper form."

The Hand That Feeds

by Kurt Newton

The alley smelled of garbage and urine. There were no windows, no doors, no way out.

"Let me see your hands!" the young officer barked. He stood at the alley's entrance, his face flushed from the chase, his gun drawn.

Out of breath and out of options, Kevin Schrader turned, his heart hammering in his chest. His left hand balled into a fist, fingernails digging into the skin of his palm. "Please... just forget you ever saw me."

"I said, let me see your hands!" The officer now called for backup.

"I don't want to do this. Please, don't make me do this..." Tears stung the corners of Kevin's eyes.

But it was already done.

Kevin felt the swell, like a seismic wave of electrical current, moving upward from his chest. When it reached his left shoulder, it turned the corner and headed downward, gaining strength, building momentum, surging through the narrow straits of his elbow and continuing into his wrist. Kevin closed his eyes, aware of what was going to happen next but also detached from it, as if his own consciousness had to momentarily exit his body for the event to occur. He felt his palm open up like a gate. His arm was raised, aimed at the young officer, hand open, fingers splayed, as if he were about to stop an oncoming vehicle. Only he wasn't stopping anything, he was setting something free. Kevin's breath caught in his chest as a rush of cold suddenly roared through him, chilling him to the bone. And then it was over.

Moments later, Kevin ran past the young officer, who now lay prone upon the alley's slick pavement, not dead, but not really alive, his two-way radio smoldering at his collar. The young man's eyes stared up at Kevin as if they had just seen God.

Kevin stepped out of the alley and onto the city sidewalk, the smell of burned plastic clinging to his clothes.

I just want you to be happy...

Kevin awoke with a start. He lifted his head up off the cold kitchenette table, his cheek wet with drool. He stared at the half-empty bottle of gin in front of him and the plastic tumbler beside it. He shook his head.

So this is what my life has come to?

The motel room was dingier than the last. But it would have to do.

He was on the run. Again. It wasn't long ago that he had all the good fortune in the world, including a perversely high paying salary at a brokerage firm. He could walk into any auto showroom and drive out with the car of his choice, and the women he could attract... beautiful women he would have never dreamed possible. In a little over a year's time he had acquired a rock star's lifestyle.

But there was a hitch. There was always a hitch. A hitch he didn't find out about until things began to go wrong.

Not wrong for him. No, he was spared all manner of misfortune. In fact, his good luck was a little too good, his decisions a little too insightful. He should have known when he felt that first twinge of *rightness* when his hand passed over the Dow Jones Averages on its way to the sports section and seemed to hover over one stock in particular. Sports and stocks, they were virtually the same, you played your hunches. And this was one whopper of a hunch.

BioPharma: a med-tech stock. Its price: twenty-five bucks a share. Kevin didn't know the first thing about stocks. But his mother's life insurance had left him twenty-five hundred dollars. In fact, the check from the State of Connecticut pension fund had arrived that morning. Money he hadn't planned on having. So why not throw the dice? Play the hunch?

He did. One hundred shares. In less than a week the price had doubled. And once again he checked the papers. Another twinge, another winner. Each time he invested twenty-five hundred. Lucky twenty-five. In a few weeks he had turned that twenty-five hundred into twenty-five thousand. His trader offered him a job, and in a few months time he was running the place.

I just want you to be happy...

In the beginning, he was. He was ecstatic. Kevin accepted his run of good luck as a long-overdue tip of the scales in his favor. Life was suddenly like a train that had pulled up one day and he just got in and let it take him to wherever it was headed.

But while Kevin was having the time of his life, the people around him began to suffer. Co-workers, girlfriends, even his own sister began to fall victim to one bad circumstance after another. Bad investments, car accidents, drug addiction, or worse. The same train that had stopped to pick him up appeared to be mowing down the people he cared for left and right.

And then came the incident with Anginette Reyes. He had just wanted to shut her up. What happened next called into question everything he had believed to that point. God, in the form of fate, luck and circumstance, wasn't the one smiling kindly upon him; he was the one performing the miracles. He was the one robbing the good fortune from everyone else.

I just want you to be happy...

Kevin felt another twinge.

His hand grabbed the TV remote and clicked it to life. The audio came on before the television picture. A female news reporter was detailing the day's events.

"The young officer appeared to have suffered a stroke while chasing this man, Kevin L. Schrader, an investment broker..."

Kevin saw his picture hovering over the reporter's left shoulder like a devil whispering into her ear:

"Officer Connelly was called to the scene of a disturbance at Johnson Memorial Hospital earlier today, where Schrader was allegedly irate over not being allowed to visit a patient. After a brief scuffle with security, eyewitnesses said Schrader took off on foot when the young officer arrived. Officer Connelly was later found in an alley, two blocks from the Hospital, an apparent victim of a stroke. No charges have yet been filed, but Schrader is wanted for questioning.

Schrader is also wanted for questioning in an alleged domestic abuse incident that occurred last week involving his ex-girlfriend, Anginette Reyes. The patient Schrader had tried to visit today was Ms. Reyes, who is still recovering from her injuries."

The television went dead. Kevin set the remote back on the table and began to weep.

He grabbed the gin bottle and hurled it against the wall, where it shattered, leaving a wet stain and a dent in the thick plaster. In the room next door, a fist pounded on the wall. A voice shouted for him to keep it down.

Kevin rubbed his face. He stared at the stain on the wall as it continued to run.

I just want you to be happy...

He checked his watch.

There was someone he needed to see.

The late afternoon sun streamed through thick oak trees as Kevin drove his Mercedes up the long entrance drive leading to the Brookside Retreat. The two-hundred-patient healthcare facility was situated on over a hundred woodland acres in the southern part of the state. As healthcare facilities went, the Brookside Retreat was one of the best.

"I'm here to see my sister."

The receptionist smiled. "I'm afraid our visiting hours are nearly over."

"I realize that. Please, I've just spent two hours on the road."

The receptionist hesitated.

"I'll make it quick, I promise." Kevin felt his hand begin to tingle.

Perhaps the receptionist sensed a hint of desperation in his voice. "I'll see what I can do," she said. "Please have a seat."

Kevin sat in one of the cushiony chairs in the lobby. He watched the receptionist phone the ward. His hand wanted to reach out in her direction. The skin of his palm burned, so he crumpled it tightly into a fist. Perspiration trickled down the side of his temple. His arm trembled, so he shoved his hand under his thigh and sat on it.

The receptionist looked up and smiled. Kevin smiled back.

He actually hated coming here. It only served to dredge up what he had worked so hard to leave in the past.

"Mr. Schrader. Someone will be with you shortly."

"Thank you," Kevin replied. He took a deep breath. His hand relaxed.

Minutes later, he and Dr. Tarabishy walked down a long, carpeted hallway to the ward. The good doctor offered a sobering evaluation. "Christine is not doing as well as we had hoped."

The dinnertime smell of food made Kevin's stomach churn. He said nothing. His sister's worsening condition did not surprise him. He realized now that no one he came into contact with did well afterwards.

"Perhaps a familiar face will bring the light back to her eyes," the doctor added optimistically as he keyed open a security door and they stepped into a glass-walled foyer. The doctor waved to the desk and an attendant came over to let them in.

"Are you carrying any pens, pencils, pocket knives, matches, cigarette lighters?" the attendant asked.

"No," said Kevin.

Patients milled about the ward; several eyed Kevin as Dr. Tarabishy showed him to a private room. Inside, Kevin's sister sat at a round conference table.

"Christine, your brother is here to see you." The doctor spoke slower and louder than necessary.

Kevin's sister stood almost mechanically. She held out her arms and greeted Kevin with a hug. When they were growing up, she had always towered over him. At five-feet ten-inches she was literally his big sister. But now she appeared less tall and felt frail in his arms, as if the life had been siphoned from her, leaving nothing but a brittle husk.

"It's good to see you," he lied.

"You too," she said. She sat back down.

Satisfied with Christine's initial reaction, Dr. Tarabishy stepped out and closed the door behind him, leaving the two of them alone.

The brightly lit room looked out into the neighboring hallways on two sides. A television sat in the corner, the sound turned low, a cooking show in progress.

"Sorry to interrupt your dinnertime. I had to promise them to keep my visit short."

Christine stared at him, her expression one of abject innocence. She was more like a child now than a woman reaching middle age. Perhaps that's what happens when your mind cannot cope with the present; it leapfrogs back to a time when there were no worries, no pain. Or maybe it was just her medication.

"So how are you?"

Christine's shoulders hitched. What was supposed to be a shrug looked more like a spasm. "I'm okay."

Looking at her, Kevin could tell that she clearly was not. He wished he had forced himself to visit her more often, maybe then this wouldn't be so awkward.

"Chris, do you ever think about Mom?"

"Mom?" She said the word as if she were trying to understand its meaning. "Mom?" She said it again and her unblinking eyes began to flood with tears. "Mom's dead. I saw her. She sat up like this --" Christine sat up straight in her chair and looked off into space. Then her eye's refocused on Kevin. "She was talking to somebody. But nobody was there. I said, 'Ma, I'm right here.' I got right in front of her. Just like this." She leaned in close to Kevin momentarily, then retreated. "But she looked right through me. Then she died. She sat back and she just stopped breathing. But her eyes were still open. Staring."

"I know, Chris, I'm sorry you had to see that. But listen to me. Can you remember what Mom said? Who was she talking to?"

Christine shook her head slowly from side to side, her expression as blank as her understanding. And then a light did appear in her eyes, as if the frayed wires of her psyche had momentarily made contact with each other. Her back stiffened as she stared at Kevin, suddenly adopting their mother's voice.

"I'm ready now. Remember the hand that feeds."

Christine's shoulders softened. Her eyes looked away, the light now gone.

"What did Mom say? What about the hand that feeds?"

"Mom? But Mom's dead. I saw her. She sat up like this --"

"I know. Stop it." The tears were back in his sister's eyes. "It's okay."

Kevin wanted to grab her by the shoulders and shake her. He wanted to make her repeat the words she had said just so he could confirm he had really heard them. Why didn't she call him the morning their mother died? Didn't she know something was different that day? He could have been there and maybe all of this could have been avoided. But he hadn't been there. Not until after the hospice workers had taken his mother's corpse away and it was just he and his sister left alone in the apartment. Their mother had lived here for the last twenty years of her life, the last year of which was consumed slowly, painfully, by a cancer she had waited too long to see the doctor about. Just he and his sister sat there surrounded by the sudden emptiness, left to catch their breath in the vacuum caused by their mother's death. That was when Kevin had to get up, for fear of being sucked into that void; get up from the very couch his mother had died upon, placing his hand near the spot where his mother had sat in the final moments of her life. His hand came away wet. Wet with urine. His mother's urine. And he nearly got sick as he hurried into the bathroom to wash it off, but by then it was too late.

I just want you to be happy...

And now, feeling the dampness of that awful moment still clinging to his palm, Kevin stared at his sister, her eyes large, tears collecting like dew drops on her lower lashes. He could see how she struggled to stay in the here and now. If he could, he would take away those memories that haunted her; take away that last year of their mother's life when his sister had moved in to tend to their mother's needs, only to watch her slow disintegration as helplessly as a child watching a sand castle crumble beneath the tide; take her back to a place before all this had happened. But Kevin knew, as he reached up and placed his hand upon his sister's forehead, it was impossible to selectively destroy her memories without destroying everything else.

A surge of energy coursed through Kevin's body and he felt his sister sigh beneath his palm.

He left her sitting peacefully in the room with a smil on her face like a child seeing the world for the first time.

They say in order to truly finish something you have to go back to where it all began.

By the time Kevin arrived in Willimantic, the sun had nearly set. He drove through his mother's old apartment complex and parked, his Mercedes looking out of place among the second-hand cars and brightly painted low-riders. It was a warm August night. Salsa music floated on the air.

He stared out at the tan two-story building in the fading light and remembered all the good that had come out of his mother's apartment, not simply memories of a mother and her son but the special moments shared by two adults who had a genuine love and respect for each other. He remembered Sunday morning conversations over tea, talking about the current state of politics or the future state of the world. He remembered watching tennis matches and Red Sox baseball games. He also remembered her penchant toward the unexplained mysteries of life -- her interest in palmistry and the afterlife. She shared so much of herself but, like the mysteries that interested her, she also kept equally as much hidden. There were incidents and events, choices she had made, things she had done before meeting their father -- things that Kevin knew little about -- that she seemed to never forgive herself for, and which, on occasion, plunged her into an emotional abyss, as if her past was a black stain that left the rest of her life somehow tainted, and to share these things about herself would have somehow made her an awful person, one unworthy of love. In the end, of course, Kevin couldn't help but believe that she was eaten up by these dark secrets, some of which may have been handed down -- quite literally -- to him.

I just want you to be happy...

Kevin hung his head as tears fell from his eyes. He felt them land in the palm of his hand, except they didn't feel liquid. The tears subsided and he opened his eyes. He brought his palm close and turned it toward the streetlamp. Instead of tears his palm held miniature mounds of dust -- gold dust. As he tilted his hand, the dust fell in a shower of magic sparkles. He laughed, a laughter laced with sadness and truth.

He had put it off long enough. He knew what he had to do.

Kevin cut his headlights as he drove between the stone columns that marked the entrance to St. Joseph's Cemetery. He followed the narrow dirt drive, navigating by moonlight, until he reached the newer section of the cemetery where he pulled over and parked beside a large group of cedar trees. It was far enough away from street traffic for him not to be seen. He grabbed the shovel, sledgehammer, and pry bar out of his trunk -- newly purchased, price stickers still attached -- and went in search of his mother's gravesite.

Kevin had his own theories about his gift. Maybe his hand had become a divining rod, able to tap into some kind of future stream of events that let him know what was about to happen. And like a diving rod, capable of gathering energy, maybe he was also able to create an event just by redirecting that energy toward the object of his intent. He knew an ex-girlfriend and a young police officer that would testify to the latter, if they could. There was also a host of near-acquaintances over the past year that suffered from the collateral damage of just being in the wake of his all-too-fortunate presence.

Kevin really didn't know how it worked, but as he walked over to his mother's grave and sunk the shovel into the dirt, he was finally going to get to the bottom of it.

Overhead, the moon hung in the damp haze like a pale grey ball, nearly full. Kevin stopped to catch his breath. His shirt was sweat-soaked, his hair matted to his forehead. He stood shoulder-deep in his mother's year-old grave. He leaned against the shovel's smooth handle.

The stars were lost amid the city's cumulative glow. Nothing moved. Even the trees that stood like sentries amid the cemetery grounds were entombed by the thick night air. In the distance, Kevin heard the revved-up whine of a motorcycle hurtling down Main Street, reminding him there were still people up and about at this hour. He worried that a young couple, looking for some privacy, might choose St. Joseph's to park and grope in the dark. Or perhaps some local teens, in search of a nice quiet spot to pass the bottle around.

He continued digging.

Ten minutes and another foot deeper his shovel struck the concrete casement.

Kevin hoisted himself up out of the pit. He grabbed the sledgehammer. His hands shook.

The casement shattered with the first blow. Dirt and concrete fell on top of the casket beneath. Moonlight reflected off its shiny surface. Kevin bludgeoned away more of the concrete until there was enough room to open the head of the casket. He got on his knees, reached down, and tried the cover -- and it opened. He wouldn't need the pry bar, after all. He lifted the cover and pushed it to the side -- and stared.

In the soft moonlight, his mother lay peacefully be   him, her eyes closed, her face as sleep-still as the day of her funeral.

But this can't be, Kevin thought. *It's been over a year.* Embalming only forestalls the decaying process; it doesn't prevent it. The weight of the casket lid might provide some kind of waterproof seal but it wasn't airtight. Neither was the casement. Perhaps it was a combination of all three.

Kevin sat back. His muscles felt weak and once again he began to sob. The past year's events flashed through his mind... the sudden rise of his success; the money, the cars, the women; the exhilarating feeling, better than any drug he had ever experienced, a feeling that he could do anything, be anyone, a reach-out-and-grab-the-fucking-gold-ring-from-the-nose-of-the-universe kind of happiness where everything was glitz and gloss and gold dust... he saw Anginette, the only woman he ever loved, the only person he ever told his secret to, her face contorted, screaming how she was going to tell everyone he was a fake, a cheater, unless he let her in on the action; this was followed by her beautiful face bursting into flames as his hand was open before he knew it, the energy inside dispensed in a preemptive strike... and, finally, the hospital, a last ditch effort to set things right, only to make matters worse, always worse, because once his intent was made clear, like death, there was no taking it back.

But, now, as he sat on his mother's unearthed casket, he wondered: *Maybe, just maybe, I can give it away...*

He leaned forward and placed his palm on his mother's cold forehead. "Take it back," he said quietly. Then his voice rose and echoed in the night. "I don't want it anymore. Take it back, dammit! Take it back!"

Nothing happened. At first. Then the skin beneath his hand began to warm.

His mother's eyes suddenly opened. She sucked in a violent breath, her body arching in the narrow coffin space. Kevin recoiled but kept his hand steady. After several moments of searching in the moonlit dark, her eyes finally settled upon his, and with a motherly smile she said, *"Kevin, my son... I just wanted you to be happy..."*

Kevin looked into his mother's eyes one last time -- so kind, so loving, so full of secrets. He thought of all the lives he had touched for the worse, all the pain and suffering he had imparted. Whatever dark legacy he was supposed to carry, he didn't want any part of it. "Goodbye, mother," he said, and the fire that began to build in his chest was the most powerful yet.

His arm felt as if it had been suddenly dipped in ice as the energy surged through him. His hand became momentarily fused to his mother's skull as the grave filled with the pungent odor of burned flesh. He could hear someone screaming and realized it was his own voice caterwauling in the night. At last he was able to pull his hand free.

When he did, it was as if an invisible string had yanked the soul from his mother's body. Her eyelids drooped shut and her body seemed to shrink as it settled back into the casket. Blotches of long overdue decay slowly covered her skin like lichen, and a ripe stench filtered up from her rotting corpse.

Kevin closed the casket lid, and with the strength he had left he climbed up out of the open grave and filled it back in, sealing a chapter in his life he wanted to forget but knew he never could.

Kurt Newton is the author of two short story collections, one novel, and five collections of poetry. His short stories have appeared in *Weird Tales, Space & Time*, and *Dark Discoveries*. He is currently at work on his next novel.

What the author writes about this story:
" 'The Hand That Feeds' sprung from an actual event. I received a phone call at work from my sister telling me our mother had just died. She had been battling cancer for nearly a year. I left work to be with my sister while the necessary arrangements were made. After our mother's body was taken away I sat on the couch where my mother had died. When I got up, pushing off the couch with my hand, I felt a dampness. It was where my mother was sitting when her final breath left her lungs. Apparently, what was in her bladder had also left. Needless to say, I was a bit disturbed by the incident. Of all the gifts my mother had given to me this was indeed the strangest, and quite possibly the most lasting. I dedicate this story to her."

The Central Coast

by Jason V Brock

Alex was cold.

Wistfully observing the now silent ambulances and police cars pull away into the darkness, red and blue lights painting the black grass with glowing streaks, he thought: *Man, I hate that yellow crime scene tape...*

He swallowed hard, head buzzing, and turned around. A warm breeze caused the palm trees to rustle, but it did little to change the icy mercury of dread creeping up his back as he stood on the sidewalk facing his house. Staring ahead, blood crusting on his shirt, sticky on his hands, his thoughts were confused, jangled. He felt removed from life: a dreamless somnambulant.

Entering the living room, Alex paused in the shattered doorway, a strange metallic aftertaste on his tongue. At the edge of his awareness, he heard women quietly weeping: some of the last remaining guests, they looked up at him from blood-drenched seats, coated with gore and bile themselves.

As he surveyed the demolished remnants of his home, Alex regarded his visitors, still mute with astonishment; slowly shaking his head, he shrugged imperceptibly, at a loss as to what to say. *Hell of a party...* he mused. *Damn Crime Lab left the place more of a wreck than before they arrived...*

And those police interviews... Those really *killed the mood...*

The migraine pulsing in the center of his cranium made him grimace. Stumbling toward the kitchen, he contemplated what he should tell the survivors.

Maybe 'Thanks for coming -- I'm relieved the rest of you are going home in one piece...'

He paused near the threshold of the closed kitchen door, head pounding, face warm. *No, too direct...*

Mentally bracing himself, he slowly pushed on the door. His breath was shallow: he was afraid of what might still be on the other side.

Perhaps, 'Glad you could make it -- that was quite the dessert course...'

He shut his eyes as he inched the door open. *That's no good,* he reflected, *Too morbid...* Sweat caused his shirt to cling to his body; his heartbeat grew louder in his ears, crowding out the whispers starting to emanate from the living room.

How about: 'Next time, let's just play Twister and forget the drinks...'

Eyes closed, Alex smiled half-heartedly at the thought that any-one on earth would ever play another party game -- or even *go* to a party -- after what had happened tonight. His legs were unsteady; the door felt as though it weighted a thousand pounds.

Probably best not to say anything... pretend nothing happened...

Thank God *someone cut off the stereo...*

The door was fully open at last; Alex reluctantly opened his eyes, his face twitching involuntarily.

"Jesus..." His voice was weak, constricted. Stomach lurching, eyes watering, he sagged against the doorframe, fighting vertigo. Un-consciously holding his breath, he exhaled with a sob.

At least the paramedics took the bodies away...

The room was coated in a thick syrup of coagulating blood. The coppery smell of carnage was nauseating. Broken platefuls of ripe cheese, overturned bottles of alcohol and shattered wine glasses -- all covered in the fine black grit of fingerprint powder -- completed the surreal montage. Distantly, he felt more than heard the scurrying of the former revelers as they departed, leaving him alone to clean up his destroyed residence.

Guess it's not every day you see people slaughter each other at a social gathering...

Something slid under his shoe. Pulling his foot up, Alex realized the popping sound he had heard was one of Jordan's eyeballs.

He screamed.

"I'm tired."

Alex's eyelid spasmed at the sound of Jordan's whining.

"So am I," he said, glancing at the gas gauge. "We're making good time." Changing the subject, he continued: "We should be hitting Paso Robles in about fifteen minutes, and you know what that means..."

"Wine tasting!" Jordan exclaimed, squirming in the passenger seat. He smiled at her childish clapping.

"Olives, too," Alex reminded her.

"Yes! Mmmm..." she said, smacking her lips.

The drive from L.A. was long, but they needed to get to San Francisco the following day for an industry seminar. He was annoyed that the *en route* visit to her mother's had kept them so late; ever since reading that creepy Etchison story, Alex found stopping at rest areas disturbing -- especially after sundown.

Upon returning, they were scheduled to finish some pick-ups for the movie: reaction shots and a scene with Jordan's erstwhile best friend, Krystal. Afterward, the plan was to have a nice week or two of vacation on Kauai. In spite of all the traveling, it would be fun to get out of the rat race: *No helicopters, no high-speed police chases, no junk mail from realtors, no credit card offers...*

At least temporarily...

"I think we should re-fi the house," Alex said, breaking out of his thoughts.

"Yeah -- I was thinking that, too. We could get a better rate and use some of the equity to remodel the guest bath," Jordan said, squeezing his hand.

He looked at her. She was tan, healthy. Her skin was clear, eyes alert. He had always liked her hair, which she kept shoulder length these days, and more blonde than when they first met. She also seemed more confident, more relaxed. *I have to admit: the increase from B cup to DD was a good move.*

Alex had first met Jordan on the set of one of her early films. He was dating Krystal at the time, and it was she who had suggested him as a replacement for the prima-donna European director that had bogged the whole production down. Alex's first feature film break after too many commercials, endless numbers of music videos, and a good deal of episodic television, the movie's success catapulted him into a lucrative new career: the go-to director able to bring a tough project in on time and under budget. Jordan -- a rising starlet at the time -- was very personable and pleasant: not the sneering, preening monster some of these people could be.

For Alex and Jordan it was love at first sight, and he had to end his two-year romance with the fiery Krystal. Unfortunately, Krystal had been unable to come to terms with the dissolution of their relationship. Even after all this time there was tension between the two women on-set, although they were always consummate professionals once the cameras started rolling. Alex secretly felt that the animosity and competition only added to their performances, especially during spanking, or girl-on-girl action.

Jordan's intense performances had interested Alex from the beginning, and he had been glad to get the chance to work with her. Even when being pounded in that bare vagina after five other positions, Jordan was still top notch: the hottest breasts, ass and legs in porn.

Some actors popped practically the second they started doing her: that face; those eyes; the sweaty hourglass body -- it all just worked. She obviously relished her ability to milk the studs dry, and was game for new challenges: DP, anal, even strapping on to teach the guys a thing or two.

Fortunately for Alex, she was familiar with his work. He had especially enjoyed getting to know her after hours. It was a slow process, as she was cautious about dating people "from the industry". He found her to be a down to earth girl, very liberal, and fascinated by insects.

Everything was going well: married for nearly two years, they were prepping Jordan for "retirement".

"*I want to go out on top!*" she always joked. He was glad for her; soon he would have her just to himself.

The sign post up ahead read: 'Entering Paso Robles.'

"We're here!" she squealed. "Let's find some wine and get buzzed!"

Alex felt wobbly; perhaps it was the long drive -- or the fact that the heat was more than he expected for late September on California's Central Coast -- but it was probably due more to overindulgence during their wine tasting odyssey.

"You're drunk!" Jordan teased, tickling his side. "You're supposed to taste, then spit -- not drink it all: you'll get hammered!"

"I'm a swallower," he slurred, crooked grin on his unshaven face. Both of them laughed as they got into the car.

"Are you OK to drive?" she asked, looking at the map.

"I'll be fine... We picked up some killer wine, huh? Let's do one more for the road; how about that Spanish-sounding place?" Alex pulled the car onto Highway 101, which was strangely deserted.

"Oh yeah! They were closed last time..." She glanced at her watch, then toward the sky as the vehicle jostled down the road. The scent of wet earth was strong, fresh, comforting; the landscape was rustic, romantic: sunlight dappled cypress trees, gently rolling hills, the sky fading into a gorgeous rust and blue mélange in the early twilight.

"Doesn't this place remind you of Tuscany? Kind of near *Firenze?*" Jordan asked at last.

Alex nodded. "I was just noticing that. It's the quality of the light, I think."

She smiled, looking down to study the atlas once again. "Here it is: *Sotanos Negros del Diablo.* It's about three miles north."

"Let's hit it, then on to San Francisco," he said, gently touching her thigh.

In the distance, lightning flashed.

"You see," the vintner stated, "my grandfather came from the Old Country to South America on a steam ship as a young man. Who knows why, eh? Adventure? Women? All the things that make life worth living, no?" He winked at Jordan. She blushed, giggling as she inhaled the full, sensuous aroma of her first taste: a Nebbiolo.

His gentle brown eyes glinting, the old man continued: "Later, Grandpapa moved up here, but only after a long apprenticeship with a Master Winemaker -- *Señor Azura* -- and began our family vineyard on a small plot of land with old vines from France and Chile."

The proprietor gave a sweep of his arm toward the windows.

"As you can see, we have grown! We have our own lines of Merlot... Chardonnay... Petite Syrah, and this huge Zinfandel Port -- as good as any you'll find in Napa or Sonoma, we feel. Try it." He pushed a glass toward Alex, then poured Jordan another sample.

Swirling the taste of Port in his glass, Alex savored its sweet, dark, cinnamon fragrance. *Look at the legs on that! The nose is phenomenal...* He took a sip, relishing the lush, velvety texture as it spread over his tongue -- liquid divinity. While they conversed, Alex studied the luxurious mahogany counter top.

The tour of the vineyard had been educational. Alex loved the process of planting, tending, harvesting: the nurturing aspect appealed to him; perhaps that was why he preferred directing to performing.

The elderly winemaker was full of stories: about the vineyards, the history of the area, his family, and viticulture in general -- the whole process of winemaking. He seemed to be a nice man, but something about him made Alex just a little... *uneasy*.

"Awesome! Chocolate!" Jordan chirped, remarking on the Port. "Wonderful bouquet." She cleansed her palate with a slice of ciabatta dipped in extra virgin olive oil, pouring the remaining sample into a reservoir on the table. The old man nodded his approval, the smile under his mustache causing his dark, weathered skin to crease.

They were the only patrons; as Jordan continued to try other varietals, Alex wandered over to the exhibition area. The prices escalated the higher the bottles -- all resting sideways -- were placed in the elegantly rendered showcases. The impressive furnishings, deeply carved and artfully arranged, displayed several winemaker's medals, framed sepia-toned photographs, and various other spirits, from 125 year-old French wormwood *Absinthe* and dessert liqueurs, to the present vintage of the estate's premier Meritage. Behind him, Jordan mumbled to the owner about taking a couple of the Ports, the Nebbiolo, a Baco Noir and a Pinot Grigio. Just then, he noticed a lone, ornately tagged bottle, cloaked in shadow, at the top of a huge tiered shelf.

"What about that one?" Alex asked, transfixed.

The wizened merchant stepped from behind the wine bar, wiping his hands on his apron, looking to where Alex pointed. As the light slowly faded outside, the room was getting dimmer. There was a sudden chill; the thin old glass of the huge bay windows overlooking the vineyards was no match for the cool air of the approaching storm.

"That, *señor*, is the last bottle we have of our special *Estate Reserva*... It was depleted years ago, except for a few we kept as... mementos. It is highly prized by collectors."

"Must be good," Alex replied, curiosity piqued.

"Of course... the best! It is one of the first wines vinted by the Manor, grown from the original old-world vines."

The aged man paused, looking up at the bottle. "It... We only made it one year... Grandfather said we should only make more once the last bottle was gone. We call it *'Absentia Anima'*. It's a wonderful 1917 vintage: truly beautiful -- so I have been told. We have so few that I've never even tried it myself! Right before the great wine reviewer Pierre Cocteau disappeared, he gave it a Platinum Medal and Five-Star critique in his prestigious *Wine Connoisseur* magazine."

Alex's gaze locked momentarily with the winemaker's. "So it's for sale?" he asked, mentally calculating the funds in his wallet. Glancing at Jordan, he pursed his lips. Her eyes were wide with excitement: she loved wine and was always after him to beef up their modest cellar.

The old man looked again at the bottle. He made a face as if tasting something bitter, then straightened.

"Yes, yes it is. *Si*... it's quite expensive, *señor*. To be sure, it's no ordinary bottle of wine; at 100 years old, it can remain bottled for many more years..."

"I understand: it's extraordinary. That's what we're looking for. How much?" Lightning flashed, but there was no thunder. As the proprietor stared at him, eyes narrow, Alex could swear -- if only for an instant -- that something changed on the man's countenance. It was strange. *Macabre*. It seemed almost -- subliminal. *Probably just a trick of the lightning...,* Alex thought.

"Promise me," The owner said finally, "that you will share it with your friends, *señor*? This exceptional wine -- it is *meant* to be shared."

Alex nodded, hypnotized by the intensity of the old man. They were practically whispering.

"Let me get it for you, *por favor*. Wine is truly a gift to be enjoyed by all..."

The vendor stepped away. Alex and Jordan watched him retreat into a curtained doorway behind the bar. From the back room, there was faint clanging and thudding. Alex strained to hear.

"How exciting!" Jordan quietly mouthed, softly clapping her hands.

"It is..." he agreed. The exchange with the owner had Alex a bit spooked. *That guy is* strange, he thought. More noise from the back, followed by swearing in Spanish, then silence.

"At last!" the old man exclaimed, appearing in the doorway with a rickety wooden ladder. He waddled across the cavernous room, propped the ladder against the dust-covered shelves and began his slow ascent, wheezing as the ladder groaned under his weight. Reaching the top, the proprietor hesitated. Lightning flashed again, brilliantly illuminating the room for a split-second; thunder growled in the distance as rain began to tap at the windows. It was nearly dark, and the storm seemed to have settled in for the evening.

"You're sure you want this, *señor*? It's *very* expensive." His hand was on the bottle as the winemaker peered down at them, his eyes like pits.

"Yes, we want it -- we're looking forward to it," Alex replied, voice tight. *Bet he thinks I can't afford it...* The vintner nodded, pulling the container from its housing.

Once back on the ground, he handed the bottle to Jordan, beaming proudly, his forehead dewed with sweat. Alex gazed over her shoulder, admiring the engraved image on the cobalt glass. Wiping away the dust and cobwebs, they turned the bottle to read the back label:

Aged in the finest American and French barriques,
this unique vintage is nearly impossible to grow in
North America.
Potent, powerful and specially crafted
from only the finest and rarest of ingredients,
an ancient recipe and exacting standards imbue it with
wonderful color, intense aroma, and piquant taste.

These characteristics give us our name:
Sotanos Negros del Diablo.
Enjoy with friends and family.

Vintage 1917
Absentia Anima
Estate Reserva

"Nice bottle," Alex said, looking over at the vintner. The man seemed mentally preoccupied, pensively staring from the rain-streaked windows into the darkening yard. Thunder rattled the old window-panes. The owner turned to face them.

"Let me wrap it for you, *señor*..."

"That guy was a little odd, huh?" Alex said as they pulled away from the winery.

"You think? He seemed pretty nice to me," Jordan replied.

Alex frowned in response, watching for cars as he pulled onto the rain-slicked road. The downpour nearly overwhelmed the robotic synching of the wipers.

"Acted to me like he thought we couldn't afford his precious wine --"

"Don't be silly! Maybe he just wanted to keep it for old time's sake... You know: kind of like you and your books even though you never read them..." Jordan said.

Lightening up, Alex smiled. "I suppose... I just get tired of being -- judged."

"Well, doesn't everybody judge everybody all the time? Anyway, you pushed him -- you made your point and got what you wanted, so be happy about that."

This practical, laid-back aspect was one of the things he found so endearing about his wife. *That, and she's hot.* "You're right -- I'm being a jerk: guess I'm just ready to get to Frisco and chill."

Jordan caressed his thigh. "Maybe we can do some stress relief later," she said, smiling impishly.

As rain daggered the ground, a runny red sunset smeared the dark horizon.

The stopper was obstinate.

The last thing I need to do is break the fucking cork off in it...

Alex had -- finally -- retrieved the cherished, dusty bottle from the basement. Resisting the temptation to imbibe the special *Estate Reserva* for over three years, it seemed the perfect choice for Jordan's "retirement" party.

The time has arrived...

Alex patiently worked the corkscrew, slowly pulling the plug; at last, there was a satisfying 'pop'.

The strong aroma from the bottle made him smile. *Excellent: needs to breathe a little.* From the living room, he could hear the festivities getting lively: toasts being given, music thumping, laughter.

Jordan came up behind him, encircling his waist.

"Oh -- this is wonderful," she said, sniffing the cork. Alex poured several glasses for their guests; he was still working on his first glass of the Baco Noir.

"Could you finish pouring the rest of the *Reserva* for everyone while I take these out?" He asked Jordan as he took a tray of the wine to the living room.

She kissed his cheek as he passed. "Of course! How yummy looking..." She took a sip of the *Reserva*. "Wonderful -- I *love* it!"

As he was about to exit through the kitchen door, Krystal walked in.

"Jordan, darling, do you need any help?" she asked. Alex smiled at her on his way out, pleased that they all got along again.

"Krystal!" Jordan exclaimed, still pouring. "Do come in..."

Vino rosso: the blood of the vine.

Alex relaxed for a moment in the living room, delighting in the last of his Baco Noir. He was looking forward to his share of the *Absentia Anima* when he heard a demented cacophony erupt from the kitchen. The party was suddenly quiet, except for the stereo. Again, another anguished howl from the kitchen. Rushing into the room, Alex was dumbfounded by the gruesome spectacle unfolding there beyond the door:

Jordan was hunched over on the ground, stabbing Krystal repeatedly in the crotch with a huge knife. In the corner, Krystal's surprised face stared up from the floor; she seemed to observe the mêlée with detached reserve, vertebrae sticking out of the ragged ruin of her neck, bloody lips twitching, before her eyes finally fluttered closed.

"Jordan!" was all Alex could exclaim; yowling in response, she turned to kick and slash at the bewildered Randy, Krystal's husband, who had suddenly appeared. As Alex remained frozen in shock, Randy attempted to disarm Jordan, but it all seemed to be in agonizing slow motion, like some dreamy, gore-streaked ballet. Behind him, a chorus of screams rang out from the living room... It was then Alex that realized his friend Terrence was lying next to the stove, swimming in a virtual ocean of hemoglobin and lymph. Though his vision had tapered to a blurry tunnel, Alex could still comprehend: *Jordan eviscerated Terry as he was returning from the bathroom...* Vomit and blood slicked Terrence's chin as he held his sanguineous intestines, looped in his shaky hands; after a few dry heaves, he collapsed, his face drained to the color of a sheet of paper.

"*What the fuck?*" Alex screamed, hoarse with disbelief, cold sweat breaking on his body.

As if in the grip of some demented chorea, Jordan leapt forward, nearly severing Randy's upraised hand. He regarded his new injury -- which swung impossibly from the meaty, spurting stump -- in silent amazement, paying no heed to Jordan as she descended on him. Biting his throat, she tore out a great chunk, the carotid artery spraying the room in a grisly red mist; Randy blurted out a final gargling scream as he fell to the ground, eyes bulging.

Now everything seemed impossibly fast: finished with Randy,

Jordan turned her attention to Alex, blade flashing in her bloody, athetotic fist.

Everyone in the living room had panicked by now, but the front door refused to budge; a few of the guests began to jabber, some wailing like Jordan. Just prior to turning on one another, they were afflicted by the same weird facial contortions, the identical outlandish dyskinesia.

In the kitchen, Alex dodged Jordan's knife, observing that she was no longer clothed: just stained head to foot in offal and excrement.

"Jordan! Stop! Jesus!"

His spouse lurched toward him in a spastic St. Vitus's dance, slicing the fetid air. Her discolored, twisted face was writhing, covered in what looked like small blisters.

"Stop, please!"

The commotion in the den was now fever pitch: a riot exploding the small confines of the house...

Far away, Alex thought he heard sirens...

Still screeching, Jordan pulled her eyes out. She threw the orbs and the bloody knife at Alex: her mushy, gaping sockets streamed garnet tears...

In a burst of adrenaline, Alex grabbed the nearest object at hand and beat her; grunting like a wild beast, he bashed Jordan's head until it was an unrecognizable mass of pulp, hair, teeth. At long last her congested whimpering stopped; Alex was hyperventilating, blood warm and salty on his lips.

As he sank to the floor, the police kicked the front door in -- their stunned demands immediately swallowed by the crush of screaming and noise. Once the assaults started on them, their warnings yielded to a barrage of gunfire. In the end, there was only a smoky, expanding silence, attended by the reek of sulfur.

"Yeah, we got it now," a young black cop said into his walkie-talkie, out of breath. He lowered his weapon, sweat beading on his bald head as he surveyed the tableau: "Holy shit..."

Alex slumped in the entryway of his destroyed kitchen. Oblivious to who might be left alive, he barely acknowledged the reinforcements asking if he was okay. He waved at them without looking, then picked up the object that he had used to murder his wife: an empty wine bottle. He focused his eyes on the back: *Estate Reserva, Vintage 1917, Sotanos Negros del Diablo, Absentia Anima.*

Great, I never even got to fucking try it...

So this is what the French mean by "terrior", I guess...

More like "terroirism"...

In the distance, Alex heard more sirens. Growing in intensity, they seeped under the wash of crying, then drowned out the pulse of *Sympathy for the Devil* playing on the stereo in the living room. He was afraid to look, knowing what he would see, and continued to study the bottle.

Nice artwork. Alex admired anew the shape and dark color of the clot-encrusted receptacle; the front image -- a graven bas-relief of an orange-irised eye weeping a single red tear -- gave him pause. He turned the vessel upside-down; its last claret trickle fell to the floor, blossoming in the blood.

It's like egg-drop soup...

Many years later, Alex was a saggy old man.

Giving up the movie business long ago, he had semi-retired to Europe on Jordan's life insurance after leaving the mental institution. He picked up part-time work here and there as a waiter; it was enough with Disability and Social Security to meet his meager day-to-day existence, and was really all he could muster psychologically.

Alex enjoyed the human contact and the work could be fun; it offered relaxed schedules, free meals and nocturnal diversions to keep his mind busy. Between the medicine and lifestyle, it almost permitted him a respite from that horrible night, so distant, yet so fresh in his memory. He never remarried.

During the weeks -- and the interminable police interrogations -- that had followed, Alex explained that there must have been something about the wine. To his way of thinking, the alcohol and the violence had to be linked -- though the toxicology reports were all negative for ergot poisoning or anything else.

He spent several years trying to find the winery again, to no avail. The place seemed to have vanished -- almost as if it had never existed to begin with. Of course, Alex knew better.

On his final stay in Rome, he served a young American couple a fine Tuscan Chianti with their dinner. He smiled at them, knowing heartbreak was probably inevitable.

"*Buona sera!* Join us for a sip, *signore?*" the young man asked. "We just got married, and we're touring Europe on our honeymoon. It's wonderful here!" He hoisted his glass in a gesture of salutation.

Alex only gave him the same melancholy look he gave all newlyweds.

"Wine?" he asked, then shivered. He looked at the fading sunset, rheumy eyes shining. "Sorry son -- I can't drink it anymore..."

Jason V Brock is an award-winning writer, artist, composer and polymath. He has been published in the U.K., Australia, the U.S., Canada and Europe, and served as the Managing Editor/Art Director for *Dark Discoveries* magazine. He is a liberal and an atheist with Hindu and Buddhist leanings, as well as a strict vegetarian with an unnatural affinity for reptiles and amphibians…
His wife and soul mate, Sunni (a talented writer, film editor and cook), live with their brood in Southern California and Vancouver, WA. A filmmaker in addition to writer, he has done three documentaries (about Charles Beaumont, Forry Ackerman and Fantastic Art, respectively), and has been a cover model for J.K. Potter. He is currently deep in the production of a short story collection (*Grotteschi*); three comic book projects with William F. Nolan for Bluewater Productions (*Logan's Run: Lastday; Dark Universe; Sam Space*); a follow-up to this anthology (*The Devil's Coattails*), as well as an extensive bibliography/companion to the works of Charles Beaumont (*The Dark Fantastic*), both with Nolan; compiling CDs of his former prog-rock/avant-jazz/noise-punk band *ChiaroscurO*; multiple screenplays and a few novels. Visit his website at *www.JaSunni.com*.

The author writes about this story:
"My wife and I were in the California wine country, and I had a 'What if…' moment. It was my attempt at commentary regarding violence in society, and its possible root causes. Does the wine simply lower inhibitions, or is there really something sinister about it?"

OMNIVORE

(Formerly titled *They Bite*)

(An Illustrated Screenplay Excerpt)

by

Dan O'Bannon

Registered: WGA West. 1975

Omnivore

Scenario: An isolated university-sponsored archeological dig in the Uinta desert of northeast Utah, with our hero, Brian, arriving at an already established community of scientists, students, and their family members.

Location: The dig site, and also the permanent encampment, both in a remote part of the desert.

Cast List:

Brian Alcott

Mike Bacon

Bonnie Lee Stein

Heather Camilla Charles

Sewell Davies

Jack Chance

Andy Chance

Mary

Kimby

Milo Cole

Harry Emerson

Claire Fujii

Eve Kendall

James White Feather

EXTERIOR - THE FOOTHILLS - NIGHT, RAIN

A jeep bounces to a halt. Leaving the headlights
on, Brian and Mike climb out into the rain and
start walking up a slope. They click on flashlights. Their ponchos glisten wetly.

                    MIKE
            Up this way.

They wade uphill into blackness.

                                        CUT TO

EXTERIOR - THE DIG SITE - NIGHT, RAIN

After a moment, their flashlights reveal a worked
area of ground, marked off into squares with
stakes and full of deep pits, partly tented. Small
torrents gush into the excavated holes.

Mike hurries forward and picks up a tripod-like
thing with a little telescope on top.

                    MIKE
            Left the damn thing right
            out in the open.

Brian shines his flashlight upward, exposing a
stratified cliff face.

                    MIKE (cont'd)
            That's the formation. Really beautiful
                    sedimentation.
            Right back to the Jurassic.

Mike brings his flashlight up to join Brian's, and
they stand in the rain a moment, gazing up at the
layered rock face.

Suddenly Brian turns his head, in a listening pos-
ture.

                    MIKE (cont'd)
                       What?

                      BRIAN
          I thought I heard something.

As we strain to catch any little sound, there's a
DEAFENING THUNDERCLAP/SIZZLING BURST OF LIGHTNING
(intended to scare us out of our wits).

                       MIKE
          (gestures with the theodolite)
          Better get this back to the jeep.

They start picking their way back down the slope,
slipping in the oily mud.

                    MIKE (cont'd)
                 What did you hear?

                      BRIAN
                  I don't know.

Brian stops, grabbing Mike's arm.

                   BRIAN (cont'd)
                  There! Hear it?

They listen, but the sibilant din of the rain ob-
scures any other sound.

                       MIKE
          No. Let's get back to the jeep.

They resume walking, briskly. Suddenly Brian stops
again, and points his flashlight into the darkness.

                      BRIAN
                There! Look at that!

Mike looks.

Illuminated in the beam, a small, circular MOUND
OF SAND is rising up out of the ground, bubbling

as it comes up. The rain batters little holes in it. Slowly it inches up, a soggy plug of clay & gravel.

> BRIAN (cont'd)
> What is it?

> MIKE
> (shakes his head)
> I don't know, Brian. Some burrowing animal...?

But the plug is still RISING. The deeper clay just breaking the surface is filled with small rocks and shale. It moves upward in lurches, as if being pushed up from below.

> BRIAN
> What kind of an animal does that?

> MIKE
> (a different tone)
> I don't know.

The plug, still coming up, is no longer loose sand. It is a tightly packed cylinder of earth and stones, six inches in diameter. It has now reached an unbelievable height of three feet. The weaker topsoil crumbles off, splattering into the liquid mud, but the plug continues to extrude itself from the soil. The rain bounces off it in a spray.

> MIKE (cont'd)
> Jesus Christ! What is that?

Suddenly Brian realizes ... the gloppy, scraping NOISES are coming at him from more than one direction ... in stereo. He swings his flashlight around, searching.

> BRIAN
> Look over there.

A few feet away, ANOTHER PLUG is rising from the

ground, and it is EIGHT FEET TALL and ringed with
strata. Thick fluid spills out from around the
base, like lubricant being pumped up from below.
It sizzles and smokes.

> MIKE
> I don't believe that.

The second pillar BREAKS OFF and FALLS to the
ground with a heavy, wet thud. But more of it continues to grow from the rain-soaked ground.

> MIKE (cont'd)
> They're coming up all around us.

They swing their beams in wide arcs. NUMBERLESS
COLUMNS have begun to ooze up out of the slime.

> BRIAN
> Find that big one,
> the one that broke off.

They scan with their flashlights, locating the
plug. Still rising like a petrified fecal bolus,
it is now composed of basalt, from deep down.

> BRIAN (cont'd)
> What is this, some kind of ...
> geothermal activity?

> MIKE
> I don't know; maybe we better get
> out of here.

Suddenly the obelisk TOPPLES ponderously into the
sand, leaving a small HOLE, black and circular,
where it was.

> BRIAN
> Wait -- look!

SOMETHING ... BEGINS CRAWLING UP OUT OF THE HOLE.

It is PALE and SLIMY and it WRITHES, struggling to pull itself out of the hole, bulging in-and-out with tensing muscles.

> MIKE
> (revolted)
> My _God_!

The THING vibrates and lunges from side to side, trembling as it strains to squeeze itself out of the tiny opening. It appears to swell as it emerges, and several kicking LEGS come free. It scrambles frantically at the ground with pearly, stick-like limbs, trying to get a purchase and yank itself free.

It is like watching something being born.

With one last convulsive effort it disgorges itself onto the ground and lies, pulsing. It is the size of a house cat.

> MIKE (cont'd)
> Jesus! Jesus!

> BRIAN
> The legs! Look at the legs!

Shakily, the thing climbs to its several articulated legs. Wobbling, it crawls on the mud, barely able to support its own weight. They follow the naked monstrosity with their lights as it totters slowly across the soil. Its skin -- veined, waxy, translucent -- gleams slimily in the rain.

As they watch, spellbound, it grows sturdier on its feet, and the whitish-green coloration deepens rapidly to a mottled brown.

Now we can hear chitinous SCUFFLING NOISES from the darkness on all sides.

                    MIKE
        Jesus H. Christ, these fuckers
             are all around us.

They scan their lights in a circle, catching MORE
pale, flailing things in their beams.

Then Brian's beam falls on one that looks ... ma-
ture.

                    BRIAN
                    Look.

This specimen has a hard, brown carapace with
ugly purple markings, and it looks STRONG. It
moves quickly back and forth on powerful-looking
legs, testing them. Rain bounces off its back in a
spray. It vibrates, thumping the ground with new-
found energy.

                BRIAN (cont'd)
        I think -- look -- I think
           that one's developed.

The thing spins toward them.

                    MIKE
                 Oh, fuck.

It begins to DRONE.

                    BRIAN
                 Let's go!

Too late. The thing RACES TOWARD THEM. MIKE steps
back, dropping the surveying instrument. Before
either of them can react, the creature CRAWLS UP
MIKE'S ARM, buzzing voraciously. Mike SCREAMS and
drops his flashlight.

Mike dances and shrieks, trying to fling it off,
but it clings, thrashing, piranha-like. Brian
BEATS at it with his flashlight -- the BEAM wipes
across the rain and their struggling bodies -- the
thing DRONES, there is a horrible sickening CRUNCH

like wood splintering and Mike SCREAMS several
more times, in a shrill falsetto.

Brian strikes repeated blows at the creature with
his heavy metal flashlight, CRACKING its shell.
Buzzing stridently, "it" drops to the ground. Brian falls to his knees and POUNDS the thing into
the mud. Again and again, bursting it open like a
coconut until it stops convulsing and is still ...

Shaking, adrenalin pumping, Brian rises to his
feet. All around him is the loud sputtering DRONE
of unthinkable numbers of nightmare things. He
turns and steps toward Mike, shining the light on
him.

Mike is tottering backward, his eyes wide and
shocked, his mouth open to say something -- but
he is speechless. A mass of shreds hangs from his
elbow and a geyser of BLOOD, vivid in the light of
the hand-torch, sprays from the wound. His arm is
gone at the elbow.

Brian grabs Mike around the waist and drags him
toward the jeep.

EXTERIOR - JEEP - NIGHT, RAIN

The headlights are still on ... beacons in the
blackness, toward which Brian struggles.

LIGHTNING ILLUMINATES THE AREA BRIEFLY - REVEAL-
ING DOZENS OF CREATURES around the jeep -- mostly
green and wobbly and unsure. Brian steps on one.

Brian shoves Mike's bulk into the passenger side,
and runs around and jumps in the driver's seat. He
grinds the key in the ignition.

> BRIAN
> Start, god damn you!

He stamps the gas pedal.

A THING, glossy brown and fully developed, scrambles up onto the hood of the jeep. At the same moment, the engine CATCHES, and with a roar, Brian accelerates out of the area. The creature drops from the hood.

                                        CUT TO

INTERIOR - JEEP - NIGHT

Brian's foot is pressed to the floor. The motor throbs. Rain blasts against the windshield. Mike sits very quietly, his face white, staring straight ahead.

                    MIKE
                 (in shock)
       Take me home. I want to go home now.
            Please take me home now.

                    BRIAN
          We're getting you to a doctor,
            Mike, just please hang on.

                    MIKE
          Take me home now, you guys.

                    BRIAN
               Just hang on.

Mike looks down at his elbow: blood pumps from it, in rhythmic spurts.

                    MIKE
               Is that my arm?

Mike reaches over with his left hand and closes his fingers over the pulsing wound. The flood subsides to a trickle.

Suddenly, up ahead, through sheets of rain -- the LIGHTS of the camp.

                    BRIAN
          We're there, Mike, we're back,
               there's the camp!

MIKE
Camp? Where's my arm?
Did somebody go back for it?

[Continued...]

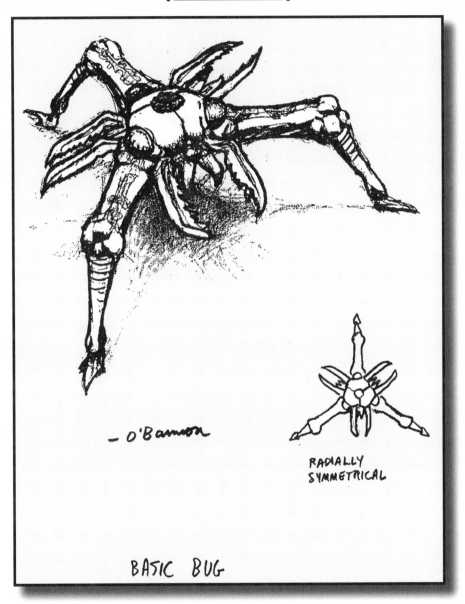

— O'Bannon

RADIALLY
SYMMETRICAL

BASIC BUG

[Later: Back At Camp]

The huge, brown bug has lost interest in them, and
appears to be consuming a chair ... ripping off
splinters and stuffing them into a cavity between
its legs ... EATING THE WOOD.

As it dines, oblivious to its rapt audience of
three, its back arches; something there is bulging, swelling up -- a rubbery, pinkish pouch.

As the pouch fills, it balloons out in irregular
lumps and becomes transparent, covered with black,
pulsing veins. Pieces of crushed wood can be seen
inside.

                    BRIAN
               What the fuck??

                    DAVIES
          It's eating, eating the chair!

Brian stands poised with his shovel, watching the
insect stuff the last morsel of hickory up between
its legs. When the chair is gone, it spins, looking for more edibles. The bag on its back wobbles.

                  DAVIES (cont'd)
               The sac! Hit the sac!

Brian steps forward and brings the cutting edge of
the shovel down on the fleshy bag, which bursts
open, spilling fluid and slimy pieces of wood onto
the floor. The insect gives a horrible chitter-
ing SHRIEK and LEAPS into the air, arcing its back
as if broken, splaying all its legs out in a gro-
tesque rosette.

They all jump back as it goes into a death parox-
ysm, stridulating and thrashing. It runs around
the room in a circle, too fast to react to, then
runs against the wall, ripping splinters from the
wood. Finally it turns and makes a dash for the
door. It tries to crawl out -- then drops in a

heap and lies motionless.

The three humans stand in the wrecked shack, quivering and sobbing. A dreadful stench emanates from the contents of the creature's pouch. Outside, the sound of the attack continues. People are shouting. Things are being smashed. Behind all this, the buzzing of the insects.

Suddenly, there is a sharp REPORT.

> BRIAN
> What was that?

> DAVIES
> I don't know.

> BRIAN
> Sounded like a gunshot.

> DAVIES
> We have no guns here that I
> know of.

Immediately, they hear the REPORT five more times in succession.

This is followed by the sudden, vicious SNARLING and BARKING of Killer, the camp dog. She is nearby, and it sounds like a fight to the finish.

> HEATHER
> Killer.

> DAVIES
> Oh, no.

Brian goes to the back and peeks out through a hole in the shutter. Davies and Heather come up behind him.

THEIR POV - OUTSIDE

Killer is circling and slashing with an insect. So far they are just racing and snarling around

each other, but the bug is clearly on the offen-
sive.

> HEATHER
> Killer! Killer! Run! Here,
> girl!

Davies squeezes her shoulders tightly.

Stiff-legged, Killer advances on the insect. They
half-circle around each other, Killer growling and
feinting, it pulsing and flexing its pincers.

Then Killer makes a lunge, teeth slashing. The bug
rears back on its hind legs like a spider, raising
its foreclaws and HISSING. The dog pulls back before the claws SNAP back down, but at that moment
a 2ND BUG comes up from behind and leaps on her
hindquarters with a sickening CRUNCH.

The dog lets out a pathetic SHRIEK and dances
away, snapping at the thing on her tailbone. While
she spins in maddened circles, the 1ST one jumps
on her and wraps its legs around her head.

Killer goes down under a writhing mound of chitinous legs. She utters one last, long MOAN, which
terminates abruptly as her windpipe severs ...
followed by a long, whistling wheeze .

Inside the shack, they are silent. Heather has Davies' hand in a painful grip. Gently, he pulls her
face into his shoulder. She sobs bitterly.

Brian is a little green around the gills but he
continues to watch.

BRIAN'S POV - THE BUGS

The two eating-machines are squabbling over the
carcass of the dog, stuffing the flesh up under
their thoraxes, where their mouths are located.
Terrible CRUNCHING noises are heard as they break
up the bones. As they eat, their external stomachs

begin to swell. They chirp, contentedly.

The humans' expressions show how hard this is to watch.

> BRIAN
> They're consuming it complete-
> ly. Bones, teeth.

> DAVIES
> The strength in those jaws.

> BRIAN
> That expandable bag must be
> the stomach.

> DAVIES
> Stomach outside the body.

Davies shakes his head in amazement.

> BRIAN
> Seems pretty vulnerable to me.
> The stomach exposed like that.

> DAVIES
> Yes, but look at the <u>feeding
> capacity</u> it gives them.

The insects' stomachs are now so full they have become top heavy. Flabby and sloshing, they flop over onto their backs, resting on their bloated belly sacs, and continue to stuff the remnants of the dog into their beaky mouthparts.

> DAVIES (cont'd)
> Look at that. They're eating
> so much they're immobilizing
> themselves.

Finally they are gorged. Their twitching legs curl up toward the night sky. They stop moving entire-ly, comatose on their swollen bellies.

Suddenly we realize that it is QUIET outside. The rain has stopped, leaving a deathly hush. No insects running around, nothing. Silence and the drip of water.

> HEATHER
> (listens)
> Has it stopped?

Brian cups his hands to his mouth and calls:

> BRIAN
> (shouts)
> Hellloooo ... !

> DAVIES
> (chiming in)
> Can anybody hear us?

A VOICE floats back from the darkness.

> VOICE OUTSIDE
> (calls)
> Have they stopped?

> DAVIES
> (calls)
> They're not attacking here anymore. Are they attacking out there?

> VOICE
> (calls)
> Not here. They quit. Do you think it's safe to come out?

The voice is that of Jack Chance.

> DAVIES
> (calls)
> I don't know. Not yet. Let me phone for help.

Davies turns and stoops by the desk, picking up the phone he dropped. He puts it to his ear. He listens for a second, then hangs up.

> DAVIES (cont'd)
> It's dead.

Outside a boy begins to SOB violently.

> BOY'S VOICE
> Oh <u>nooo</u>, <u>oh</u> <u>nonono</u>! <u>They</u> <u>got</u>
> <u>her</u>! <u>They</u> <u>got</u> <u>her</u>!

Davies looks at Heather, at Brian. They go to the
door of the shack. Brian shovels the dead bug
aside, and they scramble out through the jeep,
which is jammed up close against the door.

> CUT TO

<u>EXTERIOR - THE CAMP - NIGHT</u>

The three climb hesitantly out of the jeep and
stand looking around.

Now that the rain has stopped, the compound is
still and expectant. Yellow incandescent light
spills from ends of quonsets, across the soggy
ground, into black pools of water. Overhead, scud-
ding clouds obscure the stars. The only sound is
the boy (HARRY) sobbing.

Their eyes glisten with fear. Brian grips his
trench shovel.

> DAVIES
> (squaring his shoulders)
> Well.

Davies starts across the camp, Heather and Brian
following.

JAMES WHITE FEATHER appears in stocking feet, his
square face peering around suspiciously. In his
hand is a PISTOL, a .22 peacemaker with a hogleg
grip.

                    JAMES WHITE FEATHER
                 Where are the god damned
                          things?

                         DAVIES
                    (eyeing the pistol)
                 Was that your gun, James?

                         JAMES
                         Yeah.

                         DAVIES
                 I didn't know you had one.

                         JAMES
                     Now you know.

They arrive at the Student Union.

The screen has been ripped off the front of the
quonset, leaving it gaping. On the ground in front
of it lies a crushed insect. Dead.

Standing silhouetted in the entrance, her shadow
thrown long, is pregnant Andy Chance, holding a
BASEBALL BAT. The bat is black and drippy. Behind
her stands her husband Jack.

They all look at each other wordlessly. Davies,
Heather, Brian, and James enter the hut.

                                            CUT TO

INTERIOR - "STUDENT UNION" QUONSET - NIGHT

Inside, Bonnie and Claire Fujii crouch next to
Mike, trying to hold him up onto the table, which
has lost a leg and is tilted crazily. Bonnie sobs,
quietly.

Davies and Brian help prop the table back upright.
Davies bends over Mike, whose face is frog-belly
white. His ravaged body is limp as a rag.

> DAVIES
> Mike?

> MIKE
> (whispers)
> Doctor.

> DAVIES
> (pats him)
> We're going to get you to a
> doctor.

Heather starts bundling blankets around Mike. Davies turns his attention to Bonnie, who is being comforted by Claire.

> BONNIE
> (shaking)
> They tore all the screens off
> the doors.

Davies takes her by the arms.

> DAVIES
> Bonnie, I need your help. I
> need you to take care of Mike.
> Can you do that for me?

She nods.

> DAVIES (cont'd)
> Good.

He ruffles her wiry blonde hair. Then he gives Claire a squeeze of the arm and a reassuring smile.

> DAVIES (cont'd)
> We've got to be strong.
> (looking around)
> Who's not here?

Davies walks outside and starts CLAPPING HIS HANDS loudly.

CUT TO

EXTERIOR - STUDENT UNION - NIGHT

                    DAVIES
         (calling to the whole camp)
         Okay, everybody, we've got to
         have a head count! Everybody
         to the Student Union! On the
                    double!

Milo Cole emerges from Darwin Hall, looking
around.

Mary emerges from the Women's Dorm, carrying
Kimby. They hurry toward Davies.

                    KIMBY
         Mommy, what were they?

                    MARY
         Shh, baby.

Brian comes outside with a flashlight, clicking it
on and off. Davies starts counting heads.

                    DAVIES
         Okay, there were fourteen of
         us here before this started.
         And, uh, now there are ...
         (ticks off on his fingers)
         Okay, first, I'm here. That's
         one. And Heather.

Everybody looks around to see who's missing.

                    BRIAN
         Me.

                    DAVIES
         That's three. Bonnie is in the
         Union with Mike. And Andy is
         here. With Jack. That's seven.

                    JAMES
                 I'm here.

                    MILO
                 Milo Cole.

                   CLAIRE
                 Claire Fujii.

                   DAVIES
                 That's ten.

                    MARY
              Mary and Kimby.
        (looks down at her daughter)
          We weren't scared, were we?

                   KIMBY
          What were they, Mommy?

                    MARY
                    Shhh.

                   DAVIES
              That's twelve...
               (looks around)

Harry Emerson wanders up, his face streaked with
dirt and tears. Davies goes to him.

               DAVIES (cont'd)
             Harry. Where's Eve?

Harry just shakes his head. He can't say it.

               DAVIES (cont'd)
                  (repeats)
             Harry -- Where's Eve?

                   HARRY
                   Eaten!

              [Continued...]

[Later: The Camp]

THEIR POV - THE BUGS

The bloated STOMACHS of the two insects are no
longer soft and transparent, revealing their
blurred contents. Now they are hard and opaque ...
varnished brown melons.

> BRIAN
> They were feeble and trans-
> parent in the beginning. Then
> they got hard. Then they at-
> tacked.

> HARRY
> Couldn't we kill them while
> they're like that?

At that moment, with a loud POP, a CRACK appears
down the side of one of the stomach casings.

> JACK
> Look out!

Involuntarily, Brian takes a step back from the
wire. There is a startled chorus of gasps and
cries from the others.

They all stare in terror, as more cracks appear in
the hardened stomach wall. What was formerly the
legs -- now curled pitifully on top of the pod-
like shell -- SPLIT apart. With much struggling,
something soft starts to crawl out.

> HARRY
> (in tears)
> Oh, Jesus, is it starting
> again?

Shaky hands grip weapons.

Davies studies the creatures with intense concentration.

                    DAVIES
          They're shedding their cuti-
                    cles.

                    BRIAN
           (disgusted, fascinated)
             Eat -- then molt?

The mucid, pale thing pulls itself out of its old
skin and drops to the ground. Weakly, it drags
itself across the damp sand. Meanwhile the SECOND
one is struggling to break free of its dead husk.

The students draw in closer toward one another.

                    DAVIES
          Don't they look a little ...
                  different?

                    BRIAN
              Different how?

                    DAVIES
          From the way they looked be-
                    fore.

                    BRIAN
            No, that's exactly the way
          they looked before. Green and
            transparent and weak.

                    DAVIES
                I mean ...

The creature's silhouette and gait seem different.

                    Heather
          It's a metamorphosis ... like
          a caterpillar turning into a
                butterfly ...

                    HARRY
            That, is no butterfly.

The 2ND one is now struggling free of its shell.

The FIRST one is stronger, its pale green color
changing.

> HEATHER
> The second stage is really
> different ...

> CLAIRE
> (shrilly)
> What's wrong with you people?
> You're analyzing it like a
> bunch of goddamned professors.
> You're really _enjoying_ this!

> DAVIES
> We're not enjoying it, Claire.
> It's important that we study
> them, for our own safety.

Heather moves to calm her.

> DAVIES (cont'd)
> (sotto voce, to Brian)
> However, they _are_ extremely
> interesting.

Meanwhile, the first insect is eating its discarded shell. Crunchcrunchcrunch. It has turned
a strange, glossy striped YELLOW and is running
back and forth, drumming its legs and testing its
strength. The second-born, wet and soft, struggles
to its feet.

> BRIAN
> The others turned brown when
> they dried out. This one is
> sort of ... yellow.

An intake of breath from Davies.

> DAVIES
> Oh, Lord, it's mimicking the
> dog.

Mimicry or mockery: the thing looks like a sick,

disgusting imitation of a dog -- a dog made of
fiberglas. The "coat" is suggested by pigments in
the shell. The collie's "mane" is represented by
a big, waxy mantle. Two insectile forelimbs are
tucked up into the mantle by way of concealment,
giving it the appearance of having only four legs.
The head looks like a painted dog skull. An abomi-
nation.

Andy belches, starts to choke. Jack reaches for
her, but she pulls away and runs into the lava-
tory, slamming the door. Inside, she can be heard
retching.

> BRIAN
> (mesmerized)
> Like those moths ... the ones
> that look like owls.

> DAVIES
> Or stick insects. Or leaf in-
> sects.

A silence.

> HEATHER
> What are they mimicking for?

Another silence.

> DAVIES
> (his eyes grow abstract)
> Damn. What ...

The bathroom door opens and Andy emerges, looking
pale. Davies looks over at her with concern.

> BRIAN
> Davies.

> DAVIES
> (spins back)
> What?

> BRIAN
> They're looking at us.

Davies runs and stares out the screen. Most of the people move back.

The two DOG-MIMICRIES have turned to face the quonset. Each is roughly one-half the size of the original collie. They are not identical. There is a distortion based on what part of the dog each ate the most of.

They're as motionless as lawn ornaments. Through the steel screen, their EYESPOTS seem to return the humans' gazes.

Simultaneously, they begin to DRONE.

Kimby SCREAMS in terror and starts to cry. Mary drops to her haunches and crushes the little girl to her breast.

> MARY
> Don't look, baby!

> KIMBY
> What are they going to do to
> us, Mommy?

[Continued...]

###

-O'Bannon-

Dan O'Bannon is the well-known screenwriter behind the classics *Alien, Total Recall, Lifeforce, Heavy Metal* (two segments), *Dark Star* (which he did the special effects for and starred in as well; this led to a stint on *Star Wars* as a special effects designer) and *Return of the Living Dead* (which he also directed).

A St. Louis native, he was inspired at an early age by horror movies, EC Comics, and weird fiction to pursue a career in film. A Lovecraft aficionado, he was the person to bring brilliant Swiss surrealist H.R. Giger to the attention of Hollywood. A talented artist himself as well as a great writer, O'Bannon is currently involved in a variety of film projects, and a book version of *The Necronomicon*.

What the author writes about this screenplay:

"In 1975 [pre-*Alien*], I wrote the first draft of 'They Bite' -- presently entitled 'Omnivore'. It developed a good reputation around town, but since I insisted on directing it, it was repeatedly given a pass. In addition to an institutional coolness toward me filling the director's chair, the studios thought the bugs were undoable -- this was before 'Star Wars' brought special effects back into vogue. Too bad; 'They Bite' would have been a groundbreaker if it had been made back then. Over the years, I have revisited this screenplay from time to time, revising it to keep up to date, but the characters, and the carefully crafted narrative structure, remain unchanged. Since then, many elements that made it unusual in 1975 have appeared in other films; it was inevitable that sooner or later other writers would think of these devices. Even though it is no longer altogether unique, I hope that our readers will find it enjoyable to spend a little time with a screenplay for which I still have great fondness."

De Mortuis

by John Tomerlin

"I can assure you, ma'am," said Captain Aikman, putting down his teacup, "we are not dealing with another Jack the Ripper."

He waved away her offer to refill his cup; he hated tea.

"The Ripper committed his crimes in London the 1880s -- over thirty years ago -- and three thousand miles away from New York... No, the chap we're after has a completely different methodology: his victims are nearly all men. There have only been two women, thus far neither of them -- ladies of the evening."

"Prostitutes," Madame Dragovich corrected.

"Uh -- right."

Ladies of the evening, for Chrissake! Aikman thought. He glanced at Sergeant Walczak, sitting beside him, and saw the big man smile. Aikman felt like a fool visiting the Dragovich home; he'd only done so at the Coroner's insistence.

"I still don't understand how I can help you," the woman said. "I'm a doctor, not an expert on crime."

She is quite handsome, he thought, *for someone in her sixties.* He'd had Sgt. Walczak look up her background: she'd been living in the city just over a year, having arrived shortly after her husband, a famous surgeon and minor royal, had passed away. Aikman had never met a woman doctor before.

From the looks of the room they were in -- gilt crown molding, mahogany wall panels, marble and gold floor inlays -- she'd been left very well off.

He went on: "We haven't told the public everything we know about the murders. By no means do we wish to start a panic. You see, we're dealing with what could be called a *repetition killer:* seven victims that we know about, so far. And he doesn't just cut their throats, he -- er, *removes* things."

The woman stared at him, gray eyes slightly widened. "*Removes* things," she repeated.

"Heart, kidney, parts of a liver. Last time, it was something Doc -- that's Doc Strickland, the Medical Examiner -- called the spleen." Aikman waited for some reaction, but getting none, continued: "I guess you and Doc have met?"

She nodded.

"He thought you might have some idea what this loony was doing with the parts."

She blinked, then stood abruptly, face flushed with anger. "How *dare* you! My husband and I are -- were -- respected members of the medical profession. How could you come here and --"

"All we're asking, Doctor," said Sgt. Walczak calmly, "is if this madman might be doing some -- *experiments*. Like the ones you and your husband --"

"Certainly *not!*"

"No offense intended, Doctor," said Aikman. "We're only doing our duty."

She sat down.

"Excuse me, gentlemen, I've been under some... There have been personal matters... You're certain you wouldn't care for more tea?"

Before he could refuse, Aikman saw a door open on the far side of the room; a young man rushed in. "*Maman*, I beg of you --" the man exclaimed, but broke off, staring at the visitors.

He was in his early twenties, of moderate height and slight of build, with large, deeply shadowed eyes and a pale complexion. He wore a purple dressing gown over a shirt with open collar, dark pants, and leather slippers.

"I- I'm very sorry; I didn't know you had guests," he said, and backed from the room, pulling the door closed.

There was a moment's silence. "My son, Adam," Mme. Dragovich explained. "You were saying, Captain?"

"Uh -- nothing important, I guess. Just an improbable notion."

"Surely not. I imagine you have to consider all the possibilities in your line of work. Just let me think... vital organs..." She closed her eyes, and after a moment opened them again and shook her head slowly. "No, nothing that I can conjure. One cannot simply re-attach an internal part of the body the way one would a finger or a toe -- as my late husband and I were able to do. There would be no way to immobilize the subject. Too much loss of blood. Oxygen starvation. Shock... *impossible*, I'm afraid."

"I suspected as much," Aikman announced, and started to rise.

"A more likely explanation would be something ceremonial," the woman went on, "perhaps a- a *blood rite:* a form of *voodoo*..."

"Thank you anyway, Doctor." He motioned to Walczak. "We've already taken up too much of your time."

"I'm sorry I was unable to help." She rang a bell on the table beside her; the same door opened, this time to admit a very large man wearing a collarless white jacket.

"Cyrus, see the gentlemen out, please."

✦✦✦

"What do you mean she doesn't *have* a son?"

They'd taken the trolley back to headquarters in the Lower East Side. They sat, now, on either side of Aikman's desk. There was a map of Manhattan on the back wall, marker pins stuck in it in several places.

Walczak, consulting his notes: "Married 1868 to a Vachislav Saltsman, deceased November 1878. Married Dr. Ivan Dragovich 1900, deceased 1910. No children, either marriage." He looked up to grin suggestively. "Likes 'em young, you think?"

"You've got a dirty mind, Sergeant. The boy could be adopted for all we know."

Niklas Walczak, known as "Nick," seemed unconvinced. "You can never be sure with these foreign dames. Old family -- royalty of some kind -- they've got peculiar tastes."

"We're wasting time, here! It's been almost a week since the last killing, our man may be ready to do it again. At least if the past is any indication." Aikman stood and turned to study the map. "The question is, *where?*"

Walczak came over to him. "I've noticed one thing, Chief. We know he does his dirty work in parks -- either downtown or on the riverfront -- right?"

"Yes, and a different park each time, which doesn't help us much."

"Maybe it does. There's something else I noticed: always a bar or gin-joint not far away." Walczak pointed to the pins, then the neighboring streets. "A dive called *Dooley's* here, another called the *Blue Dog* there... *Sommerset's... Angelo's...* All walking distance from where a killing happened."

Aikman considered. "I get it. He picks a victim, then stalks them to someplace dark -- instead of waiting in ambush. Damn it, Nick, you may have something!"

"Course it could be just coincidence."

"Or, you may well be right. It would answer one question: why are all his targets so similar? All young to middle-aged, well-dressed respectable types... It's because he picks them up in the same kinds of places." Aikman made up his mind. "Let's check it out. Draw up a list of places you can get liquor that are in walking distance of the parks -- here, here, and over here," he said, pointing to the map, "-- all the ones he hasn't been at, so far as we know. Assign a man to each from 10 PM through the latest time we know the killings have happened."

Walczak continued studying the map. "Something else a little odd. Look --" he drew a circle with one finger to encompass the murder scenes, then pointed to a place in the center. "That's where the good

Dr. Dragovich lives..."

✦✦✦

Aikman rode up to West 39th, to *Bustanoby's Restaurant*, which was his favorite eatery. A captain of police generally couldn't afford to dine in such an expensive place, but Aikman had done several favors for the Bustanoby brothers, including breaking a workers' strike, and here his money was no good.

After being seated by Dominic, the *Maitre d'*, at his customary table -- outfitted with an expanse of white linen, and festooned with silver flatware and bone china -- he ordered his usual: oysters, followed by a T-bone steak and fried eggs, a selection of braised vegetables, and a schooner of the house ale -- all finished off by a thick slice of strudel and a pot of coffee. Having drunk a brandy with the coffee, he was about to get up to leave when he noticed the occupants of a table farther back in the room: one face in particular seemed familiar. Aikman stood and walked closer, recognizing the same man he'd glimpsed briefly that afternoon.

"Evening, sir. Mr. Adam Dragovich, is it?"

"I beg your pardon?"

"We haven't actually met..." *He's seems even paler than before,* Aikman thought, *eyes more deeply set, lips thin and bloodless.* "I was at your home earlier today."

"Ah, yes, the *Copper*." It was almost a sneer. "Found the killer yet? *Maman* told me about your -- *inquisition*."

"No, sir... not yet,"Aikman replied stiffly. The man definitely did not look well... almost corpse-like, in fact... "But you may rest assured, we will."

A young woman was sitting across the table from Dragovich. She was of similar age, and also a bit washed out: dressed in sheer white organdy with a fur stole draped over the back of her chair. *Attractive enough,* Aikman thought, *if you like that type; I prefer my women with more meat on their bones...*

Adam Dragovich appeared to control himself with an effort. "Do forgive me, Officer; where are my manners? I should have introduced my fiancé, Lil -- that is, Lilith. Now, please, don't let us keep you."

The detective nodded and turned to leave. As he did so, he saw Mme. Dragovich's servant, the man she'd called Cyrus, seated alone next to the wall, watching the constable through narrowed eyes.

✦✦✦

Aikman's telephone rang at two in the morning, a raucous summons from the adjacent hallway. He stumbled from his bed, failed to locate his slippers, and lifted the earpiece from its fork.

"Aikman," he said, still partly asleep but already expecting the worst. He listened awhile, rubbing his eyes, then suddenly stood straighter. "Where are you now?... Have you called a doctor?... I'll be there immediately."

It took him only minutes to dress and arm himself; he left his apartment, turned west, toward York Ave, hailed a hansom cab, and gave the driver the address Walczak had supplied. It proved to be that of a private park, one they hadn't staked out, in a tony section of the East Fifties. They might easily have missed their man, but luck had been on their side: the killer had been interrupted at his grisly task by a beat cop making rounds. The assailant got away, Walczak had said on the phone -- but not before being wounded by the officer.

As Aikman stepped down from the cab in front of an enclosed area of turf, trees, and hedges, he was suddenly conscious of the neighborhood and his surroundings. They seemed familiar, and no wonder: he'd been here earlier in the day -- *no, yesterday, now...*

"It's our man, all right," the Sergeant said, "same *modus operandi* as all the others."

"You said the victim was still alive?"

"Yeah, barely, but can't tell us anything, yet. Got hit on the head; still out cold. M.E. is on his way with the ambulance."

Aikman reached a decision. "Stay here and keep an eye on things, Sergeant. I think I know where to find the killer."

"You do?"

"Let me have your torch." Walczak was carrying one of the hand-held electric lamps recently acquired by the Department. "When you checked out the Dragovich place, did you find out whether any of the servants lived in?"

"I don't think any do, but -- Listen here, Aik-- I mean Captain -- it's not such a good idea to go barging in there without a warrant." Walczak seemed more angry than concerned.

"Maybe not, Sergeant Walczak, but I'll take that chance."

Aikman's determination grew at the sight of bloodstains on the sidewalk outside the Dragovich apartment building. A night watchman, asleep at his desk in the lobby, awoke to swear that no one had got past him that night: but after seeing the policeman's identification, he agreed to take Aikman up to the doctor's suite.

The service elevator opened onto a carpeted vestibule: the thick, maroon Bukhara floor covering showed no further signs of blood, but there was a smear of it on one of a set of entry doors, which yielded to Aikman's touch.

He could feel his heart; almost hear its rapid beating as he moved cautiously across the marbled hallway and along the corridor to the room he'd visited yesterday. It lay in stillness: dark, save for a faint illumination through the windows to the street. A sliver of brightness shone at the bottom of the door on the far side of the room, and he made his way toward it, careful not to stumble on any of the furniture. He took his gun from under his coat, and upon reaching the door turned its handle slowly with his free hand. He threw it open with all his force...

He was unprepared for the intensity of the light that filled the room; it momentarily blinded him. He was just able to make out the shape of a table with something lying on it -- *A man!* -- attached to several machines by tubes.

Aikman saw now that he was in an operating theatre, an all-white chamber lined by shelves and cabinets filled with jars of colored liquids, vials of strange powders. As vision returned, he was shocked again by the discovery of a figure seated on the other side of the table. He swung his gun toward it, shouting, "Police! Don't move!"

"Go ahead and shoot," Mme. Dragovich said quietly. "I beg you, Captain, kill me. I have no further reason to live."

He took a step forward. "What the devil is going on here?" He finally recognized the body as that of Adam Dragovich -- motionless, eyes closed beneath purple lids. "Is he...?"

"Beyond help?" She shrugged. "A vein above his heart -- the *vena cava* -- ruptured. I had hoped to replace it in time, but..."

Aikman sought comprehension. He looked at the network of scars and welts across young Adam's chest and abdomen, and began to understand at last. "Are you admitting all those people were killed for... for..."

"For my son. Yes."

The captain's head started to throb. "You don't *have* a son!" he cried.

"A birth child, no, but my son nonetheless. One that I created as surely as if I'd carried him inside me." She rose and took a step toward the table. Aikman leveled his pistol. "I told you don't move!"

She seemed not to hear.

"He was from our village, near Piatraneamt. That's in Moldava, Captain, very far from here. He had been a peasant hunting on the grounds of our estate when my husband shot him. It was an accident, that's all.

"Ivan brought the body back, and we worked to revive him. It was extremely difficult: the damage was severe. Fortunately, we had all the equipment we needed at the chateau."

"Go on," Aikman said, repulsed by what he was hearing, yet mesmerized.

"In those times my husband and I had done a vast amount of

research; devised equipment capable of sustaining the life functions for a limited time. All experimental, but even then we were able to restore smaller creatures: rabbits, mice..." She gestured at the machines near the table. "Sufficient, as it turned out, to revive a human being. A donor was needed, of course -- a male -- and there was only one possibility..." She turned her eyes to him as though seeking understanding. "There was no other choice. After all, it *had* been Ivan's fault in the first place."

The Captain had heard enough. "Either you're crazy, lady, or I am. Anyhow, I'm taking you in... hold out your wrists." He retrieved a set of handcuffs.

"As you can see," she went on, unheeding, "our -- that is, *my* -- efforts were successful. And yet --" She frowned, looking at the figure on the table. "He was never strong afterwards. Everything I'd done to save him had to be done again, and again -- organs replaced, blood supply renewed. More donors were needed and, eventually, the people in the nearby villages became suspicious. It was time to come to your country."

"Time to come with me, you mean. Your wrists, madam!"

"Fortunately," she continued, "I've had more success with my most recent creation."

"*Your what?*"

" Adam's fiancé, of course -- Lilith." The woman smiled, looking past him. "I think you've already met?"

He sensed rather than heard the movement behind him, and spun around. The sight of the girl striding toward him -- clad in white, but with crimson gore spilling down her face, neck, and shoulder courtesy of the terrible wound inflicted by the park policeman -- paralyzed him.

Only an instant, but too long: the girl's hand, clutching a surgical blade, descended once -- twice -- then again.

Aikman fell to his knees and rolled onto his side, sight fading, consciousness departing. He lived just long enough to hear Mme. Dragovich say:

"That's enough, my dearest. Mustn't harm the *vena cava!*"

John Tomerlin was born in Los Angeles on March 26, 1930. He has lived in Laguna Beach, Napa, and Long Beach, California, as well as New York, and Nice, France. His television and film credits include *Wanted, Dead Or alive; The Lawman; Thriller; The Twilight Zone* and the ABC Circle Theater adaptation of *The Picture Of Dorian Gray*, by Dan Curtis.

Publications include ten novels, four of them for young adults, plus short stories in magazines such as *Playboy, The Magazine of Fantasy and Science Fiction, Dark Discoveries* and numerous anthologies. His non-fiction has appeared in more than two dozen national publications, including *True; Woman's Day; McCall's; Motor Trend; Road & Track* and *Car and Driver.* John lives in Southern California with Wilma, his wife of more than fifty years.

The author writes about this story:

" 'De Mortius' is a sly tribute to several styles of dark fiction at once. Detective Aikman may be no Sherlock Holmes -- And Sergeant Walczak certainly isn't Watson -- but the evil genius they pursue is a worthy successor to Dr. Frankenstein.

De mortuis nil nisi bonum:
'Of the dead speak nothing but good.'
But can the same be said of the undead?"

I, My Father and Weird Tales

by Frank M. Robinson

I never met my father until I was four years old. It was the start of the Depression and my mother had gotten a divorce. She, my two brothers and I ended up at the Lawrence Hall Home for Boys in Chicago, where she was lucky enough to have a job as a matron.

One morning I was called down to the library and introduced to my father, a complete stranger. (He and my mother had divorced when I was two.)

At four, I knew that meeting him was supposed to be a Big Deal but I might as well have been meeting the postman. An average man, medium height, reddish hair and a little on the heavy side. I felt no emotion toward him and I imagine he felt little toward me beyond a certain curiosity. He was a Canadian, I was told, which didn't mean much to me. I didn't owe him anything and I suspect he felt the same way.

Years later, I discovered that I owed him everything.

My mother remarried when I was eight years old and for a while we lived in Forest Park, a suburb of Chicago. I had taught myself to read at the Hall -- *The Red Book of Fairy Tales* and *The Blue Book of Fairy Tales* (name your color) by Andrew Lang were in the Hall's library and I read them all, looking up the words I didn't know (which was most of them). Discovered Jules Verne and H.G. Wells in the suburban library and at Christmas a friend of the family gave us some Grosset and Dunlap Burroughs books. My brothers loved Tarzan; my favorite was *The Moon Maid*.

It was about this time that an older brother discovered pulp magazines, namely *Dime Sports* and *Sport Story Magazine*. He usually entrusted me with a quarter to pick up issues he hadn't read, though occasionally I got away with a copy of *Argosy* with a sport story cover.

One fateful day I couldn't find any he hadn't read but I *had* discovered *Astounding Science Fiction* (the first issue I'd ever bought -- February, 1939, containing Jack Williamson's "Crucible of Power" and the first installment of "Cosmic Engineers" by Cliff Simak -- that's from memory, science fiction buffs *never* forget the first magazine on which they broke their cherry).

I promptly became a convert. My brother, on the other hand, detested the stuff and promptly hit me for wasting his quarter. (My brother and I were made for each other -- he was a bully and I was a snitch.)

It wasn't long before I discovered the reader's columns and started to make friends all over the country -- a godsend for a lonely kid. Close friends in the Chicago area included Ronald Clyne (a young artist) and Charles McNutt (in later years to become better known as Charles Beaumont). Walt Liebscher and Neil de Jack, other Chicago fans, and I became collectors.

Chicago at the time was a happy hunting ground for old pulp magazines. W.F. Hall and the Cuneo Press, both located in the area, printed most of them. Initially publishers took full copy returns, soon to be superseded by returns consisting only of torn off covers, and that superseded by issues with a small star punched in the covers to indicate they were second hand, and even *that* was succeeded by publisher's certified returns. Meaning the publisher went to a notary public and made out a sworn statement that the issue had sold only so many copies.

The unsold copies eventually ended up in magazine dumps -- stores on West Madison street that dealt in returns. It wasn't unusual to walk into one and see copies of *Amazing Stories* and *Blue Book* stacked in rows from the floor to the ceiling -- all coverless. One exception was *Golden Fleece*, published in Chicago, whose returns only had a small star punched in their covers. The magazine had a run of nine issues and the dump sold them for a nickel a copy. I promptly made friends and influenced fellow fans by buying up complete runs for 45 cents and gifting one and all with a set.

The last time I bought a set, it cost me a thousand bucks.

By the time I was sixteen the war was well under way and my mother had a job in a defense plant -- the first time in her life she made any kind of decent money. Walt and Neil and I were stalking the city for old magazines and one day we hit the mother lode: a large store on Chicago's south side had tables piled high with all kinds of pulps -- *The Shadow, Doc Savage, Adventure, Argosy, Terror Tales, Sport Stories, Wild West Weekly,* etc. We started thumbing through the piles, not especially interested by any of the titles, when one of us spotted a locked glass-front cabinet in the back of the store.

We promptly dropped the magazines we were holding on the floor and ran for the glass-fronted cabinet. *Amazing Stories, Science Wonder Stories, Astounding Stories of Super Science, Weird Tales, Fantastic Adventures* -- you name it. Beautiful condition, Frank R. Paul covers, the works...

"How much?" we asked. "To you guys? They're not for sale." The owner was pissed -- we had dropped his valuable merchandise on the floor. (If you could travel back in time and buy the contents of his shop, it would be worth a million dollars at today's prices -- really.)

Once outside the store, we decided we'd romance the guy. We

came back again and again and listened to his war stories, we bought hamburgers for his dog, and never once did we look away from the cabinet.

Finally, after an excruciating tour of the trenches of World War I, he offered to sell them to us. For a hundred and fifty dollars. That was a *lot* of money back then and, even if we split it three ways, it was still fifty each. I didn't have fifty. At the time, I don't think I had five.

At home I hit up the old lady -- she had a full time World War II defense job -- but I doubted she made that much in a week. For reasons that to this day I don't understand, she agreed to lend me the money. My stepfather, I knew, heartily disagreed.

We bought the magazines, hired a cab and took them to my kitchen where we divvied up the spoils. Walt and Neil were entranced by anything with a cover by Frank R. Paul. I, on the other hand, was fascinated by the *Weird Tales*, many of which dated back to 1926 and 1927.

After an hour of picking-and-choosing, my mother came out to the kitchen to see how I had wasted her money. She took one look and turned pale. Back in the late '20s, my father -- an improvident sort -- tried to make a living by painting portraits from photographs. He had the ambition, but was never a very good painter. While he applied paint to canvas, my mother read stories to him from his favorite magazine -- *Weird Tales*. In the kitchen, my mother was looking at the covers from the very same issues of the magazine.

To this day, I'm not sure of the connection: I had no idea of my father's reading preferences; I wasn't aware that he was an embryonic horror and science fiction fan. I wasn't aware that he collected Burroughs and after the divorce donated his entire collection of Burroughs (all Grosset and Dunlap's, I'm sure) to the Hall.

A little questioning of my mother, and I filled out the rest of his persona: he was a womanizer (a talent he never passed on to his sons); my grandfather liked to dress up in woman's clothing (an acquired taste, I'm sure); but the most important thing about my father was his taste in literature. Later he developed a limited ability in writing -- the names of other family members on checks (a streak of larceny to go with his improvidence and womanizing). He was promptly deported back to Canada and my mother got a divorce on grounds of desertion.

But there was one thing I'd inherited from him, and that was his love for *Weird Tales*. It was obviously genetic and along with it came a limited ability in writing and painting.

Aside from my mother, he was the only member of my immediate family that I had ever met. A streak of talent, a love of the same reading matter that I loved, and a broad swash of larceny. I enlarged on his ability to copy two or three words in a signature and later started stealing money from Publishers.

I owed the old man a lot, and even today I wish I had been old enough to listen to his accounts about the old *Weird Tales*, which Burroughs books he preferred and why the hell he went off the rails at the end.

The only real connection I had with him was his love for *Weird Tales:* it immediately became my favorite collectible. The one thing I was sure I inherited from my mother was her liking for things that were new. When she went antiquing, the only thing that caught her eye were those cups and saucers that were obviously just off the assembly line.

As a consequence, in collecting old *Weird Tales,* the only copies that really interested me were those issues that were brand new. Not an easy task to collect them. The 'Number One' issue I bought in an old magazine store in Chicago. The owner read the avarice in my eyes and promptly charged $25, a week's salary. But it was, very nearly, mint...

I ended up picking and choosing from collections that came up for sale and gradually filled out a compete run -- all 279 issues. The price of my first issue was a mere pittance to what some of the other issues cost. I once made the mistake of lending my treasured first issue to a magazine historian who promptly dismantled it, made Xerox copies that he sold for $25 each, and gave the remains of the magazine to his wife to put back together. The issue was ruined -- she got the pages mixed up and used a glue on the spine that never dried.

Years later, at an auction in San Jose, the first issue was bid in at $3,000 -- it was a pristine issue but I didn't have the money. A little later, a story sold and I promptly contacted the successful bidder. It was all mine -- for $4,000 plus a file of Gernsback's *Radio News* (Science and Invention?) in which Gernsback was fond of reprinting stories by Ray Cummings. The owner wanted to reprint the stories in his own fan magazine of the period.

Done deal. I ran over to the historian who'd ruined *my* first issue and got a file of *Radio News* (his penance for ruining my first issue). The auction copy remains the best conditioned first issue of *Weird* that I've ever seen.

There's one more collecting story re: *Weird Tales* that's worth retelling. At a comic book convention here in San Francisco, a kid showed up with a cardboard box full of... something. Since he wasn't buying anything it was obvious that he must be selling something. He circled the huckster room and gradually a line of dealers formed up behind him.

When he finally put down the box and opened it, I caught my breath. After the first two issues in pulp size, *Weird Tales* had switched to a "flat" sized format for eleven issues. The kid had all the flat-sized issues in 1924 -- brand new, never been opened. The young seller came from northern California, dealt in collectibles and bought the magazines from a local old lady. Turns out, she was the sister of John Martin

Leahy, an early contributor to *Weird Tales*. She'd bought two copies of every issue in which her brother had a story. One set, she bound with fine wire nails. The other set she put in her hope chest -- and there they sat for generations.

The greedy comic book dealers in the huckster room were willing to pay the kid ten cents on the dollar. I told him I'd give him a hundred dollars plus my copy in trade (my copies weren't shabby but come on, these were *new*).

He was willing -- except for one issue with an Indian on the cover. For some strange reason he didn't want to part with it -- maybe because it had an article by Harry Houdini, ghosted by H.P. Lovecraft. I pressed him and the kid came up with an impossible deal -- he'd trade it for a file of the French magazine *Photographie* (he was obviously fond of French nudes). Impasse -- but not quite. I was working for *Playboy* at the time and was friends with the man who handled the foreign editions. He, in turn, was friendly with the editor of the French edition.

Within two weeks, the kid had the file and I had the *Weird Tales*. I meant it when I said the issues were mint -- their only flaw was the faint odor of moth balls.

One last story and then I'll go away. When I was much younger I took a razor blade to the "overlap" of *Weird Tales* published in 1927-1928. At that time, the body of the magazine was trimmed on the right hand side but the cover was full size and simply pasted on the spine, a quarter to half an inch of the original cover overlapping the body. It was this overlap page that was frequently torn or bent. I thought I'd neaten them up and took a razor and cut off the overhang.

Forgive me, I was stupid back then -- I even had my file of *Air Wonder Stories* and *Unknown* bound with my name printed in gold at the bottom of the spine. Classy.

It cost me thousands to replace the magazines I had mutilated, but two issues of *Weird Tales* from 1927 eluded me. A few years ago, a Canadian collector helped me and I finally got the two issues in pristine condition. For the bargain (I'm being sarcastic) price of $3500.

I once added up the value of a complete set of *Weird Tales* in mint condition at eBay prices. A hundred and fifty grand might do it -- if anybody had them for sale.

I think an artistic streak may be genetic and manifest itself in art or music or writing and I suspect the same thing holds true for a love of fantasy.

Almost everything I have of value, one way or another, I owe to the man I'd met when I was four years old. If I'd met my old man when I was sixteen, I think we would have had a lot to talk about.

Born in 1926, **Frank M. Robinson** began his career in 1944 when he went to work as a copy boy for Ziff-Davis publications in his home city of Chicago. Frank sold his first professional story to *Astounding* in 1950, having by then acquired a B.S. in Physics and a M.S. in Journalism. He served in the Navy during World War II and in the Korean conflict. Back home in the States, he became editorially associated with *Science Digest, Rogue, Cavalier,* and *Playboy,* turning to full-time writing in 1973. He has more than a dozen novels to his credit, most famous of which are *The Power* (filmed in 1967) and, with Thomas Scortia, *The Glass Inferno* (one of five best-selling disaster novels he co-wrote with Scortia). The latter formed a partial basis for the successful 1974 film, *The Towering Inferno.*

A former speech writer for the late political activist Harvey Milk, Frank's San Francisco home once contained his amazing assemblage of near-mint pulp magazines, one of the largest such collections in the world.

The author says about this essay:

"At one time the readers of pulp magazine numbered in the tens of millions. The 'pulps' were everywhere -- more than a *thousand* titles and close to thirty-five thousand different issues. They were at the height of their popularity in the '20s and '30s, but largely disappeared in the mid '50s, forgotten by all but a few avid collectors and cultural historians. I'm happy to be one of them."

Silk City

by Lisa Morton

*A*lice parked at a broken meter, turned off the engine, and looked out the driver's side window. The six-story luxury hotel on the other side of the street had once been a marvel of architecture -- it still bore curling ornamentation on the brick sides and ornate wood frames around the windows -- but now it looked like an obsolete relic from a warzone. Rusted shopping carts lined the doorless main entrance, the windows were boarded over. Even the concrete sidewalk in front was crumbling.

She double-checked the address, then spotted the official city truck parked on the other side of the street.

This had better be worth it...

Alice scanned her equipment: glass vials tucked in her vest, gloves, miner's helmet equipped with a high-powered light-- then she climbed out of the SUV. She waited until she heard the reassuring chirp of the locks activating, then crossed the street.

A man stepped from the truck. He was thin, dark-skinned, wearing a nondescript khaki uniform. "Dr. Friel?"

Alice nodded.

The man's eyes darted nervously. She'd seen the look before.

"So you're the spider expert, huh?" he asked. His voice had a trace of accent.

"Yes," Alice answered. "Are you the gentleman who found the spider?"

He gulped and his head jerked up and down, out of rhythm. "In the basement."

Alice tried to sound soothing as she asked, "Can you tell me more about it? Sorry, I didn't catch your name..."

"Call me Arturo." He jabbed a thumb over one shoulder at the building. "I had to inspect the place, you know, the city owns it now. I went down into the basement, and I was just running my light along an overhead heating duct when I saw this... *thing*. I swear, Doc, it was this big --" He held his hands at least six inches apart.

Alice nodded, and knew damn well she'd likely find, at best, a brown recluse no more than an inch wide. "It's probably easiest if you just show me."

Arturo's eyes shot to the building and back. "Okay..." He didn't move.

She caught a quick glimpse of red-rimmed eyes peering out at her from a crack in the plywood sheets covering the nearest window, and felt a shiver of adrenaline.

"Arturo, are there people living in the building?"

"Oh, yeah."

"I thought this building was condemned?"

Arturo followed her glance and nodded. "It was. *Is*. These are homeless people."

Alice frowned. "How many?"

"A lot. The city can't kick 'em out because there's nowhere else for 'em to go. Shelters are full. Town's got no room. So we call this place Sheet City and let 'em stay here." Arturo's lip curled slightly, and he added, "Cause you rich people needed some more tax breaks."

Alice couldn't tell if the man was joking or not. "I live in a three-bedroom house I'll be paying off for another twenty years. I'm not rich."

He shrugged.

Arturo turned away from her and started towards the entrance to the hotel. Alice followed him.

The smells hit her first: alcohol and urine and an organic stench she could only label "sickness". She swallowed down her revulsion and stepped over the ruined entryway into the hotel lobby.

She could see how this ruin had once been a palace. The expansive lobby was floored in marble, still incongruously gleaming, the blocks unchipped. A staircase with brass railing swept up to the right, and off to the left, in the dusky gloom, she could just make out a registration area, backed by a huge hand-painted mural. Although the paint was peeling and cracked, the work covered in decades of grime, she could sense brilliance to the art, in the colors and the way the figures conveyed hope and desperation.

Then, as Alice's eyes adjusted to the dimness, she saw them... the old, the sick, the unlucky; alcoholics, junkies, hustlers. There were at least fifty people in the room. They lined the perimeters of the cavernous lobby. Some had created small areas for themselves from boxes, cardboard, old clothing strung on lines. And sheets. Pale linen billowed here and there, marking small territories. Bodies reclined on the hard floor, unmoving. The accoutrements of squalor abounded: gin bottles... crackpipes... plastic garbage bags stuffed with discarded food. An old man whose features were lost amid leathery wrinkles spasmed as coughs wracked his body, while near him a bent woman muttered a ceaseless stream of Spanish.

"Basement's over here, Doc," Arturo called. He was indicating a door near the registration area.

She started to walk toward him, trying to ignore the stench and the bodies she had to step around. She found herself holding her breath, hoping the air of the basement would smell of nothing worse than rot and age.

"Hey..." A hand clutched her shoulder.

She jumped and spun, only to find herself facing a man who had a tangled, filthy beard, long hair already running with gray, and a missing front tooth. "You the one who knows about spiders?" he asked.

Alice nodded.

He thrust an arm at her, and Alice saw a filthy bandage wrapped just below the elbow. He picked at the bandage, and Alice experienced a rush of both anticipation and dread.

"Goddamn spider bit me," he muttered, then pulled back the bandage.

Alice gasped.

There was a five-inch hole in the man's arm. She could see white bone at the bottom of the wound, and large fleshy blisters had formed over tissue in one area. The flaky skin around the edges of the pit had blackened; it had the characteristic spoiled-meat smell of decay.

"Dermo-necrotic lesion," Alice half-whispered. Then, loudly, she looked at the man and said, "You need to have this looked at."

The man barked a laugh. "They *did* look at it, said there was nothin' else they could do... It's a fuckin' spider bite. Got it down there." He dipped his chin towards the basement, then turned away, already wrapping the arm back up. "Go see for yourself..." Alice heard him say as he staggered off.

The area in front of the door was clear, and Arturo opened it. Alice looked in, and saw a dark stairwell leading down.

"You should probably switch that on now," Arturo said, gesturing at her helmet.

Alice reached up and flicked on the helmet light.

"And you'll probably need this one, too... Mighty dark down there." Arturo handed her an additional two-cell flashlight. "I'll wait here, if that's okay." There was a quiver in his voice, an unmistakable note of fear. Alice considered, then reluctantly agreed: "Fine. But you'll be here when I'm done, right?"

"Sure, doc... I'll be here."

If he was right, if he really had seen an arachnid with a six-inch leg span, she had to know. Twenty years ago a nest of *Loxosceles laeta* had been discovered near here, brought by South American immigrants who'd never even known they'd been carrying a deadly spider north with them. Alice had just heard some of the people in the lobby speaking Spanish, and figured it wasn't impossible that *laeta* could be here again.

She pulled on a pair of heavy gloves and glanced back at the lobby.

Everyone in the room was staring at her.

Alice stared back for a second, unnerved. The place was quiet, nothing but the muted sounds of distant traffic intruding from outside.

She was actually relieved when one man finally dropped his gaze in favor of a bottle. She looked at Arturo, then stepped into the stairwell.

The door closed heavily behind her.

She turned and started down the stairs. At least they were concrete, the footing good, the reek more tolerable in the basement's cooler climate. After twenty or so steps, she arrived at a small landing. The stairs turned left, and she continued on down.

At the bottom, she reached a doorway, stepping into the large, empty basement. Pipes and ducts ran overhead, broken furnishings and storage boxes filling much of the floor space.

She spotted some webbing draped over a stack of decrepit chairs and moved to investigate. The web was decaying, partly destroyed, and Alice couldn't identify it as either the classic circular work of the orbweaver or the more haphazard construction of a widow. A few strands overhead looked like the work of *pholcids* -- daddy long-legs -- and Alice allowed herself to smile as she imagined a large but harmless *pholcid* being the source of Arturo's fear.

Turning away from the center of the room, Alice stepped carefully past a few pools of stagnant liquid as she approached a stained and graffiti-covered wall. She saw a small pile of trash in one corner, and realized the bottles and food wrappers meant that someone had lived down here.

She turned her attention back to the hunt, running the beam of her handheld light along a crack in the wall, up to where it joined the ceiling, hidden slightly behind a large rusting tube...

There!

Something skittered at the edge of her beam, having just crawled from behind a duct. Alice caught it firmly in the light, and felt a thrill of discovery.

It was a spider, about one inch from leg to leg. Alice stepped closer, and from the reddish coloring on the legs and the size, she knew it was *Loxosceles laeta,* the South American cousin to the native brown recluse.

She followed the progress of the one her beam had picked out, and felt a small disappointment when it disappeared into a ventilation duct overhead. She moved her light down, hoping to find something she wouldn't have to strain to capture, and was rewarded with the sight of a *laeta* trudging lazily across a dusty box top. She set her handheld flashlight aside, and used the beam from her helmet as she set to work. It proved to be simple enough to guide the spider into a collection vial, and she felt the satisfaction of the treasure hunter as she secured the vial in a pocket of her vest.

In a few minutes she had four more of the spiders captured, and she realized they had been breeding.

Well, I don't know about those people upstairs, but the spiders certainly like their new home.

Alice's thoughts were interrupted by a sound from somewhere behind her. A louder sound, probably a rat. She swept the beam across the floor.

What she glimpsed was too big to be a *laeta*; it was still an arachnid, but unlike any she had encountered before in an urban environs.

What the...? It scrambled out of sight around a corner.

She moved quickly after it, dodging chairs and support pillars. The basement stretched before her, seemingly endless. The stored material became less and less distinct as she moved farther away from the stairs. Alice realized that the cobwebs were both thicker and newer in this section. She brushed a hand through some of it, and felt a light burning sensation where some of the silk met the bare skin of her wrist.

She paused, playing the light around her surroundings... and spotted her quarry.

It rested at the base of a column, as if waiting for her. The spider had a leg span of at least five inches and, as the light settled on it, it reared back on its hind legs to challenge her.

My god, how did you get here?

It was a *Phoneutria nigriventer*, or Brazilian wandering spider. Alice had seen a live specimens only once before, during a trip to São Paulo.

"You shouldn't be here," she muttered to the spider.

And then, recalling that *Phoneutria* was the most venomous and aggressive spider in the world, Alice cautioned herself: *And neither should I!* She had no way of capturing a half-foot-wide spider.

She began to back slowly away from the creature, keeping the light centered on it.

The spider advanced toward her, crawling faster than she was moving.

Even *Phoneutria* shouldn't be this aggressive. She knew that if it reached her, it could quickly climb up her leg. If it found any open skin it would bite, and although fatal envenomation was unlikely, Alice knew she could expect a painful and feverish two days.

She swept a pile of moldering rubbish into her path, hoping it would at least slow the thing down. The spider scuttled over the detritus and started toward her again.

Fuck it.

Alice turned to run. She ducked around several columns and mounds of discarded furniture, realizing she'd lost her sense of direction in this underground maze. She thought the door to the stairs was somewhere off to her left, so she turned in that direction, raced towards a huge object that might once have been a display cabinet…

…and froze when she saw at least five *Phoneutria* on the floor, blocking her path. Another half-dozen clustered on the surface of the old étagère, all poised now in that reared-back attack stance.

For the first time in her life, Alice panicked at the sight of spiders. They were already starting for her. *This is impossible -- spiders don't hunt in packs! They don't seek out human prey! They shouldn't be doing this!*

But they were.

She ran to the right and heard one crunch underfoot. She didn't slow down to see if more were around her; she fled. Once, as she ducked beneath a low-hanging pipe that had come partly loose from its ceiling fittings, she felt one of them drop onto her back, but she frantically shook it off.

Her trembling light found a corner, and she pulled up short. *A wall, that's good, I just have to follow it and eventually I'll come to the way out.* She tried to tell herself that -- and realized she had no idea which wall to follow. *If I choose the wrong one…*

She thought she saw more shadowy eight-legged forms to the left, so she went right.

Then she heard laughter.

It was low, male, wet. She couldn't tell how far away it was in the dark.

"You'll never get out if you go that way."

The voice was heavily accented, and the speech sounded strange, as if the tongue delivering it was too thick to shape the words. Her flashlight beam picked out a vague human form, perhaps fifty feet off to her right.

She edged towards the man, and felt dread curdle within her. He was obviously sick, with skin that seemed taut and papery, as if it lacked any hint of moisture. His eyes were sunken and ᵣ mmed, his nose and lips raw and cracking, his hair patchy.

His bare arms were covered with spider bites.

Several had turned into lesions, although not yet as extensive as the one she'd seen on the man upstairs. Others were small, oozing pinpricks. The arms were swollen and red, and she couldn't imagine that his hands were still usable. He was smiling.

He was obviously quite mad.

Alice tried to remain calm, tried to steady her shaking hands. "Do you know where the exit is?"

He nodded, then laughed again. "Sure…" he said, in that speech Alice could barely parse, "but you won't make it."

"We could try together. You shouldn't be down here, either."

He chuckled. "I like it here. I like them."

Judging from the man's arms, Alice knew the amount of venom

in his system must be causing delirium. "Let me help you," she offered, gesturing toward him. "Let's go upstairs."

She took one step in his direction. He moved with her, blocking her way. "Oh no. You should stay. You need to know about this."

"Know about what?" Alice could hear the *Phoneutria* scurrying up behind her.

"They came north with us. They settled here, just like we did. We've all been here for a long time now. No one notices us. And so no one notices how we are changing."

Alice felt her stomach lurch at the way the man's eyes glinted from deep within their orbits. "Changing...?"

"*Si.* The spiders change here, and now they change us." He hesitated as a thick, milky fluid seeped from the corner of his mouth, then he grinned, a few teeth still left in yellowing gums. "And we like it."

He tilted his head at an angle, his ear toward the ceiling. As Alice watched, a *Loxosceles* emerged from his half-eaten ear, moving slowly, as if drunk. It staggered over his hairline and onto his desiccated face.

Alice took off. It no longer mattered whether she was heading towards the exit, or into a web teeming with arachnids. She bounced painfully off an antique table, colliding with a pile of rotten cardboard that exploded into dust. She felt one of the vials inside her vest break, and knew that the spider held there was free now, so she shrugged out of the vest as she ran, leaving it somewhere in the blackness.

Suddenly her helmet beam picked out a doorframe, and she allowed herself an instant of exultation. Alice clutched the railing, taking the stairs two at a time. She saw a dim light above. She reached the landing and yanked the door open. The rank odors of the lobby were a relief.

"Arturo!" she cried out, lunging forward into the lobby -- and froze.

Arturo wasn't there -- but *they* were. The homeless. Clustered around the door, looking at her with strange, cold eyes. Twisting away, she blundered into one of their hanging sheets, suddenly realizing that they weren't made from cotton but silk -- *spidersilk:* strong, protective. She tore herself free. They were edging in: the whores, the winos, the forgotten. All of them shambled around her, closing the space between Alice and the exit. Arturo's face materialized near the back, orbs blank, face drawn.

Silk city! she thought hysterically.

They closed in around her.

Lisa Morton is a screenwriter, reviewer and the author of three non-fiction books, including *The Halloween Encyclopedia*. Her short fiction has appeared in several dozen books and magazines, most recently *Unspeakable Horror: From the Shadows of the Closet; Winter Frights; Terrible Beauty: Fearful Symmetry* and *Dark Passions: Hot Blood XIII*. She won the 2006 Bram Stoker Award for Short Fiction and is a two-time winner of the Horror Writers Association's Richard Laymon Award. Her first novella, *The Lucid Dreaming*, will be published by Bad Moon Books in 2009, followed by her first novel, *The Castle of Los Angeles*, to be published by Gray Friar Press. She lives in North Hollywood, and can be found online at *www.lisamorton.com* .

What the author writes about this story:

"'Silk City' was inspired in part by the work of a remarkable woman named Dr. Greta Binford, who is a leading expert on venomous spiders. I have no doubt that Greta is far happier, more compassionate and less fearful than my heroine."

Red Light

by Steve Rasnic Tem

Franklin pulled the top of his sweater higher against his neck. He didn't like the woolen scratchiness, but he liked being cold even less. He rubbed his mittens rapidly over the steering wheel, imagined he saw a spark, but knew it was just a trick his eyes typically played at night, seeing lights that weren't there, at random locations. Frank had been told the condition might not get any worse, but he wasn't feeling optimistic. He didn't suppose everything gets worse -- he wasn't a pessimist, for Christ's sake, but he was pretty sure most things do.

Something big, heavy, and fast thundered by the car, rocking it wildly on its loose springs and threatening to suck out all the air through the half-open window. In the red metallic blur ahead of him impossibly tall fins rose, whipping the dark as the huge auto fishtailed and disappeared. He gripped the steering wheel tightly, aggravating his always-resident wrist pain.

It had been like this ever since they'd left the dinner at his brother-in-law's house: larger and larger vehicles, and each succeeding driver worse than the one before. No place on the road seemed safe. People changed when they got behind the wheel. Drivers went rogue.

Some people have no business driving. That was the first thing he'd learned as a driver. Seventeen at the time, but when he said that to his friends he knew he sounded like a cranky old man. Well, now Frank *was* a cranky old man, and it was still a regularly revisited conviction, spoken loud and clear to any passenger with him. Usually to Jenny, who'd never learned to drive, who'd been too nervous about the responsibility. So he'd taken the responsibility, even when he didn't want it. He didn't always enjoy driving, in fact in recent years it had become barely tolerable -- today's drivers acted as if those were weapons they were driving, and if they got annoyed, well, watch out. They had no business. It was nerve-wracking, but what choice did he have? Somebody in the family had to drive.

The light was still red, had been red. Stuck red, seemed like. The car kept urging forward and he was tired of holding it back. He'd been driving almost two hours, so tired he was afraid he'd start crying like a child. *Some people have no business driving.* But he didn't say it out loud. Not just because Jenny was sleeping, silent and still as a big overstuffed chair. But because this time the thought was for himself. He had no business.

A scattering of homeless people with loaded trash bags over their shoulders crossed the street ahead. In the midst of the crowd he could see a little girl with pale skin, a dirty face, whispery, almost translucent hair. Who would bring their child into such an area, and at this time of night? She appeared sickly, poorly looked-after. Some people had no business trying to be parents.

He and Jenny had had no business being out tonight. That had been part of the reason he'd retired, so he wouldn't have to drive anymore. But Jenny wanted to visit her brother on the other side of town, where they used to live. I-48 and the Valley Highway crossed the city like a giant, ragged X. Each of the resulting four sections was hardly a triangle, more like a jagged shard. He and Jenny had lived in the Southeast corner, near that know-it-all brother of hers. Now they were Northwest, a little poorer, a little more run down. They'd been convinced selecting their retirement home would be a matter of finding a smaller, more manageable, yet equally nice sanctuary to spend their remaining days. But Frank had an uneasy feeling they'd traded down, in every sense of the word, for the small wooden box they would eventually die in.

Red light filled the front part of the car, as if the air itself were suffused with scarlet dye. He could see little moths flapping against the ceiling of the car, bloody little bodies attached to vermillion wings. *Stop. Just stop this.* He had no business, but what was he supposed to do? Jenny wanted to see her family sometimes. He and Jenny just had each other, and they had doctors' appointments, they needed groceries, and every once in awhile a movie or a play to go to. With that crappy bus system their taxes paid for, somebody *had* to drive. You do what you have to do. Even if you have no business driving a car. Even if you might be a danger to yourself and others. That's the way they'd say it, isn't it? When they finally hauled him into court because of some dumb move he'd made with their big old Buick? "A danger to yourself and others," before they took away his license. Well, let them. He didn't want the damn thing. If they took his license he and Jenny would *have* to figure out some other way to get around.

Something roared down the cross-street ahead. He couldn't catch the details -- too dark, and it traveled through a cloud of dust, and leaves, and trash. It could have been a very large car, maybe a limousine. It could have been a truck, it could even have been a train. Frank never knew what he might encounter at a dark intersection. That was the dangerous thing about driving at night in a strange place. That was the dreadful thing.

The light stayed red. If anything the red intensified, redder, darker. But no warmer. A perfect circle of cooling blood hanging from an invisible wire above the dark street. It was freezing in the car, but he didn't dare run the heater that long. It was an old car, and stalled if you just looked at it wrong.

Earlier that evening he'd gotten lost driving to his brother-in-law's house. How long had Frank lived in that same neighborhood? Twenty years at least. Twenty plus. But he couldn't remember ever coming from the Northwest before. It made everything look different, like he'd never seen any of it before. He'd taken the wrong exit twice, then had turned the wrong direction on his old street. The lights had thrown him off, especially those extra ones his eyes made. Mr. Bigshot had wondered why Frank hadn't called him on his cell telling him they'd be late. As if Frank would ever own a cell phone.

At least that terrible dinner was over. At least now they were on their way home.

A green wink, finally. He pushed the gas, but not too hard. This was no place to stall. Still, it was good to be moving again, the road unreeling under them like a dirty black ribbon. Then it was another light, another red. Another wait long enough for him to wonder if the traffic light was broken, but he was afraid to move because it might not be broken, and then whatever happened would be all his fault.

An old lady shuffled up the sidewalk ahead clutching a grimy suitcase in her blackened hand. She crouched and trembled with each step, chattering to herself, a portrait of frenetic dismay. A small figure appeared to be leading her, now and then twisting around to show its tiny feminine face to Frank's headlights. Frank thought this was some child, but the shadows were too thick, the figure's clothing too bulky, for him to be sure. People just didn't take enough care. Children were lost in the streets everyday and people just weren't careful enough with their young, inexperienced charges. They didn't know what it really meant to take responsibility for someone.

He and Jenny had been a half hour late for dinner and still the food wasn't ready, so Mr. Bigshot had decided to fill the time by telling them that story, that awful, awful story, right before dinner, right in front of his sister with his wife and kids in the other room. The man had no sense. The man had no business at all. Jenny's brother liked telling awful stories about the worst things human beings had ever done. Frank didn't need to hear that -- he *knew* how bad people could be. Mr. Bigshot's point, well, maybe there wasn't a point.

Of course Mr. Bigshot always *pretended* he had a point, that somehow if we knew about these things we became better people, sharing a moment in which we all agreed these were awful things. But if he'd been so damn sensitive he'd never have been able to tell such a story in the first place.

Too many lights out there on the streets. Frank knew he was supposed to turn somewhere soon. But there were always more lights than there should be. Stop and go. People doing things they had no business doing. Small children wandering the streets unsupervised.

Stop and go. Then stop for such a long time you wonder if maybe you've stopped forever.

"This happened somewhere Northeast," her brother had begun. "I don't mean *our* Northeast, that part of town -- I mean the real Northeast. New England. New York. Stop me if you read about it."

But he didn't pause for Frank's answer, and Frank knew the bigshot wouldn't stop anyway. Frank could stand up on the couch yelling "Stop! Stop! Stop!" and still this jerk wouldn't stop.

"This young couple, they've been charged with welfare fraud. And desecration of a corpse. And murder."

"Bobby," Jenny said. But that's all she said. She didn't even say stop. Frank didn't say stop, either, and he had no idea why, because Lord knows he was thinking it. He already knew where Bobby (a kid's name, and Frank's brother-in-law being almost fifty-eight) was going with this.

"What got me was the *order* of the list of charges. Like the welfare fraud was the most serious charge, you know? Then corpse desecration, which is hard for most of us to imagine anyway, right, even if you don't know the details? And murder. Do you know who they murdered?"

This would be another good time to yell *Stop*, not that it would do any good. You'd say "stop" and Bobby would apologize, then tell you anyway.

"Their little boy. Two years old." Jenny made a sorrowful little noise. But Frank knew they hadn't heard the worst of the story. "Put him on the family barbecue grill to cremate him. They buried what was left and didn't tell anybody. That's where the welfare fraud comes in, you see. They still wanted to collect checks on him."

Frank and Jenny didn't say anything. Anything they said might encourage Bobby to say more about it, which was the last thing they wanted. Mr. Bigshot had told this terrible story to his brother-in-law and his plainly sensitive and nervous sister just before they all sat down to a meal together, and with his own wife and children right there in the next room.

And when Mr. Bigshot heard the wife and kids coming in from the other room, he quickly added, "You might not understand how hearing about something like this affects a father like myself, your not having kids."

At least the dinner had been a chicken salad with no unfortunate associations, but Frank had been furious. Perhaps he would have gotten lost on the return trip in any case, but he'd allowed himself to blame Bobby for at least part of it.

Frank had made a small mistake, a turn taken a few minutes too soon which resulted in a trip alongside and underneath the interstate, the way home floating tantalizingly above and out of reach.

This wasn't necessarily a bad neighborhood, although one Frank was unfamiliar with. But it was alternately dimly-lit and blazing with those large industrial lights Frank found the most confusing. And now there was all this red light, this red atmosphere, unaccounted for even by the largest of traffic lights hanging in front of the car, telling him stop, telling him no, this isn't the right way at all.

Bobby's story had been completely true -- Frank had found it buried on an interior page of the paper several days before. It was the kind of story he tried not to pay undue attention to, to think about it as some reporter's wild exaggeration. But reading the details he knew it hadn't been exaggerated at all, and he could not stop thinking about it. In fact not thinking about it would be like committing the crime himself. Reading the story had made him feel dirty, and for that moment ashamed of being a human being. Sometimes he found it overwhelming, the insanity of people, the stupidity of what people did, and what people endured every single day. A peculiar sort of momentum was dragging him into despair.

He slammed the brakes, the next light having changed suddenly, and seemingly out of rhythm with the others. Jenny bobbed precariously in and out of shadow, her eyes closed, apparently asleep. Frank reached out a hand to steady her, then found himself snapping it back, reluctant to touch her. After all, he didn't want to wake her up. She rocked back in the passenger seat and settled there.

He roared the engine to greet the green, felt the car lurch, then settled into a bouncy rhythm across the segmented pavement. He watched Jenny out of the corner of his eye, determined to reach out and steady her if he needed to. He tried to stop himself, from looking at her, from over thinking their predicament, but sometimes you can't stop, you have no business stopping.

Frank wasn't sure when the mongrel first appeared. Sometime after his wrong turn, somewhere down in the dark beneath the interstate. That ragged, emaciated creature could have been running alongside the car for miles. Certainly Frank hadn't been driving fast enough to lose the dog, and when he had stopped, and endured these long, intolerable waits beneath the blazing red traffic lights, he hadn't thought to look down at the road beside his door.

Jenny was the first to see it, leaning forward out of the shadowed passenger seat as if something had finally triggered the life in her. But what came out of her mouth seemed self-consciously casual, or bored. "Oh look, Frank. A dog."

Frank *did* look, and saw, the dog having moved far enough out of the shadow of the car that he could view the sorry length of it. It was some sort of hound, from the shape of it, although something so disastrous had happened to its fur that any similarly-sized breed was possible. The poor thing had been burned its entire length, and random swatches of the underlying bloody muscle were exposed, as if it were some stage of butchered carcass normally kept secret from the layman. The rib cage stood out in deep-charred contrast to the rest of the torturously loping corpse, but then those black lines seemed a bit too bold, too regular.

"We should stop," Jenny said with muffled urgency. "Frank, stop the car. We're barely moving anyway."

"That," he said, gripping the steering wheel even more tightly as if his contracting muscles would keep him from making some terrible mistake, "would be a bad idea."

Then Jenny began a crooning that raked the hair up his arms. "Poor, poor puppy. Poor poor poor poor puppy. He's like somebody's child, hurt and scared and so lost he isn't sure if he ever had a home."

Frank could see the little girl's face at the edge of his headlights, confusing and unreal, just another brilliant oval among all the other oval lights his eyes invented. She had no business being out there in the darkened street. Her presence had been completely unexpected. How was he supposed to know? How could he know when to stop? There had been no warning. And that sound, so subtle, just a sigh really -- he'd heard bigger sounds just hitting a plastic trash can with the corner of his bumper, or grazing a cardboard box with his fender, or striking a curb with his front tire, or hitting a mongrel dog that had wandered too close to the car.

"Poor poor poor poor puppy."

"Jenny, don't. Stop, okay? Just stop."

"Poor, poor puppy. Didn't you ever want a puppy, didn't you ever just feel like stopping and picking up some poor damaged puppy off the side of the road? You weren't always like this, Frank. I'm sure at some point you must have wanted a puppy, some poor poor puppy to take care of?"

If Jenny had been with him that time she would have made him stop, they would have loaded the poor crooked body into the car and driven it to the hospital. It probably would have been too late, but at least they would have acted like human beings doing the business of human beings, and not mongrels with no sense of responsibility, who had no business driving a car in the first place because their eyes had gotten so bad, their attention so unfocussed, their reactions so sluggish, their arthritic hands too sore to make a steering wheel turn properly.

She would have made him stop to see what he had done, to see what he could do. At least she would have made him stop.

Frank glanced out the window at their canine companion. He'd never noticed the slight creepiness in that phrase before. Canine companion, "loyal canine companion," as if it would follow you everywhere you went, even, and especially, where you never ever wanted it to go. The dog stared at him with deep umber holes, its incredibly long tongue hanging and flapping like a torn, bloodied rag.

"Jenny," he whispered, not sure why he was whispering. Did he think the dog might hear and take offense? "Jenny, that thing's no puppy. There's nothing we can do for it -- can't you see that?"

He didn't say that the dog, even as obviously injured as it was, scared him, because how could he explain why? It was practically dead, should have been dead from what Frank could see. There was nothing it could do to hurt them.

"You have a cruel streak, Frank. You always have. You've never liked animals, ever."

"That's not true. I like some- *some* animals... Just not every animal. And that *thing*, it's hardly even an animal anymore. A child? It's not even a pet. Have you really looked at it?"

"I see one of God's creatures that needs our help, Frank. That's all I see."

He stopped talking. There was no use. The dog continued its uneven pace. It moved with a distorted rhythm, like something winding up and winding down at the same time, its own movements starting to tear itself apart. It turned its twin holes his way and appeared to be trying to grin, but the grin fell loose and lopsided. He felt foolish to think it, but the dog seemed like some kind of warning, and like the truest warnings it was completely beyond his ability to understand.

The next light began to turn, and he considered hitting the gas and blowing through the intersection, but he was too afraid of being hit, of making a mistake, so he stomped the brakes instead. The tires squealed and the car bucked, and it felt as if the rear of the car had risen off the ground, tilting the contents toward the windshield. When everything landed he heard the passenger door open and close.

The dog staggered toward the front of the car, tail vaguely wagging, claws clicking across the pavement like thoughts running away. He turned to look at Jenny who wasn't there. He snapped his head around, eyes forward, as Jenny glided into the red light bathing the hood, right in the middle of the intersection. "*Stop it*, Jenny," he whispered, his lips barely moving. Jenny's own lips were slightly pursed, and he imagined she was crooning to the ugly thing, but he could hear nothing. *Just stop.*

There's no fool like an old fool. His mother used to say that. People make mistakes, and sometimes no one knows what the right thing to do might be. The Buick rocked back and forth from the heavy passage of yet another undistinguishable juggernaut of screaming metal, the ear-splitting whine of huge brakes and the blast of the horn's cry drawing the air out of the car and even the breath out of Frank's lungs, almost as loud as the sound of his rushing blood. He jumped out, frantic to find her, crying "Jenny! Jenny!" as he ran to the front of the vehicle and fell to his knees before the hideously grinning dog.

It was a struggle to get her back into the car. Jenny had always been a stubborn woman, her obstinacy only intensifying as she grew older. She had more heart than sense and she'd always been proud of it. But all that was why he'd married her in the first place. He knew himself to be a deeply flawed man but eventually she always forgave him for things, at least for the things she knew about. She was kind when it was foolish to be kind, but Frank had always recognized, despite his complaints, that the world needed more of that. A lot more of that.

He'd gotten her away from that awful dog and she must have been quite angry with him, because she was punishing him by not speaking to him the rest of the trip. She was leaving him alone with his own thoughts, the worst punishment possible.

The car rattled across segmented pavement, the flow and stop of chilling red light a desperate beat marking the rest of his evening. Jenny pretended sleep, but Frank could see her shifting on the seat, unbalanced, drunk with fatigue. Several times he had to stretch out an arm to steady her. It annoyed him that she could continue to punish him this way yet remain so relaxed. The red light drifted through the car, obscuring her features, washing her clean.

All around him old buildings rushed the car, faded into the background and disappeared. Now and then a tattered figure pushing a shopping cart raised its short arm and waved. He had no plan for how he would regain the highway, but assumed if he only drove long enough he eventually would.

For himself, he'd always driven until he'd reached some sort of destination, even though he had no business driving in the first place. As far as he was concerned he had no business even being inside a car. What people did, generally, himself included, was unfathomable to him. And they never knew when to stop. They ignored every possible warning. They missed out on every possible chance.

They did terrible, terrible things. They loved for no good reason. They either ignored the dog in the street or they foolishly tried to pet it. They thought if they kept driving they'd find their safe way home, but in the end they almost never did. Sometimes the best they could hope for was a long drive away from the world.

All the air was leaving the car, red light rushing in to fill the vacancy. Jenny began to topple, and when Frank tried to straighten her, she fell apart all over his trembling hands.

Past winner of the Bram Stoker, International Horror Guild, British Fantasy, and World Fantasy Awards, **Steve Rasnic Tem's** most recent novel is a collaboration with wife Melanie Tem, *The Man on the Ceiling* (Wizards' Discoveries). In the Summer of 2009, Speaking Volumes, LLC is bringing out *Invisible*, a 6 CD audio collection of stories. Late 2009 will see a collection of collaborations with Melanie Tem, *In Concert* (Centipede Press). Some of his 250+ published short stories are collected in the volumes *City Fishing* (Silver Salamander) and *The Far Side of the Lake* (Ash-Tree Press). New short stories will be appearing soon in *Asimov's*, *Portents*, *Interzone*, *Postscripts*, and *Crimewave*.

The author writes about this story:

"As for 'Red Light' -- I suffer from slowly progressing drusen, an eye condition, and I can already foresee a time in which I won't be able to drive at night as a consequence. I expect to be responsible about it (and I find driving a bit of a drag anyway), but people do make bad decisions, don't they? Particularly, it seems, where automobiles are concerned."

How it Feels to Murder

(A Teleplay)

by

Norman Corwin

[NOTE: In the narrative to follow, all di-
alogue marked as (O.S.) is to be played
OVER the action, unless noted otherwise.]

FADE IN:

(PRESENT) INT. - POLICE INTERROGATION ROOM - DAY

The time is in the early 1900s.

HERBERT DOUGAL, a middle-aged man, is seated in a
wooden armchair a few feet removed from a small
table at which a STENOGRAPHER sits taking down
what he says. An INVESTIGATING OFFICER asks an
occasional question. The procedure is matter-
of-fact; the tone of the officer is polite, but
stern.

DOUGAL is stoic.

The OFFICER closes the door to the room, and, as
he seats himself opposite DOUGAL, says:

                    OFFICER
            If you're ready,
            Dougal, let's
            continue.

                    DOUGAL
            Well, as I said, I
            did not find my new
            wife, Cecile, as gen-
            erous as I had ex-

> DOUGAL (Cont.)
> pected. You see, I
> didn't have very much
> money, and that was
> why I suggested that
> we should buy a farm.
> I told her that my
> father would not live
> long, and that upon
> his death I was en-
> titled to a large sum
> of money, which was a
> lie… I further showed
> her a claim I had
> against the War Of-
> fice for arrears of
> pay due to me: I had
> made erasures and al-
> terations to the doc-
> ument, and was afraid
> she would detect
> them…

(FLASHBACK) INT. SMALL ROOM. - WALL AND SOFA - DAY

CECILE HOLLAND, 41, sits on a sofa, reading a doc-
ument DOUGAL has handed her. She is prim and ex-
ecutive, but attractive. She scrutinizes the paper
in her hand with the acuteness of a lawyer reading
a contract.

> CECILE
> When will the pay-
> ment on this claim
> be made, do you have
> any idea?

DOUGAL
Oh, when they get
around to it, I
suppose. You know
how they are at
the War Office.

CECILE
(busy reading)
Yes… well.

SHE reads on. After a moment, Dougal gets nervous
about the way she is going over the paper, and
reaches out to take it back. She pulls away from
him.

CECILE (Cont.)
No… I'm not
through… I want
to read it
carefully…

She reads further, is satisfied; then, like an in-
spector, she hands it back.

CECILE (Cont.)
Now are you quite
satisfied that the
Moat Farm is the best
of those we've seen?

DOUGAL
In every way.

CECILE
But -- it's so re-
mote… so isolated
and lonely.

                DOUGAL
But that's its charm.
We'll be able to live
there together, away
  from inquisitive
  strangers. You'll
love the farm, once
  we've settled in…

                CECILE
But do you know any-
thing about managing
     a farm?

                DOUGAL
Of course, my dear.
I once managed a
  large estate.

                CECILE
   You did?

                DOUGAL
Certainly, and I war-
rant that if we buy
the farm, I'd make it
  very profitable.

                CECILE
  What would you
    grow on it?

                DOUGAL
Mushrooms, tomatoes,
cucumbers, or perhaps
 I'd cultivate bees
and flowers. Then, by
watching the markets,
        we

                    DOUGAL (Cont.)
                 could ship the produce
                  to be sold only when
                 the demand sent prices
                           up.

CAMERA moves in to a CLOSEUP of CECILE'S thoughtful face, weighing what he has proposed. OVER it
comes DOUGAL'S narrative voice:

                   VOICE OF DOUGAL
                       (O.S.)
                 Of course, I never
                 intended to do any-
                 thing of the sort:
                 my plan was to get
                 her to buy the farm
                 and transfer it to
                 me, whereupon I
                 meant to sell it.

(PRESENT) INT. - POLICE ROOM:

                    DOUGAL (Cont.)
                 …and, therefore, I
                 did not want an or-
                 dinary farm, where
                 there would be a lot
                  of prying neigh-
                 bors. The Moat Farm
                 was just the place.
                 I thought the moat
                 would be very use-
                          ful…
                 Everything went all
                 right up to the time
                 that the farm was
                 purchased, and I
                 requested that the
                 deeds should be made

> DOUGAL (Cont.)
> out in my name. Miss
> Holland would not
> consent. I could see
> she intended to be
> master, and that she
> had been so in the
> habit of doing her
> own business that,
> even if we did make
> a profit, it would
> be she who would
> handle the money.

(FLASHBACK) INT. LIVING ROOM - FARMHOUSE - DAY

It is neat and sensibly furnished, as farmhouses
of that day go, and it reflects the frugal tastes
of Miss Holland. There is an old upright piano
in the room; chairs; the same sofa we saw in her
previous home; a small table with a decanter and
glass on it, and a desk. A door leads off to a
bedroom.

As DOUGAL'S VOICE continues his confession without
interruption, we are ANGLED on CECILE and a very
downcast DOUGAL. CECILE is at the piano, playing a
sentimental tune of the period, and now and then
looks up to see if DOUGAL, sitting nearby on the
sofa, is absorbing it.

> VOICE OF DOUGAL
> (O.S.)
> Finding she was so tight-
> fisted, I began to think
> of various schemes to put
> her out of the way; but
> I thought I would wait a
> little while and see if
> she altered. It was

> VOICE OF DOUGAL (Cont.)
> (O.S.)
> strange to find a woman
> so close, because oth-
> erwise she was not so
> bad, and she would often
> try, when I was miserable
> or down in the dumps to
> cheer me up by playing or
> singing to me…

CECILE finishes at the piano, gets up, and walks over to him with her hand extended, a gesture of comfort and consolation. He takes her hand as she sits beside him.

> CECILE
> Are you feeling
> better, Herbert?

He nods "Yes."

> DOUGAL
> I enjoyed your
> playing.

> CECILE
> (pleased)
> Do you like Mendels-
> sohn?

> DOUGAL
> Is that what it
> was?

> CECILE
> Yes -- one of my
> favorite pieces. I
> learned it when I
> was a child.

No response. He couldn't be less interested. In the vacuum, CECILE smoothes her skirt, draws his attention to it.

> CECILE
> Do you like
> this dress?

> DOUGAL
> (vaguely)
> Oh yes. Yes.

> CECILE
> You don't, re-
> ally.

> DOUGAL
> Well, to be perfect-
> ly frank, Cecile, I
> think you ought to
> buy yourself some
> new dresses, and
> wear more fashion-
> able clothes.

> CECILE
> (stiffening)
> I don't want to be
> in the fashion! If
> two people are fond
> of each other, it
> doesn't matter what
> they wear.

> DOUGAL
> That's true; but
> still, you can do
> better than that lot
> of clothing you got
> from your aunt.

                    DOUGAL (Cont.)
                You're always twist-
                  ing, mending and
                altering old dresses
                that I wouldn't give
                   house room to.

                       CECILE
                I will wear what I
                like, is that clear?
                You're very insen-
                sitive! I don't nag
                you about that foul
                pipe you smoke, or
                your fondness for
                       drink…

She flounces out of the room, slamming the door
behind her. Under the following VOICE OVER confessional narration, DOUGAL gets up, crosses to the
table on which stands the glass and decanter, and
pours himself a drink.

                  VOICE OF DOUGAL
                      (O.S.)
                I didn't mind these fits
                of temper; they gave me
                an opportunity to clear
                her out and have a good
                day, perhaps a game or
                two of billiards. I was
                drinking heavily then,
                because I had made up my
                mind to either get a lump
                sum out of her and leave,
                or put her away and have
                the lot… Only trouble
                was, I knew very little
                about her financial posi-
                tion. She kept her

> VOICE OF DOUGAL (Cont.)
> (O.S.)
> checkbook, and details
> of the shares and stocks
> she owned, locked up in
> a little desk. She car-
> ried the key on a chain
> attached to a ring in her
> pocket.

HE moves, drink in hand, toward the desk.

CLOSE SHOT - THE DESK

The hand of DOUGAL reaches in, tries a drawer. It is locked.

FULL SHOT of DOUGAL at the desk. He tries another drawer, then another. As he is at this, the VOICE OF CECILE comes in OVER the shot, startling him.

> VOICE OF CECILE
> (from out of
> the room)
> Herbert…

DOUGAL moves quickly away from the desk, bolts down what is left of the drink, replaces the glass on the table and looks up as CECILE comes through the door. She is contrite.

> CECILE
> Herbert…

> DOUGAL
> (coldly)
> What is it?

CECILE
I'm sorry
about losing my
temper.

DOUGAL
That's all
right.

She goes to him, puts her arms about him. HE re-
sponds with little interest.

CECILE
I'm afraid I
was sharper
than I need
have been.

DOUGAL
I was only sug-
gesting for
your own good...

CECILE
Do you forgive
me?

DOUGAL
Why yes, Ceci-
le, so long as
you realize my
intent was in-
nocent.

CECILE
I know it was.

DOUGAL
Then let's for-
get it.

As they continue their embrace:

>   CECILE
>   It's only my state
>   of nerves, really,
>   that makes me give
>   way to such temper.

CAMERA MOVES IN SLOWLY as, in their embrace, he
gently pats her on the back with one hand. His
confessional narrative continues OVER the shot:

>   VOICE OF DOUGAL
>   (O.S.)
>   I debated whether to
>   kill her or not. I had
>   thought about it for
>   a long time, because
>   although I had done a
>   lot of things during my
>   life, I couldn't quite
>   make up my mind to go
>   so far as to murder
>   someone. At one time, I
>   thought maybe I would
>   make it look like an
>   accident: get her in a
>   room while the servant
>   girl was present, and,
>   while I was fiddling
>   about with a revolver,
>   contrive to fire it
>   off, so evidence could
>   be given that it <u>was</u>
>   accidental. But she had
>   such a horror of fire-
>   arms that she wouldn't
>   even let me keep one
>   in the house… I hid it
>   outside.

EXT. - GARDEN BOWER - DAY

Covered with boughs and vines, with an old-fash-
ioned cast-iron bench underneath. Ivy covers the
ground, and has crept over a neglected ornamental
urn at one end of the bench.

DOUGAL comes into the scene, removes a gun from
his pocket, places it in the urn, under the ivy,
concealing it from view.

> VOICE OF DOUGAL (Cont.)
> (O.S.)
> I thought a
> very good place
> to bury her
> would be the
> ditch of the
> moat.

EXT. DITCH OF MOAT. It is filled with about six
inches of water. DOUGAL, CECILE and a laborer
named PILGRIM, stand examining the ditch. PILGRIM
tests the depth by standing a shovel in the water.

> VOICE OF DOUGAL (Cont.)
> (O.S.)
> ...and that was why
> the very first week
> we were at the farm,
> I gave orders for it
> to be filled in.

> PILGRIM
> It will have to
> be drained, sir
> -- a bit of a
> job.

CECILE
I still don't
see why it
can't stay as
it is.

DOUGAL
Well, it's not
the best look-
ing thing in the
world, is it? Haz-
ardous, too.

CECILE
How do you
propose to
drain it?

DOUGAL
Well, simply si-
phon off the water,
and then --

CECILE
Siphon? I
don't know --

DOUGAL
(icily; with strained
expression)
Cecile my dear, I
know very well what
I'm doing.

CECILE
(bristling)
But I have a right to my
opinion --
(to Pilgrim, the laborer)

                    CECILE (Cont.)
               How do you think this
               should be done, Mr. Pil-
                        grim?

                       PILGRIM
                 Well, ma'am, I think
                 the proper way to do
                 the job is to make
                 a new drain first,
                 and then fill in the
                 ditch. Don't think
                 I'd try to siphon --

                       CECILE
               There, you see, Herbert?

                       DOUGAL
                     (irritated)
               I see nothing of the sort.

HE makes a gesture to PILGRIM, indicating that he
wants him to start work on the project.

HE and CECILE glare at each other for a long moment, then CECILE turns and goes off.

                  VOICE OF DOUGAL
                      (O.S.)
                 She was getting on
                 my nerves: I had
                 made up my mind what
                 I was going to do
                 with her, so it did
                 not suit my purposes
                 to accept Pilgrim's
                 advice; I insisted
                 the work begin imme-
                        diately.

DISSOLVE TO:

INT. - LIVING ROOM - FARMHOUSE - DAY

CLOSE SHOT: DOUGAL - He sits alone, glass in hand, slowly putting away some whiskey. He seems full of dark contemplation. OVER this SHOT:

> VOICE OF DOUGAL
> (O.S.)
> I don't think I could have done it had I not been drinking heavily; but the more I drank, the more determined I became. I needed money badly then, and made one final appeal to her to let me have some money until I got my dispute with the War Office settled, but she refused, and told me that she knew all I wanted it for was to spend it on drink. She was so mean that she would not trust me with even the wages to pay the farm hands. I knew that if I didn't soon get her out of the way, more people would get to know that she was there, so I decided to shoot her the first opportunity I got.

(PRESENT) INT. - INTERROGATION ROOM - DAY

> OFFICER
> Just a moment, Dougal. What about the

OFFICER (Cont.)
testimony of the ser-
vant girl, Blackwell,
that you made advanc-
es to late one night?

DOUGAL
(grimacing)
What that servant girl
said about going to her
door is about right, al-
though I think she exag-
gerates a little. I'd
had a snootful of brandy
that night, and I don't
quite remember what hap-
pened. I knew that Ce-
cile, when she discov-
ered what I'd done,
would sell the farm, and
not live with me one day
longer…
I was correct: we had
quite a row; she ac-
cused me of a lot of
things. Of course, I
declared the girl's
story was a lie from
top to bottom, but Ce-
cile stuck up for her…
But a few days later we
made up. I told her my
claim against the War
Office had been set-
tled, and, in the fu-
ture, I should devote
myself to the farm. She
forgave me, and that
night we went for a
walk…

EXT. - COUNTRY ROAD - MOONLIT NIGHT

DOUGAL and CECILE walk slowly, hand in hand.

DISSOLVES within the walk indicate lapses of time and distance, but all is contained within the following continued narrative:

> VOICE OF DOUGAL
> (O.S.)
> It was a lovely night...
> The light of the moon
> was so bright one could
> pick out the leaves of
> trees... Cecile held my
> hand all the way.
> I should think it was
> about a quarter past
> eight when we got back
> to the farm. I suggest-
> ed it was such a nice
> night, that we should
> not go in right away,
> but sit for a while on
> the back porch.

EXT. - GARDEN BOWER - NIGHT

Still hand in hand, DOUGAL leads CECILE to the bench and they sit -- DOUGAL on CECILE's left.

> VOICE OF DOUGAL
> (O.S.)
> The wind was in right
> direction, so I knew
> that a shot would not
> be heard by the servant
> girl in the house...

Unseen to CECILE, DOUGAL reaches down to the urn at the side of bench, retrieving the pistol that we saw him place there earlier.

                        CECILE
                   (looking up at the
                        moon)
                   What a beautiful
                        night!

INSERT CLOSE SHOT: DOUGAL's hands as he slowly
passes the pistol from his left to right hand, and
raises it behind her head, the motion seeming like
one in which he was going to put his arm around
her.

TWO SHOT held on CECILE still looking up at the
moon, DOUGAL'S right hand and pistol hidden behind
her head.

THERE IS A GUNSHOT: CECILE pitches forward, falls
on her face.

                                        FADE OUT

(COMMERCIAL BREAK)

FADE IN:

EXT. - GARDEN BOWER - NIGHT

We resume at the moment where we left off. DOUGAL
stands, bends down, turns CECILE over so that she
lies face up. She is a bloody mess.

           VOICE OF DOUGAL
              (O.S.)
        If I live to be a
      thousand years old,
      I'll never forget the
      feeling as I turned
    her over and looked at
      her ruined face…

He kneels down and pulls her toward him by the
collar, eyes wild.

      VOICE OF DOUGAL (Cont.)
             (O.S.)
    Of course, I knew she was
       dead, and yet…

      DOUGAL (IN SCENE)
    Cecile! Speak to me.
    Cecile! Do you hear
    me? Can you see me?
       Cecile!!

With disappointment, Dougal lays her gently down.

      VOICE OF DOUGAL (Cont.)
             (O.S.)
    Now, I began to be ner-
    vous about the noise of
       the pistol…

He stands, puts the pistol in his pocket, starts
off.

EXT. – GATE – NIGHT

FULL SHOT – DOUGAL approaches, comes to the gate,
lifts the latch. But instead of going through, he
stands and listens.
CAMERA moves into an extreme CLOSEUP. Beads of

perspiration stand on DOUGAL'S brow.

> VOICE OF DOUGAL (Cont.)
> (O.S.)
> I had the most pecu-
> liar sensation as if
> someone was follow-
> ing me. I thought Ce-
> cile had gotten up and
> was walking after me.
> I could almost feel
> her touch me; as true
> as there is a God in
> heaven, I was ready to
> drop…

FULL SHOT on back of DOUGAL as he stands, paralyzed in front of the gate. He turns around to the
direction from which he has just come.

> VOICE OF DOUGAL (Cont.)
> (O.S.)
> I couldn't quite shake
> the feeling that some-
> thing or someone stood
> between me and the ar-
> bor. I had the impres-
> sion that someone was
> coming towards me.

He raises his pistol and holds it out, trembling.

CLOSEUP - DOUGAL tries to work his mouth, but his
tongue seems stuck. HE puts the pistol back in his
pocket, turns, and goes through the gate.

INT. - LIVING ROOM - NIGHT DOUGAL goes to the decanter from earlier and raises it to his mouth,
gulping down half its contents. He puts the decanter down, wipes his face with his hand and

moves to the door.

EXT. - HALLWAY - NIGHT
(limbo… any dark passage… DISORIENTING ANGLES ON
DOUGAL)
DOUGAL walks down the hallway.

EXT. - DOOR TO KITCHEN - DOUGAL raps on the door.

> VOICE OF SERVANT
> GIRL
> (from within)
> Who's there?

> DOUGAL
> Mr. Dougal.

The door opens just a crack -- the girl is not
ready to let Dougal into the kitchen after what
happened before.

> SERVANT GIRL
> Where's the
> mistress?

> DOUGAL
> She's gone to town on
> business. She... She'll
> be gone awhile.

CLOSE SHOT - The SERVANT GIRL eyeing DOUGAL suspiciously.

> VOICE OF DOUGAL
> (O.S.)
> I believe at that mo-
> ment -- if I had even
> a <u>suspicion</u> that the
> girl had known anything
> about what had happened

                    VOICE OF DOUGAL (Cont.)
                         (O.S.)
                    -- that I would have
                    shot her, too.

                         SERVANT GIRL
                    I think it's very un-
                    kind of Mrs. Dougal to
                    go to away and leave
                    me in the house after
                    what's happened here.
                    Most unkind -- and I
                    shall tell her so when
                    she returns.

SHE shuts the door in DOUGAL's face.

(a beat)

DOUGAL, disheveled, slowly turns away. He looks
directly into CAMERA, thinking.

                    VOICE OF DOUGAL
                         (O.S.)
                    I felt relieved that she
                    had not heard the shot.

                                        CUT TO:

INT. - LIVING ROOM:

                    VOICE OF DOUGAL (Cont.)
                         (O.S.)
                    Every few minutes I
                    broke into a soaking
                    perspiration… I don't
                    know why, but I thought
                    it might all be a mis-
                    take; maybe the bullet
                    hadn't killed her,

> VOICE OF DOUGAL (Cont.)
> (O.S.)
> that she had only been
> grazed and had fainted...
> Perhaps she might come
> to if I gave her some
> brandy...

DOUGAL staggers in, reaches once more for the brandy bottle and takes another hard pull. He grabs the decanter as well and starts out with it.

EXT. - GARDEN BOWER

CECILE is lying just as he left her. DOUGAL drags her to the bench and props her up against it in a sitting position. He then tries to force some brandy to her lips. It simply trickles over her chin; she sags limply to one side.

CAMERA moves in slowly to concentrate on DOUGAL: he gets to his feet, picks up CECILE, slings her over his shoulder, bends to pick up the decanter, and moves off. CAMERA pivots to follow him, but loses him in darkness.

CLOSE SHOT: FEET OF DOUGAL as he trudges along the path, obviously struggling under the load.

> VOICE OF DOUGAL (Cont.)
> (O.S.)
> As I carried her along, I
> wished there was a great big
> furnace that I could stuff
> her in and watch her burn.
> I dreaded getting caught.
> I thought of cutting her
> up into pieces and leaving
> her in the moat, but I was
> afraid of being interrupted...

EXT. - MOAT DITCH - NIGHT

The water has been drained from the ditch since last we saw it. DOUGAL enters the SHOT, places CE-CILE on the ground, tenderly.

> VOICE OF DOUGAL (Cont.)
> (O.S.)
> I was torn: I wanted to
> bury her out of sight,
> to forget what had hap-
> pened… yet I wanted to
> keep her beside me, too.
> It was horrible to see
> her laying on the ground,
> so vulnerable, so still;
> strangely, a part of me
> wished that she were
> alive again. In some odd
> way I guess that I loved
> her…

DOUGAL bends down very close to her and speaks. Her demolished face is turned away from CAMERA, the back of her head silhouetted against the faint light on DOUGAL'S face.

> DOUGAL (IN SCENE)
> We did have good
> times, didn't we,
> Cecile? When I was
> out of my mind with
> drink, you nursed
> me, tried to get me
> well…

He kisses her, his face smeared with blood when his head comes back into frame. He takes another pull at the bottle.

> DOUGAL (IN SCENE)
> (face suddenly hardening)
> But why did you nag me
> so? Why didn't you let me
> have that money I needed?
> Why did you show me up
> before the servant girl
> and the hired man, Mr.
> Pilgrim?

> VOICE OF DOUGAL
> (O.S.)
> The more brandy I
> drank, the more bru-
> tal I seemed to get.
> One minute I wanted
> to kiss her, and the
> next minute I wanted
> to kill her all over
> again…

He kisses her once more. His face is further bloodied. His countenance is suddenly twisted in anguish over what he's done, eyes overflowing with tears which track his bloody features. He hurls the bottle away, anger flaring, and looks at the body, his eyes cold, hard. He is very drunk. He slaps her, viciously, across the face, his teeth bared.

> DOUGAL (IN SCENE)
> Why did this have to
> happen, Cecile?

HE studies her dead body, obviously distraught.

(PRESENT) INT. - INTERROGATING ROOM:

                    DOUGAL
        (to Officer, as stenogra-
        pher continues to record
              his statement)
        I buried her and covered
        the earth with brambles
        and twigs, and then went
        back into the house and
        went to bed. I'm sure I
        aged twenty years; I never
        closed my eyes the whole
        night long. I could not
        keep still or rest for
        even a quarter of an hour.
        When the servant girl got
        up in the morning, I told
        her I'd received a letter
        from her mistress,and that
        she had gone for a little
        holiday. I was anxious to
        see the last of the ser-
        vant girl. I was pleased
        when her mother came the
        next day and took her
              home.

(FLASHBACK) INT. BEDROOM - MOAT FARM - NIGHT

DOUGAL is propped up on high pillows on an old-
fashioned bed reading a newspaper in the light of
an oil lamp. He turns out the light, sinks back on
his pillow and falls asleep.

DOUGAL gasps, opening his eyes in terror.

                VOICE OF DOUGAL
                    (O.S.)
        But no relief ever lasted
        very long. That was the way
        it was -- I'd seem to free

                    VOICE OF DOUGAL (Cont.)
                         (O.S.)
          my mind for a little while,
          but dark thoughts would keep
          crowding back in. Soon after
          the servant girl left and I
          was alone in the house I be-
          gan to have terrible dreams…
          Sometimes I'd sleep for an
          hour or two, sometimes for
          only a few minutes, before
          I'd be awakened by some hor-
          rible reverie, or I would
          fancy that I heard Cecile's
                        voice…

                GHOST VOICE OF CECILE
                     (OVER ACTION)
                      Herbert!

DOUGAL bolts up in his bed, visibly shaken. He
fumbles for a match on the bedside table, lights
the lamp, and moves out of the room with the lamp
in hand.

                GHOST VOICE OF CECILE
                     (OVER ACTION)
                  (more insistently)
                       HERBERT!

                                        DISSOLVE TO:

INT. - LIVING ROOM - MOAT FARM - DAY

DOUGAL is replenishing the supply in the decanter
from a large bottle. As he concentrates on this,
he hears the Ghost Voice of Cecile again, and is
so unsteadied by it that he spills some of the
brandy.

VOICE OF DOUGAL
(O.S.)
Even in my waking
hours, as I went about
the house, I some-
times used to hear her
voice…

GHOST VOICE OF CECILE
(in a whisper)
What a beautiful
night it was, Her-
bert!

HE slumps into a chair, and buries his face in his
hands. CAMERA moves into a CLOSE SHOT of him and

DISSOLVE TO:

(PRESENT) INT. - INTERROGATING ROOM - The exact
same head shot of DOUGAL from the previous scene,
but this time we are back in the Interrogating
Room with the OFFICER.

OFFICER
Yes, Dougal --
go on.

DOUGAL takes his hands away from his face, raises
his head and says in a dead voice:

DOUGAL
Things only
got worse from
there.

FADE OUT

(COMMERCIAL BREAK)

FADE IN:

(PRESENT) INT. - INTERROGATING ROOM - DAY

We resume at the point where we left off.

> DOUGAL (Cont.)
> No matter how clever
> one may be and how-
> ever well one's plans
> have been carried out,
> there's the suspicion
> lurking at the back
> of your head that you
> might have made one
> little blunder that
> will lead to your un-
> doing…

INSERT: CLOSE SHOT - DOUGAL's hands as he opens
several pieces of mail.
CAMERA PULLS BACK to show DOUGAL going through the
mail.

> VOICE OF DOUGAL
> (O.S.)
> I used to watch ev-
> ery post in order to
> see if there were
> any letters from Ce-
> cile's relatives.

HE opens one official looking letter, unfolds the
letterhead and reads with consternation.

                                    DISSOLVE TO:

INSERT: DOUGAL practicing CECILE's signature. He writes "Cecile Dougal" over and over. He is using a fountain pen; he dips it into an ink well from time to time.

                    VOICE OF DOUGAL (Cont.)
                         (O.S.)
                    I used to watch ev-
                    ery person who came
                    to the farm; it was
                    rather an anxious
                    time for me when I
                    sent the first letter
                    to her bankers, be-
                    cause I was not quite
                    certain as to wheth-
                    er my forgery of her
                    signature would pass
                    the bank clerks. The
                    bank sent the mon-
                    ey, but at the same
                    time, they asked that
                    a fresh signature be
                         given...

FULL SHOT - THE DITCH where DOUGAL buried CECILE. Grass has now grown over it, although there is still some sign of its original outline.

                    VOICE OF DOUGAL (Cont.)
                         (O.S.)
                    I was drinking <u>more</u>
                    heavily by this time,
                    and I could see that
                    I must be careful to
                    steady myself before I
                    imitated her signature
                    any further. But af-

> VOICE OF DOUGAL (Cont.)
> (O.S.)
> ter this, not one sin-
> gle signature was ever
> questioned.
> It's all very well to
> try and drown your
> thoughts in drink, and
> no one tried harder
> than I did to banish
> entirely from my mind
> all recollections of
> that terrible night.

SUPERIMPOSE - CLOSEUP of DOUGAL: He looks haunted and abstract. WIDENING ANGLE discloses that he
is listening to PILGRIM explain something (silent
track) without hearing a word the man says.

> VOICE OF DOUGAL (Cont.)
> (O.S.)
> It didn't matter where I was,
> or who was with me, the mo-
> ment there was a lull in the
> conversation, my thoughts
> went back to that moonlit
> evening. Sometimes I would
> walk about the farm myself…
> But there was always the
> weird feeling that she was
> going to step out of the
> grave and touch me on the
> shoulder. I also had the
> feeling that something was
> near me; someone present be-
> sides myself… yet I knew that
> was ridiculous.

The SUPERIMPOSITION of DOUGAL's face remains (CAM-

ERA moving in to a CLOSEUP again) but the background changes to the grape arbor.

> GHOST VOICE OF CECILE
> (O.S.)
> Herbert, if two
> people are fond of
> each other, noth-
> ing else matters…

Still under SUPERIMPOSITION, FULL SHOT of DOUGAL
coming up to the arbor and standing in a trance,
looking slowly about him.

> VOICE OF DOUGAL
> (O.S.)
> I never could really make up
> my mind that she was dead,
> and yet I knew she was. I can
> swear that I went to the ar-
> bor hundreds of times… Some-
> times two or three times a
> day. Each time I expected to
> see her lying on her back as
> she fell, her head shattered
> by the bullet. Nothing would
> make me believe she wasn't
> there until I had gone down
> and seen for myself.

CUT TO:

(PRESENT) INT. - INTERROGATION ROOM

> DOUGAL
> At one time drink would send
> me to sleep, and, perhaps
> for a few hours, I would
> forget all about the Moat
> Farm; but as time went on I

> DOUGAL (Cont.)
> found it impossible to get a
> decent night's rest. Even-
> tually I took to walking in
> my sleep; I thought I had
> gone completely mad when I
> realized that I was a som-
> nambulist. I remember one
> night I wasn't quite sober,
> and, after having a good
> look around, I went to bed,
> about eleven o'clock. I re-
> member quite well taking off
> my clothes and getting into
> bed, but just before day-
> break...

(FLASHBACK) EXT. - DITCH - NIGHT

DOUGAL stands by the side of the ditch with a shovel in his hand. He is in his nightshirt. The wind whips his hair and robe.

> VOICE OF DOUGAL
> (O.S.)
> I had gone to the
> grave with a shovel in
> my hand. I must have
> been standing there a
> long time, because I
> was very cold, and my
> nightshirt was moist
> with dew.

SLOW DISSOLVE:

CLOSEUP - A haunted DOUGAL, his head on a pillow.

                    VOICE OF DOUGAL (Cont.)
                          (O.S.)
            I went back to bed and lay
          awake counting the hours. I
          was really afraid of myself,
          and feared that one of these
          mornings, someone would come
          in and find me standing there.
          I figured the only way I could
                     prevent my
        self walking out to the ditch
          in my sleep was locking the
          gate at the entrance to the
                   moat bridge.
          Before I went to bed at night,
          I checked to see that it was
          padlocked. Although this would
           not prevent my walking in my
           sleep, it stopped me going to
           the ditch, because I used to
           go right up to the gate, and
           as it was locked, I feel cer-
           tain I used to turn around and
          go back to bed. I got very ill
           about this time, and I felt
                     certain
          that I should go mad if I did
           not do something to distract
          my thoughts. I made up my mind
           to get one big check cashed
                and go away for good…

DOUGAL staggers toward the CAMERA and his bulk
BLOTS out the scene, providing a TRANSITION TO:

A SHIP LEAVING PORT (stock)

EXT. - SIDEWALK CAFE - PARIS - DAY

> VOICE OF DOUGAL (Cont.)
> (O.S.)
> As I was going away,
> I felt quite happy; I
> thought I would leave
> everything, and not a
> soul should know where I
> was. But no sooner had I
> arrived in Paris, than
> a strange feeling came
> over me and I began won-
> dering what was happen-
> ing at the Moat Farm...

TIGHT SHOT: A very simple setup of a small table and chair. On the table is a bottle wine and a half-filled glass.

DOUGAL, morose and brooding, takes a last swig of the wine and puts down the glass. After a moment, he reaches in his pocket and pulls out some bills, lays them on the table, gets up and moves out of SHOT.

> DISSOLVE TO:

EXT. - GATE - MOAT FARM

A MAN (extra) comes up to the gate, sees it is padlocked, stands looking off wondering what to do. We see only his back.

> VOICE OF DOUGAL (Cont.)
> (O.S.)
> It was no good... I was
> obliged to go back; after
> I'd been in Paris just a
> couple of days, I started

                    VOICE OF DOUGAL (Cont.)
                         (O.S.)
            for home. I had some ex-
            traordinary fancy that
            someone related Cecile
            had come to the farm... and
            not finding her there,
            was making inquiry, and
            that if I didn't get back
            at once, the ditch would
            be opened, and the mys-
            tery of her disappearance
                     solved.

                                              CUT TO:

(PRESENT) INT. - INTERROGATION ROOM - DAY

                         OFFICER
                 Tell me, Dougal:
            when did you first
            begin to sense re-
            lief, or did you?

                         DOUGAL
            Yes. When Cecile's
            body was found: at
            times, as I sit in
            my cell, I think of
            what we shared. Our
            marriage -- and her
            death. In the end, I
            was only living a life
            of misery, and knew
            it would be better to
                 finish it...
                 Sorry to say,

                    DOUGAL (Cont.)
                    Inspector, it
                    wasn't you that
                    finally caught
                        me...

                                        SLOW DISSOLVE TO:

EXT. GATE - DAY - CAMERA SLOWLY CRANES TO THE SKY

                    VOICE OF DOUGAL
                        (O.S.)
                    It was Cecile...

                                            FADE OUT

                        END

                        ###

Norman Corwin launched his astounding career in 1938, with his now-classic "The Plot to Overthrow Christmas". His multitude of credits, from *Columbia Presents Corwin* in 1944, to his legendary production celebrating the end of World War II, "On a Note of Triumph", place him at the summit of his contemporaries, including the great Orson Welles. He is also a poet, playwright, screenwriter (Corwin was nominated for an Academy Award for his excellent adaptation of *Lust for Life*) and has over 20 books to his credit. Corwin has won numerous awards, among them two George Foster Peabody Medals, an Emmy, and a Golden Globe. Although he will turn 100 years old in May, 2010, Corwin is still very active, attending plays staged by his old friend Ray Bradbury, writing and teaching.

The author says about this teleplay:

"My teleplay for *The Bleeding Edge* is based upon a true story. I converted the facts into a radio drama, 'The Moat Farm Murder', in 1944, and revised it for my television series in the 1970s, *Norman Corwin Presents*... This is a refinement of that program. A rather bizarre tale, I think."

At the Riding School

by Cody Goodfellow

ONE

"**C**ome quick," she said, in a voice so leaden each word took a year off my life. "Bring the black bag... There's been an *accident*."

The call woke me up, and I knocked over a water bottle getting out of bed. For an instant, the glimmer of my ex-husband's terrified countenance flashed through my murky thoughts. Shaking his horrible visage off, I realized that the cabin was freezing, then I began to worry about what really mattered: getting to Madame fast enough...

I had only been in town six months, struggling to make a name for myself when Madame Dioskilos had called the first time. I had already heard that she owned a large barn and twenty-four horses, but that she was a rather difficult client, and stingy. She and her charges did all the routine medical work, and she'd had the same blacksmith since opening the Academy.

I found her to be demanding, but fair; I kept her secrets, and she -- so far -- kept mine.

I was all packed before I woke Tonio. He had only been with me for a few months, and I was afraid of spooking him, but he got dressed and helped me load the truck, then climbed in with his sketchpad and box of colored pencils. I told him only that we were going to see a sick animal. A ward of the state for almost all of his ten years, he was well trained to follow directions. I knew Madame Dioskilos would become irate about the boy -- no men were allowed on the estate after dark, unless sent for -- but I was more worried about him waking up alone in an empty house.

Anyway, it was time, if this was what I thought it was, for Madame to see --

I brought my special kit bag, though I doubted if it would do any good. She would have the only sure cure loaded and propped beside the stable door, like always.

We didn't pass any cars going through town to the coast road. My windshield was frosted over, and it was freakishly cold for Big Sur, even in winter. The lights were out at the Yogic Retreat at the end of Main Street and the few streetlamps lit only coronas of sleet, but I had to keep myself from driving too fast. The road spilled out of the trees and clove to the sheer cliff over the Pacific. The state hadn't replaced the guardrail where the last car had gone over, only a week before. Nearly ten years prior, I'd learned, Greta Spivak, a local vet who'd worked for Madame Dioskilos before me, drove over the edge during a winter storm. They found no body in the truck, only a shark tooth embedded in the steering wheel.

Tonio fell asleep, rocked by the swaying, serpentine highway. I turned the radio on as loud as I dared to keep myself from thinking.

Only four other emergencies had called me up to Madame Dioskilos's house after dark in the whole seven years that I had worked for her. That first time, she had explained our situation: she had found me out, and we both understood that her leverage meant that I could be trusted with what I must do.

There are many veterinarians between Big Sur and Monterey who would have done the work and had no qualms about it -- bitter, middle-aged divorcees; born-again pagans; misanthropic bull-dykes... but, they were all too clean for her. Just as I needed her, she needed someone like me.

The entrance to her estate is nestled in one of the box canyons that the highway wanders into, seeking an escape from the sea, only to veer away in a panicky hairpin turn. The gate itself is formidable, shrouded in veils of coastal live oak and laurels, wrought-iron barbs ten feet high, a press conference's worth of cameras fixed on the road.

I always paused to look at the sculpture in the grove, just outside the gate. Most thought it was a modern piece, the angular severity shaming the mathematical fascism of the Italian Futurists; but the sculpture was symptomatic of Madame Dioskilos herself: so easy to completely misread. Like her, it came from the Cyclades Islands, and was a forgotten relic before Athens had erected its first temple.

It depicted a lithe blade of a human figure -- somehow, undeniably a girl -- riding the back of a rampant chimerical beast Madame told the curious was a centaur, though its hindquarters seemed to be broken off and lost to posterity. It might have been Nessus's abduction of Alcmene, the bride of Hercules, but when you got to know Madame Dioskilos, you figured it out. The centaur was not broken, and it wasn't a centaur, and the myth depicted was not in any storybooks.

The gates were swinging open as I turned up the drive, braking cagily on the slippery driveway, one arm out to brace Tonio. They'd let me adopt him with no problems, glad to empty a bed at the struggling group home in Oakland where we met. Though they did a thorough background check, the authorities never found any red flags in the short, happy life of Ruth Wyeth. Of course, they hadn't dug half as diligently as *she* had...

TWO

Artemisia Dioskilos, Madame's mother, was a fiery vamp and celebrated equestrian from a tiny Greek island. She married an ancient Italian Count who died in WWI, then fled to California with his wealth and title. The Countess ran a riding school in the Hollywood hills until 1926, when she retreated from society under a shameful cloud and purchased an estate on the Central Coast of California to raise her only daughter, Scylla. No inquiry was ever made into the identity of the child's father.

Alone on the estate with her mother and servants, the young Scylla Dioskilos must have pined for friends as a child. When her mother died in 1960, she went back to the Old Country to live for three years. When she returned, Scylla opened a new private school.

For forty years now she'd run the Delos Academy, and if there were problems with the state, no one had ever raised an eyebrow. She boarded no more than twelve children at a time, taught them to read, do sums, and shoot arrows at deer from the back of a horse. She could have charged ten thousand a semester to the snots in Carmel and gotten it, but she didn't need money, and she avoided publicity like the plague.

She selected abandoned and orphaned girls from Bay Area cities, and she didn't discriminate by race, so they tried to stuff kids into the trunk of her Rolls Royce as she drove away. They were all smart, strong little girls; the rest she could make over.

A certified teacher educated the girls, who had only each other for society. Most stayed through puberty, and came out fearless, aglow with eerie confidence and destined for bright futures. The whole West Coast was peppered with Madame's prodigies; a sorority that had helped girls obtain scholarships and entry into ivy-league schools, interviews with Fortune 500 companies, and even temporary financial assistance once they graduated university. Counted among the Delos alumni were many powerful women: one of San Francisco's most successful defense attorneys; a sitting Assemblywoman in Sacramento; even a U.S. junior Senator. They also help keep the secret. Madame Dioskilos wanted no awards, no media attention; most people in town thought she practically ran a nunnery.

THREE

I rolled up the drive and past the whitewashed Cretan villa with its showcase equestrian stables, over the ridge at the top of the canyon and around the front of the austere pine-log hunting lodge. The garage was locked down, motion-detector lights and security cameras triggering each other. Seeing no lights on, I drove on down into a stand of oaks, where I knew she would be, in the other stables...

I parked under the awning and told Tonio to stay in the truck. I gave him my cell phone and told him what to do if it rang, then got out and stumbled through the dark to the golden glow of a lantern over the stable door.

Only the oldest girls at the school came anywhere near here, the ones who had been initiated into what Madame called "the Mysteries". I didn't pretend to know what she meant, but I sensed what lay at the root of her fanaticism.

I pushed open the stable door and stepped into Mediterranean heat and the awesome stink of Madame Dioskilos's steeds.

"Ms. Wyeth?" Her voice, from the tack room. I responded and went to the little door beside the corridor that led to the indoor arena. If there'd been an accident at this hour, it would have happened there. I didn't see the shotgun anywhere about, and was both more and less uneasy as I ducked into the tack room.

Madame sat in a rocking chair in a corner of the tack room, beside a mountain of dusty blankets. She was wiry and much stronger than I was for her age and size. Her hands clutched each other, shaking.

"What happened?"

"An accident," Madame Dioskilos murmured, "an ill omen."

"Which one was it?"

"I was a fool to trust her with him! I thought, in her, I saw something... Ah! Actaeon," her wounded voice faltered, and I felt my own heart race with distress. *Her prized stallion --*

"Well, where is he? What can I do for him here?"

"He is... unharmed. I will deal with him later, myself. But I need your help with another matter... It is not for him, that I call you." She leaned forward as if to get up again, and pulled back the top blanket from the pile.

A girl lay curled up on her side with her knees tight against her chest, and bound up by her arms. She wore a few rags of the short white chitins that the girls always wore when riding. Blood smeared the inside of her legs down to her knees, soaking the blanket under her.

"Oh God!" I screamed. "What do you want me to do?" I felt sick to my stomach with the tragedy of it; I say tragedy, because it was so inevitable.

Clearly, she'd already been sedated, or was in shock; her eyes half-lidded, her tongue protruding out from her teeth. She was twelve, maybe thirteen, with caramel skin, and straight, shiny black hair in a boyish bob. Her elbows and knees were torn and blotted with sawdust, her lip split, and bruises bloomed on her neck and shoulders. The horrible wound between her legs still bled. She was ready for an ambulance --

One had to look very long and hard to see her breathe.

I wasn't breathing at all. "He -- *he* did this?"

"Trista is a vigorous rider, a natural hunter... When her first bloodletting came, she embraced the Mysteries, and hunted the hunter. She rode Minos like a high priestess -- but she trained too hard. Such girls, one cannot always see it, they are wanton..."

"*Where is he now?*" I demanded. It was only for the girl's sake that I didn't shout. "Where is the shotgun?"

The other ones had never done anything like this, but the others were all geldings. They'd only wounded each other or been lamed in accidents. Although they were bred for the steep terrain and rocky cliffs of Greece, there were other dangers here. One was bitten by a rattlesnake; another snarled in razor wire. Madame always went back to Greece and got more, though how she got them into the country always puzzled me.

The lights were dim in the arena, but I heard him, snorting and pawing the muddy turf. I couldn't find the shotgun, but I wasn't to be denied: I found a shovel.

In the Greek myths, Actaeon was a hunter who stumbled on Diana bathing in a sacred pool. For stealing a glance at her divine nakedness, the hunter was transformed into a stag, and ripped to shreds by his own dogs.

I went into the dark faster than I could see through it, with the shovel cocked over my shoulder. I followed the wall of the big round arena, wary of the hidden obstacles the girls jumped to train for the Hunt.

I heard him before I saw him, chains rattling as he came charging out of the shadows, but it gave me no advantage. The chains ran back to stout rings in the wall, giving him more than enough slack to get me. I swung the shovel as hard as I could, but he ducked under it and drove his head and massive shoulder into my gut. I fell hard on my back and lost the shovel.

I curled into a sobbing ball, with no breath to do anything else. His eyes reflected the moon glow from the skylight as he looked me over, trying to decide what he wanted most.

He was still saddled. His bridle was twisted around so it hung from his muzzle, which he'd already half-chewed through. His silver fighting spurs glittered in the moonlight.

A whip cracked between us, the tip raking his face so he leapt back and barked, submissive.

"Is not his fault!" she cried. "Trista rode him too hard... Her sisters say there is -- *carnality* -- in her, but I pay no heed; they are jealous, naturally. She rides him too hard on the course, driving with her hips, but with ulterior motivations: she pleasures herself upon the saddle! Such girls often break their maidenhood on the pommel, and this she did... nature ran away with them both. It is not his fault -- the blood --"

"*Well, what the fuck did you expect, Madame?*" She looked as if she'd never been screamed at before, so I resolved to make it memorable for her. "He's a *man*, for God's sake!"

"No!" She shouted, and crossed her arms in negation between us.

"*Not* a man: a *beast...*"

"*All* men are beasts," I said. *And most women*, I thought.

"Let me tell you," she growled, and approached Actaeon. He shifted from foot to foot and studied us both. They'd always been sedated or sequestered when I came before. I had no problem killing them. I did not see their faces in my dreams. Thanks to them, I hardly ever dreamed about my husband.

Madame Dioskilos coiled the whip taut around one gloved fist as she spoke. "When my ancestors came to the island of Dioskilos three thousand years ago, they were set upon by beasts in the shape of men, who killed and ate our men, and raped our women. The drunken gods often rutted with animals, and sired monsters such as these, here and there in the dark corners of the earth.

"The goddess Diana heard our prayers and appeared to the girls of the tribe, who alone could tame them, so long as they remained chaste. And they did tame them, Mrs. Slabbert, but they have ever been beasts."

Throwing my real name in my face, Madame untangled Actaeon's reins and tugged his huge anvil of a head down to the dirt. He bowed with a snort, one sturdy knee extended out, and Madame stepped up on it, swung her leg over the saddle and sat erect with her boots in the stirrups. At a clipped shout from Madame, Actaeon rose to his full height. His hooded eyes leered at me over his bloody muzzle.

She could make a good argument for her case without words. Though he stood on two legs and had hands, he had no thumbs, whether from selective breeding or post-natal surgery, I didn't care to guess. His barrel torso was rudely muscled, covered in sleek black hair like a goat's, and his shoulders were broad enough to carry a full-grown woman up a mountain on the elaborate saddle perched upon his slightly hunched back. That those mighty shoulders produced such puny, almost flipper-like arms screamed selective breeding over hundreds of centuries from proto-human stock, perhaps even the last Neanderthals. A Greek myth that Bulfinch left out, for better or worse, though Madame's ancestors might've been the grain of sand that grew so many pearls: the Amazons, who made impotent slaves of their men; Circe, who made pigs and asses of Odysseus's crew; satyrs and centaurs --

"This one, you will not kill." From the saddle, Madame reclaimed her regal bearing. The whip uncoiled, now, for me. "It is his nature."

"How many girls will you let him *rape?*"

"This has never happened before... It will never happen again. The girls will be trained --"

I raised the shovel. "Get down off him, Madame --"

"When you kill them, Phyllis, do you imagine that they are your husband?"

That stopped me cold, but I didn't take the bait. I could see where she was leading this, and I brought it back. "What's to become of the girl? When's the ambulance due?"

Actaeon took a few hopping steps, stalking in a lazy, tightening spiral around me. He balanced himself and Madame effortlessly on the balls of his feet -- splayed, talon-tipped toes like a mountain lion, the heels augmented with curved stiletto spurs; and, peeking out of the blood-matted black thicket between his powerful legs -- the weapon. He couldn't have gotten his chastity belt off by himself -- *nature ran away with them both...* His monstrous appendage bobbed and lengthened visibly as he circled; slavering and twitching to have done with Madame's games.

She dug her heels into his scarred flanks and tracked my eyes with hers, stroking the back of his head. "She ran away from us, went back to the city, where -- small surprise -- she was attacked. We will be heartbroken, but resolute. She brought this upon herself. The heart of it is the truth."

"So I -- you want me --" It was beneath words. "But when she talks --"

"You are not to hurry, Mrs. Slabbert."

Actaeon gave a gibbering gurgle from deep in his throat and strained with his stunted forelegs to stroke his cock, still crusted with Trista's blood. I tried to stare him down. Menopause makes you think you can pull shit like that.

He shook his head. His muzzle slipped off. He grinned at me. Each yellow tooth was the size of a big man's toenail, and the moray eel of his tongue lurking behind them. His breath raised welts on my skin.

I still had the shovel. "Hey, cut this shit out! I am not going to help you kill that girl!"

"Of course not, but you are going to get yourself out of what we are both in, no?" She snapped the reins and Actaeon reared up, his spurred feet kicking in the air, flinging sod and sweat. He bent down low, craning his neck until his head was between his knees to sniff my crotch. Madame dismounted to stand between us. "I know that what you have done for me in the past, was not wholly out of necessity. You knew how others would judge you. You are a part of the Mysteries, now."

I stepped around her and reached out to stroke Actaeon's bristly black mane. He twitched and unfolded warily from his rigid dismounting stance, and an alarmingly powerful musky scent suddenly filled the arena. Madame gripped his reins in one hand, the whip in the other.

I scratched behind his ears and the base of his skull, where all animals like it. His jaw went slack, but his eyes never left mine. I leaned in closer, holding my breath. I knew what I'd find, but it was the least dangerous way into the subject.

"What do you do?" Madame Dioskilos demanded, jerking his head back by the reins.

"Nothing... I was only counting his teeth. You told me once that they have four more than us --"

Actaeon obliged by baring his fierce dentition. The extra bicuspids and molars were there. Along with the outsized mandible muscles and projecting palate, they were made to crack open seeds, shellfish and bones. I wondered who had given him his four gold fillings.

"Like jackals," Madame said and led Actaeon away from me. She didn't know where this was going, and so it had to stop.

"Eskimos and American Indians have different dentition from Europeans. How much 'less human' does that make them?" I should have gone to the girl. Madame trusted me to let her die, it would have been so easy to save her and deliver her to the hospital, and we would both get what we deserved. But first, I had to show her --

She flicked her whip at me by way of dismissal and led Actaeon to the grooming stalls. I went to look at the girl. Her breathing was shallow, pulse shocky, and she still bled. If I dumped her out in the cold somewhere up the coast, like Madame ordered me to, she'd never revive. Madame would never dirty her patrician mind with an explicit request that I help her along, but when you work for someone long enough, you learn to read them.

Cruel, surely, but in Madame's world, nature was a serial rapist, and unfit children were left out for the wolves.

I tried not to think about it. I had treated Madame Dioskilos's livestock -- her *men* -- for seven years, and put down four of them, and I knew that what I did wasn't the worst of it. I knew about the High Hunt at the vernal and autumnal equinoxes, and what they hunted. Drifters, illegal aliens, men nobody missed. Anybody with a gun would have killed all of them because they were less than human, but I had let her use me to kill only the useless ones, because they were *men*.

Madame's school -- the Hunt and the Mysteries -- made these cast-off girls into women the rest of the world respected, envied. It empowered them to reach for undreamed of heights, and liberated them from ever becoming a man's creature. And I guess I was one of them, from the day I killed my husband.

We had a thriving vet practice in Maryland -- clients in Chevy Chase, contracts with stables that bred Triple Crown contenders. For such a smart man, Dan Slabbert got very, very stupid around money. He did things for it, just to get close to it, to dream of belonging to it. They let him think he could someday be one of them, so he started doping horses for them. Whatever they promised him was enough that eventually, he killed a champion thoroughbred for them. Insurance paid off, and Dan must've got a healthy cut in a hidden account. He started getting consultant work across the country from rich friends who could afford to fly in a witch doctor to see to their sick investments.

He killed three more before I found out, but I didn't do anything. I found out he was fucking call girls the clients threw his way, but I said nothing. Then I found out what they'd promised him, in return for becoming their equine hit man: they were going to make him a rich widower.

I confronted him with the insurance policies and the rest of it, and he took it like a man; he tried to kill me himself. We fought; I won.

I left the country, laying a convincing trail to nowhere, then quietly snuck back in under an assumed name I'd bought with Dan's blood money. I knew my new identity wasn't airtight when somebody deposited fifty thousand dollars into Ruth Wyeth's new checking account. I suppose, in the end, I did the horsey set a favor.

In Big Sur, I was just another dumpy misfit who had sublimated her miserable lack of sex appeal into a gift for animal husbandry. I thought I could start over. It took Madame Dioskilos to show me how fucking mad I still was, how many times I still wanted to kill him.

I packed surgical gauze into Trista's wound and wrapped her up in a blanket. I left the tack room and found Madame locking her prize stallion in his stable. I hit the speed dial on the spare cell phone in my coat pocket and went to meet her.

"I'm ready to take her," I said.

The barn door creaked and a solemn ten-year old black girl in a spotless white tracksuit slipped in through the crack, a big flashlight in one hand, my phone ringing in the other. Looking back at someone outside, she bowed and whispered, "Madame, there's a *boy* --"

Madame Dioskilos hissed in outrage and reached for the bullwhip coiled on the wall. I moved to stop her.

"He's mine, he's just a little boy. I adopted him. Leave him alone -- " The girl swung the flashlight at me. It smashed my forearm and the arm went limp.

"A *boy,* here?" Madame Dioskilos spat, eyes locked imperiously on mine until I looked away. "And on *this* night, of *all* nights!"

"I didn't know I'd be dumping a --" He was on the other side of the barn door. I begged, "Oh God, let me see him, please!"

"You *know* my rules!"

"You must've rubbed off on me," I pleaded. "I took him in to have somebody to teach the trade... I couldn't leave him at home, could I?"

"If you have taken in a boy, you have learned *nothing* from me." Her strong-gloved fingers worried at the silver lunular clasp holding her long white hair. She never looked so old to me before. I thought it was fear over what happened; it had never occurred to me she was *disappointed* in me.

"Let him come in, please, Madame. I want you to see him."

The door opened wider and Tonio crept in, hugging his pad and pencils to his chest. He looked scared to death, and I started to cry, but when I went to him, the girl brandished the flashlight. A lithe little Latina girl came in with a bow stretched and a silver-tipped hunting arrow nocked.

I screamed at them to back off. Tonio cried, and I hugged him. "Tonio, it's okay, honey, you scared them as bad as they scared you."

I turned him around to face the old woman. "Tonio, I want you to meet Madame Scylla Dioskilos. She's one of the ladies whose horses I take care of. She runs a school for girls, kind of like a foster group home, but... nicer. Madame, this is Tonio. Smile big for the nice lady, Tonio."

Scared, Tonio yet managed a thin smile at Madame Dioskilos, who barely glanced at him. "Hi," he whispered.

"Show her your drawings, honey," I said, but he only hugged the pad tighter.

Madame scowled and made some ancient cursing gesture with her fingers.

"You see, Tonio was born with severe cognitive disabilities, so bad that his mother surrendered him to the state when he was two. He grew up in a special group home in Oakland. I had a hard time tracking him down. There are so many, many children that nobody wants. I wanted you to meet him --"

"You have defiled my house with this --"

"They're beasts, then, and can never be more?" I demanded, and Madame nodded.

"What is your point?" she snapped.

"Please, Tonio, show her your drawings, I want her to see what a good artist you are."

Tonio looked warily around the barn, then slowly unclenched and opened the pad. Shy, slow, autistic, whatever the ignorant might call him, he could *draw*. Horses leapt across the pages like a storm, filling and spilling off the paper, rendered in every color in his box, and some others he'd cleverly blended by smudging them with his little fingers.

"So you were wrong," I started, "and you lied to me before..."

Madame made a gesture of water flowing off her face. "You did the right thing bringing him," Madame said. "You must be made to see." She advanced on Tonio until she stood between him and me. Something she took out of her belt made him scream.

From somewhere in the barn came an answer. The lowing roar and crash of wood and metal froze the room. My heart leapt into my mouth. The jaundiced whites of Madame's eyes gleamed all around her violet irises. The knife flashed in her hand.

"Chandra, go and see to the beasts!" Madame ordered. "Marina, shoot her if she moves." The black girl edged around the awkward scene and stalked into the stables. The girl behind Tonio aimed the arrow at me and drew the string back. Tonio sank to the ground, took out a pencil and began to draw.

Madame hovered over Tonio, the knife behind her back, intrigued. "You adopted this boy? Do not talk to me of lies, Phyllis Slabbert."

"You lied to me, when you said this had never happened, before..."

Madame blinked at me. Tonio whimpered and sketched. The bowstring creaked.

"Look at him, Madame: I want you to count his teeth."

Madame whirled on me and brought the knife up to my chin so quickly I couldn't even flinch. *"What is this game?"*

My muscles locked up and I just stared at her. "Actaeon's done it before, hasn't he? Maybe you even let it happen, part of the 'rituals', or a breeding experiment? And you made Greta Spivak, your old vet, dump the girl --"

"Who is this? I know no one of this name!" Madame's wounded innocence was silent movie acting at its finest.

"Bullshit! She worked for you! I think it was because you both knew the girl was pregnant --"

"You lie!" The knife slashed at my face. I ducked away, but the edge flayed my scalp. A big flap of skin with hair on it came away in my hand as I cradled the wound.

Sobs of pain welled up in my throat, but I gagged them back. Whether or not I could go on, it had to come out. "The girl was only twelve, you remember? She couldn't keep him, so they put him up for adoption, but nobody wanted him. He'd retreat and draw on everything, then have violent fits of rage. His hormones are all screwed up and no one's ever tried to reach him, let alone love him, but he's a sweet, sensitive little boy."

Madame looked from Tonio to the bloody knife in her hand. "Look at his teeth, Madame. He's a strange little boy, no doubt, but is he an animal? Do you want to put a saddle on him?"

Madame bent down and took Tonio's jaw, almost tenderly, in her gloved hand. Tonio was too far gone to resist her. Still looking into his mouth as the silence dragged on, she called out, "Chandra, come here."

In the stables, a metal pail hit the ground. The stable door groaned as it swung open. The darkness beyond yawned, absolute. Marina's fingers grew sweaty and tired on the bowstring, and she lowered it. Blood stung my eyes, soaking my hand when I wiped it away. I needed to lie down. I had to get Tonio out of there. I wanted to show her, but I never meant for things to get so out of hand --

Madame seemed, all of a sudden, to decide. She rose and turned on Tonio with the knife out: he didn't see it coming.

I dove after her, screaming. I grabbed her arm, but she slipped out of my blood-slick grip to stab him.

The knife scythed through Tonio's down parka and came out amid a flurry of feathers. I'd fouled her attack, but she cocked her arm to stab him in the throat. I stepped inside her reach and shoved her as hard as I could. Tonio rolled away shrieking and threw his pad at her. Marina shouted, "Madame!" and raised her bow at me, loosed her arrow.

It never hit me. Sailing past my eyes, it hit Actaeon in the shoulder, but didn't slow him down.

He came so fast I could only fall to the ground. Leaping over me, he dealt Marina a brutal kick to the chest. The girl slammed into the barn door and slumped to the ground. Almost in the same movement, he lunged after Madame, in turn, dove after Tonio. His jaws snapped at her and she hung, howling, in mid-air, caught by his teeth in her long white hair.

Tonio crab-walked backwards into a corner between two walls of hay bales. Hanging by her hair, Madame roared commands in Greek, but Actaeon stood frozen, unable to parse the sticky situation with the stunted brute mind his mistress had given him.

Sounds of shuffling feet behind me made me turn, and I gasped. The rest of them had broken loose, and skulked out of the dark like madhouse inmates on Judgment Day, knees skinned and spurs bloodied from kicking down their stable doors. Their big black eyes rolled and they began to hoot, deep in their barrel chests, nostrils flared as they scented blood on the air.

Tonio's blood. A trickle stood out on his green parka, studded with white down feathers, radioactive in its effect on the beasts.

I knew, then, why Madame Dioskilos had always had someone else treat and put down her beasts. The smell of their own blood, the sounds of their pain, drove them mad. I thought, then, that I would die, and I laid still as death on the ground, but I did not exist for them. They stampeded over me and converged on Madame Dioskilos.

I got up, pointedly not looking at them as I crawled along the wall to Tonio. He pressed his face against the wall and chewed his lips, too scared to make a sound as I bundled him up in my arms and shuffled with my eyes closed for a thousand years to the barn door.

I raced home and packed bags in a panic. Tonio had fallen asleep in the truck. I was ready to flee again, when exhaustion set in. I had enough strength to bring Tonio into the house and lay him in his bed, before I passed out myself.

I awakened at dawn, and no sirens wailed, no police broke down the door. We would leave, but not in a hurry, not as fugitives. I couldn't understand how the world couldn't sense something so wrong happening, but then, how could it not have sensed how wrong things had been, all along? The sisterhood would smother it in secrecy, and that would be best. No one needed to know --

I only went back once, that morning. Of the beasts there was no sign, nor of any of the girls. Trista was gone, and there were opened pill packets and gauze bandage wrappers on the floor of the tack room. I still worry about them, but I think they will make out all right. After her fashion, Madame Dioskilos prepared them well to face the world.

I won't detail what they did to her body, or where I found the head. The bloody paintings they made on the walls of the barn, in their stables, in the chapel of the Goddess at the barn's heart, were what I will always remember. Though they had only one color to work in, the delicacy of the shapes of centaurs, satyrs and nymphs sporting across, filling and spilling off the cedar beam walls, spoke as no words could of what they might have been, in another life.

I burned the place down. I buried what I could of Madame Dioskilos in a grave beneath the laurel tree behind the fire pit beyond the hunting lodge, what I could find of her. I said a prayer for her over her remains before I filled in the grave.

And after I counted her teeth.

FIN

Cody Goodfellow has written three and a half novels: *Radiant Dawn, Ravenous Dusk* and *Perfect Union*, and *Jake's Wake* with John Skipp. His award-shunning short fiction has appeared in *Cemetery Dance, Black Static, Dark Discoveries* and (with Skipp) in *Whispers V* and *Hellboy: Oddest Jobs*. He lives in Los Angeles.

The author writes about this story:
"My wife told me once that many girls who ride horses rupture their hymen in the saddle. Few human activities are quite so charged with repressed sexuality as riding, and few are so overwhelmingly feminine. Ancient cultures like the Greeks drew hard distinctions of taboo between men and animals -- and men and women -- very sharply out of necessity, while their myths freely acknowledged and fetishized the universal kinship of living things. Enlightenment has done away with the barriers, but the hunger for ritual survives. The taboo part's alive and well, too. From now on, my wife's only allowed to ride mares."